PRIDE AND PRIVILEGE

By

Les Pendleton

For Docty & Peggy

Great Freinds

Essie Press

ESSIE PRESS

Palm Coast Services, Inc. d/b/a Essie Press

Contact Essie Press at
P.O. Box 6684
Raleigh, North Carolina 27628-6684
Or
Email Address: <essie-press@lespendleton.com>
Phone: 919 632-9748

Cover Photo Credit

"The images used herein were obtained from
IMSI's Master Photos Collection,
1895 Francisco Blvd. East, San Rafael, CA 94901-5506,
USA."

Library of Congress Registration Number: TXu000692015

Pride and Privilege is dedicated
to my wife

Susanne Harrison Pendleton

Were it not for her support in every way
I'd still be chained to a desk in some
obscure corner of the world.

Pride and Privilege
By Les Pendleton
Copyright 1994 (c)

CHAPTER ONE

By three p.m., everyone on the floor of the South Carolina Journal was doing double-time trying to finish their particular task for the six p.m. deadline. This outpouring of journalistic adrenaline had been a narcotic for Oscar Phipps for forty years. The faces and names of everyone he worked with had changed a thousand times, but the focus and rhythm of the collective task remained constant. Even though, as editor-in-chief of the state's largest daily, he had more than enough deadlines of his own to meet, he nonetheless took a few minutes about this time every day to savor the mental pictures that had been his lifeblood for so long. There were editors with completed articles stacked deep in front of them, checking each for its merits and shortcomings with a bold red pen. Corrections in place, the articles would be given to one of the young apprentices who earned the right to staff a keyboard by running from desk to desk and between departments, keeping the large wheel rolling.

The building was turn-of-the-century southern, with rough-faced brick walls on the exterior and plaster on the inside. The pressed tin ceiling he had admired for so many years had been covered by much lower and drabber white acoustic tiles. It lacked any of the real architectural substance of the decorative embossed tin, but it undoubtedly saved considerable expense in heating the place. In a compromise attempt, some of the antique woodwork details had been spared and the floor was still the heart-pine planking that had been too rough and uneven for the bean counters to cover with a low maintenance tile. The one "given" was a computer terminal in front of everyone, eliminating the rhythmic clicking of old mechanical typewriters, and replacing it with silent percussions on the keyboards of dozens of computers. All said, it was a nice blend of the old and new South.

The thing that pissed Oscar off the most about this transformation into a twenty-first century operation was the politically correct concession to health mongers, who demanded that no smoking be allowed in the building. They had even gotten the Fire Marshal to conspire with them. This meant Oscar's prized cigars could not be lit, depriving him of the cerebral impact nicotine had on his creative process. Their loss, he determined. Just to show them he hadn't been put in his place, he kept an unlit stogy in his mouth most of the time. That way, he could still gather a little of the taste he cherished and he had something to chew on when his own adrenaline got pumping. That didn't happen as often as it used to. He had pretty much seen it all.

Amidst all of this organized pandemonium, two dark-suited visitors looked out of place. Oscar spotted them immediately, and followed their progress from the main entrance of the editing floor to a runner who pointed them in his direction. His years covering the gamut of stories in South Carolina had made Oscar adept at determining people's occupation from their appearance. These two were not newspaper types... most likely government hired hands, and not locals. He surmised they were either from the Governor's office or one of the myriad federal agencies he had grown to despise. Professional problem originators he had deemed them. With an air of over-importance, they marched briskly towards him. Their trained countenance had been developed like so many other bureaucrats in an attempt to intimidate the general public into believing they held some kind of innate power over them. They should be respected, feared and responded to immediately. To Oscar, they were comical. He had walked in the presence of the most powerful men of his time and been treated as an equal. His reputation as an upright journalist, one who kept his integrity in a time when that was not the norm, had earned him the respect of everyone in his industry. The Pulitzer Prize he had picked up along the way did not hurt his stature either. These two intruders were obviously not aware of his history and approached him brusquely. The first to enter through his open door without knocking asked,

"You Oscar Phipps?"

He threw out the question as if he were owed an answer. Oscar played with them.

"Could be. But before I take any questions, I have a few

of my own that need answering. Who are you? Who do you work for and don't you think it's rather rude to come bursting into a private office without knocking, overlooking the courtesy of calling beforehand and asking if I had the time to see you?"

Taken back, the older of the two men, only about thirty, replied.

"I'm sorry, Mr. Phipps. You're right. I'm David Jernigan and I work for Senator Morton. He's ill and may not live. He's in a D.C. hospital and told us to come get you immediately, that is of course if you are Mr. Phipps."

"I am. Keep on with your story."

"That's pretty much it, sir. He had a stroke last night and the doctors said with his advanced age and condition; his chances at recovery are not good. He's very fragile, but this morning he called me in and said to come down here and bring you back with me no matter what it took."

Pleased with the young man's retreat to civility, Oscar continued to direct the impromptu meeting.

"Dwight Morton is an old friend of mine and if he needs me I'll certainly take the time to go see him. I know him well enough to gather that there's more to this than just his needing to tell me good-bye. You fellas get a coffee and park it here for an hour. I'll run home and pack a bag and be back shortly. There's a flight out of here to Washington at 4:30 p.m. everyday that we can make. You call and get me a ticket and I'll be ready to leave in time to catch it."

Jernigan reached in his coat pocket and produced an airline ticket.

"You're already booked, Mr. Phipps. Here's your ticket. Seat 17C- window."

Oscar smiled and as he hurried out, replied. "I'm convinced you work for Dwight now. Just stay here and I'll be right back."

"We have a rental car outside, sir. If you don't mind, how about we drive you to pick up your bag and then go straight to the airport? Less chance for a foul-up that way."

"I swear, you young government types are something else. Hitler would have felt right at home here. All right, let's go."

They exited through the swirling office, stopping only long enough for Oscar to fill in his Assistant Editor, Esther, on what was happening. That accomplished, they all hustled to the waiting car.

Oscar's small-framed house was dark and cold. Since his wife left, he devoted himself to his work and was home only a couple of nights a week. The high degree of cynicism he had developed by reporting the news for so long had been amplified by the bitterness of divorce. Aside from the paper he had no life. The truth of the matter was, he had always been married to the newspaper business and his wife just got tired of being the other woman. There was a couch in his office and had grown to feel at home there. He considered selling the house dozens of times but could never bring himself to completely let go of a time when there was more to his life than just putting words on paper. It had grown disheveled over the years, and gave him a depressed feeling when he spent much time there alone. He entered quickly, picked up a couple of clean shirts and pants, and threw them into a small overnight bag. He then retreated to the waiting car.

As they drove towards the airport, Oscar studied the narrow streets of Florence. It remained a wonderful time capsule of the old South. As the car went from block to block, the noise generated by its tires would alternate between the smooth, continuous hiss of contact with asphalt and pounding on sections of road still paved with cobblestones. They were brought over from Europe as ballast in the holds of sailing ships. Though he had seen most of what the country had to offer, Oscar still preferred his sleepy hamlet and the nostalgic feelings it gave him. Even though there were newer sections that could be interchanged with any commercial street in the United States with no one the wiser, there were still rows of general mercantile stores that had remained constantly in use since the turn of the century. There were many scenes from the ancient South that still remained and they always brought him back to his youth spent in such territory.

Ahead, half blocking the road, workers from the Royal Chicken processing plant were picketing as they had been for months. Several dozen protestors, mostly black, stood outside an eight-foot chain-link fence that surrounded the dirty red brick building. To the casual observer, it could easily pass for a prison. Nestled on a lane of old cedars and Spanish moss, the factory looked the same as it did eighty years earlier, with the exception of many layers of dirt and grime. The paper had been covering the strike and its occasional splattering of violence. Oscar asked Jernigan to pull over alongside the largest group of workers for a moment so that he could speak with one of their organizers.

As they pulled to a stop, Oscar got out and quickly walked over to the group's spokesman, Alonzo Chavis. Now in his seventies, Alonzo had been an activist for many years. He and Oscar met many times when Oscar was a reporter covering the volatile affairs of the civil rights movement throughout the South. Alonzo was always nearby. He was an eloquent speaker and even though he was often associated with more outspoken activists, Oscar considered him to be a moderate, with a reasonable frame of mind. They shook hands warmly and Oscar inquired as to how things had been going.

"Any progress yet? Everybody still talking?"

"Well, Oscar, after two months of getting nowhere, I'm afraid this is one battle we're going to lose. Most of our people just can't hold out much longer. The union is out of strike pay and management won't concede anything. I guess the struggle will just have to go on a little longer. Why don't you cut us some slack down at the Journal and look out for the black community on this one?"

The sparkle could be seen in Alonzo's eyes as he saw the possibility of working on Oscar's conscience a little bit. Though old by most people's standards, with a head of thick gray hair, Alonzo was large and robust, and the vitality he still possessed was directly attributable to his involvement in the civil rights movement. It had been his inspiration, foremost in his thoughts all of his adult life. He had a great laugh and enjoyed using it, punctuating every other sentence with samples, even when the topic was serious. He was hard not to like. By trade he was a pastor, as could be told by his black suit and clerical collar, but by avocation he was an activist. Here he performed his finest sermons.

Though friends for many years, their view of the

"struggle" differed greatly. Oscar never failed to address the issue as if his view couldn't be said too often.

"Alonzo, this is not a civil rights issue; it's an economic issue. The people who run this place could care less what color their workers are. Hell, they live in Connecticut. They just want the cheapest labor they can find, even if they're green. That's why they built this factory down south to start with, looking for low overhead."

"Brother, you ain't ever going to see it, are you? There aren't any green people out here on the picket line, now, are there? They're every one black with the exception of Hector and his family, and they might as well be."

"Well, old friend, you and I have been going round on this for a long time. I sympathize with anyone trying to get by on minimum wage, and there's no doubt in my mind that they're pushing the workers here, but it's not because of their race. Look, I'm going out of town for a short while to see Senator Morton. He's had a stroke and wants to see me. When I get back, you come down to the office and I'll see what we can do to get both sides back together and your people working again. What do you say to that?"

"Any help will be appreciated. That's too bad about Dwight Morton; I hadn't heard. Is he all right?"

"From what I've been told, he's in bad shape and might not make it."

"I hate to hear that. Now there's a white man who understands what it is to be black and poor. We never had no friend any better than him. You tell him that we will all be praying for him, you hear me?"

"I do, Alonzo. Well, I better run before these youngsters working for the Senator have a hernia. See you next week."

They shook hands once more and Oscar jumped back in the car. With Jernigan growing more concerned about time, they sped to the airport. It made Oscar chuckle to see sweat breaking out on the foreheads of his young chaperones. He felt most young people were tied up in a knot worrying too much about being successful. He knew because he had been there himself. At their age he could only have been described as "driven."

From the small airport in Florence, they caught a commuter plane to Charlotte. Oscar liked the boarding procedures in large airports over the smaller one in Florence. The more sophisticated docking ports had large snake-like tubes that protruded from the terminal to the door of each plane and it was easy to forget that you were getting ready to go thousands of feet into the atmosphere in a man-made machine. At the small airports you boarded by means of a step-like ramp that was literally pushed out to the plane. Oscar always tried to not look at the great quantities of grease and oil smeared on the wings in the areas near the engines. It gave him too much to worry about on the flight, as he never felt comfortable in the air.

Once in Charlotte, they'd connect with the main carrier for the rest of the flight. By the time they arrived there and made the connection, a heavy rain had started. Coupled with the approaching darkness, it lent a dreary atmosphere to the entire trip. Oscar planned on catching a nap on the way to D.C., but the stormy night was producing enough turbulence to cancel that prospect. So, in a half-awake mode, he let his thoughts drift back to his first meeting with Dwight Morton.

In the summer of 1947, the Broad River overflowed its banks. It ran southward towards Columbia, and just north of there, in the small town of Peak, the black community was completely washed out. Several residents drowned and the rest had no place to live. At that time, there was no mixing of the races; not socially and certainly not by living in the same communities. People of each race had their own section of town where they lived as if the other didn't exist. With no housing available to them, their plight was becoming quite serious. Oscar, working for a small daily in the area, was sent to cover the story. The whole question of civil rights was still an embryo at that time, and there were very few champions for such an unpopular cause, especially in the rural South. Dwight Morton was a wealthy farmer and merchant from a small town near Columbia. His family had been one of the first to run a large plantation in the area and their fortune had not only survived the Civil War, but the Great Depression as well. In fact, they seemed to prosper even when all around them, others faltered. The entire Morton family was an institution in the area, well known and respected. Dwight had inherited his father's share of the fortune while he was still very young. His father had passed away when Dwight was twenty, leaving a green kid to oversee huge farming and mercantile interests in the state. He was, however, cut from the same cloth as his predecessors and was up the task. He did have a peculiar side to him, though: he felt the calling to raise the flag of civil rights, even though it could possibly ruin his business. There were lots of folks being hung in effigy, and many crosses being burned by their neighbors in the Klan. Dwight's friends and associates tried to dissuade him from this course, but to no avail. Once he started in a direction, he rarely stepped aside.

He was disturbed by his neighbor's unwillingness to share their resources with the besieged black community, and decided to help them out himself. First, he had large tents brought into the area, and set up a temporary housing base, where black families could stay dry and watch out for their children until he could figure out the best course of action. It was there Oscar ran into him, under the canvas of an imported circus tent where they both found shelter from the continuing rain.

The first thing Oscar noticed about him was how tall and thin he was. He had a bushy head of white hair and thick eyebrows the same color. In manner and appearance he could easily have passed for a relative of Mark Twain. He walked a little stooped over, and had the warmest smile and most inviting personality of anyone Oscar ever met. Being one of two Caucasians beneath the tent, Dwight noticed Oscar's presence quickly, and walked over to him, hand outstretched. One would never have guessed he was one of the wealthiest men in the state. He was frank and engaging.

"Dwight Morton here, and you are, sir?"

"Oscar, Oscar Phipps. I'm from the Lexington Banner. I came to see how things were going here. It looks like they're making a little progress. Is the tent your idea?"

"My idea, my tent. And this is just temporary. I'll figure how to help these nice folks and, before long, this little flood is going to be the best thing that ever happened to them. We're going to make some big improvements in this community."

"If you don't mind my asking, why are you doing this? What's in it for you?"

"Peace of mind Oscar, nothing more. You a God-fearing man?"

"I'm a Baptist."

"That'll work. Are you not your brother's keeper? That's what the Good Book says we should be."

"Well, you just don't see people crossing color lines to accomplish that very much."

"Just stay here a few days and you will. That's a promise."

And so he did. Oscar remained long enough to watch a very unusual man undertake the impossible. The tents were soon replaced with a dozen or so small-framed houses and the beginnings of what would become Morton, South Carolina. To keep the town going, Dwight purchased land in the area and sharecropped with many of the families he saved. On a gamble, he dug out a large lagoon and dammed it up beside the Broad River. He imported thousands of baby catfish and began what would become Flood Catfish Farms. Very few would ever have seen the opportunity there. Later he explained to Oscar.

"Hell, in every misfortune there is opportunity. I'm just willing to consider misfortune the first step in an otherwise very sound business proposition."

Oscar suspected, despite the philosophical explanation, Dwight's real motives were purely humanitarian. He seemed to have a real affinity for the underprivileged, especially the black community.

As time went by, their paths crossed many times, primarily during tumultuous political upheavals. Dwight soon found that with few friends in the government, he would have to get involved himself, if any lasting changes were to be made. Two terms in the State Legislature were followed by victories in the United States House of Representatives and then the Senate. His political career made his name a household word. Even though many die-hard racists and segregationists despised him, he prospered in all he did and shared it with those less fortunate than himself. Oscar never questioned his motives.

Oscar's pleasant memories were interrupted by a sudden jolt. The plane had begun its descent. After a young stewardess gave him a polite reminder, Oscar put his seat in its upright position and buckled his seat belt. Through the window he could see very few lights on the ground. The stormy weather had the Capital shrouded. As the descending aircraft bucked its way through the storm-tossed sky, Oscar repeated his flight ritual. Even though he had flown hundreds of times, he always found himself making the same promise to his Creator: if He would just let him get on the ground this one time, he wouldn't violate the beautiful atmosphere with his presence in the future. Five minutes later he was on the ground. They bypassed the baggage area, Oscar having only a carry-on bag and his escorts a briefcase between them, and went straight to a waiting car. Through the slick, rainy streets they sped to the hospital.

Washington Metro Hospital was bursting with activity. In an area so dense with every manner of humanity, it was the norm. Senator Morton's being there, coupled with his high profile and the lack of current information on his condition, had resulted in a large contingent of news crews. In the parking lot, several media vans with satellite dishes mounted on their roofs stood out above the rest of the vehicles, and in the hospital lobby were at least two-dozen reporters waiting for a briefing on the Senator's condition. Jernigan showed his credentials to security and escorted Oscar through the halls, towards the room where Senator Morton was being treated.

It was not hard to pick out the Senator's room. Outside the door stood a uniformed Marine Corps guard and a Capital staff police officer. They were carefully regulating traffic in and around the hall. No one, especially the press was allowed near the entrance to the room. Jernigan and his cohort approached the guard, who recognized them, and explained who Oscar was. Jernigan's assistant turned out to be not such a bad sort, actually a very reserved and polite young man named Tom Bohring. Oscar kidded him that with his quiet nature and such a name, it was pretty obvious what his moniker must have been growing up. He followed them to the door of the room. As Jernigan entered, he was met immediately by a stern-faced nurse. She informed him that a team of doctors was examining Dwight at that moment and the staff would be attending to him for a while after they were finished. They should wait in the critical care waiting room until they were called. She was a woman not to be trifled with. Jernigan pointed out Oscar to her and asked if she would notify him when it was permissible to see Dwight. She agreed and the three men went back to the small lobby.

"Mr. Phipps, if it's OK with you, we need to run back over to the office and see what's happened since this morning. If the nurse calls you, just go on in. We'll be back before too long. And Mr. Phipps, don't expect a lot. It's a miracle he's still here at all."

"I understand. See you fellows later."

Oscar walked over to a small row of hard-backed chairs, grabbed a six-month-old magazine off a table and sat down. The chair was not much of an improvement over the airplane's gravel-stuffed corduroy stool, he thought. As he sat, he noticed the only other occupants of the small cubicle. They were two young black boys, one around sixteen and the other much younger, maybe five years old. They were ragged-looking with dirty sports jackets and blue jeans, and the usual set of oversize, unlaced, high-topped tennis shoes. These were also in pretty dismal condition with more than one hole in each boy's pair. He spoke to them.

"How are you young men doing tonight?"

The older boy didn't acknowledge that Oscar had said anything. As is so often the beauty of children, the younger boy sheepishly looked at Oscar and replied,

"Fine. My Momma's getting sir-gery now."

"Is that right? What's your name?"

"I'm Cody and this is my brother Marcus. He's fifteen. He plays football."

"Is that right? Do you play too?"

"No sir, I just watch."

"Me too, Cody. Have they told you anything about your mother, Marcus?"

Oscar directed the question to the older of the boys. It was clear that he was upset and nervous about the situation.

"She'll be fine."

The answer was curt. Here was a bitter young man. Cody spoke up again.

"My Momma's heart wasn't working right so the doctor is fixin' it. Ain't that right, Marcus?"

Marcus remained silent for an extended breath and then replied,

"She's gonna be fine."

Cody sorted through the magazines beside Oscar and his eyes lit up as he recognized a character on the cover of a children's book. He carried the book over to Oscar.

"Mister, Can you read this to me?"

Oscar was taken back by his trusting innocence.

"Sure, I'll be happy to....at least till a nurse calls me. Sit here beside me."

The young boy jumped quickly up on the adjacent seat and Oscar started reading to him. Once again, Marcus ignored them. Every so often, Oscar caught him sending a glance their way. The youngster sat quietly and took in every word intently, demanding to see the illustrations accompanying each page. After nearly an hour, Jernigan and Bohring returned.

"You still haven't been in yet, Mr. Phipps?"

"Not yet, but Cody here has been keeping me company."

Jernigan went over and spoke to the guard and came back over to join Oscar and Bohring.

"He says it won't be long. Just one nurse in with him now and she's just checking his blood pressure."

After another ten minutes, the Marine Guard came over to where the group was seated.

"Mr. Jernigan, you may go in now. They've finished working with the Senator."

Oscar stood up and handed the book to his young friend.

"Here Cody, save our place and maybe we can read some more later."

"Thanks mister.....what's your name?"

"I'm Oscar."

"Thanks Oscar. Me and Marcus will be right here if you need to read some more."

"OK, I'll see you fellows later."

Dwight Morton was in bad condition. His body was attached to numerous hoses and monitors and if his eyes had not followed the three men as they entered his room, it would be easy to assume that he was already on life support. His wife Dorothy had died many years before and with no children of his own, there were no relatives there to comfort him. With all his worldly accomplishments and fame, he was getting ready to take his final journey alone, with no loved ones there to see him off. Oscar studied the sadness of such a scene for a moment as he moved over to the bedside. Dwight's eyes fixed on his, and the old man gamely lifted his hand several inches in the air for Oscar to grasp, which he did.

"Hi Dwight, it's Oscar. I've come to see how you're getting along. You don't look so bad. How are you feeling?"

Dwight shook his head weakly in a negative response. The bushy head of white hair was still there, but the bright blue eyes were dimmed and the pallor that accompanies the elderly during their final hours had descended upon him serving notice to those around him that these were his last hours. He was thin and the skin on his arms looked as though it were stretched over his skeleton. His complexion was waxy and his body was cold to the touch. There was no need to try and cheer him up. He knew the prognosis of his situation only too well. He squeezed Oscar's hand a little tighter and began to whisper. Oscar leaned over to try and hear. There was an urgency in his frail whisper.

"Oscar, thank you, thank you for coming. I need to talk with you before they carry me away from here. I'm not going to make it this time and I need you to help me set a few things right."

"I'm here, Dwight. Whatever you want, old friend. What do you need to tell me?"
Even in his weakened state, he searched his mind for the right words.

"Get a chair and some coffee."

He looked at Jernigan as he said it and the look was enough. David had worked for the Senator long enough to almost read his mind.

"Can I get you anything else, Mr. Phipps?"

He shoved a chair towards Oscar as he spoke.

"Just ask, one of us will be here around the clock."

"Coffee and a sweet roll sound good. I'll be talking with Dwight while you're gone."

He fumbled around in his overnight bag and produced a pad and pencil and a small cassette recorder.

"OK, Dwight, is there anything we can do for you before we get started?"

He shook his head again and Oscar could see the tension in Dwight's gesture.

"All right Dwight, what do you want to talk with me about? I'm gonna take notes and record you if that's OK with you."

Dwight slightly nodded yes. Oscar set the recorder beside the pillow in an attempt to pick up as much of the conversation as possible. The Senator, slowly and with the faintest of voices, began to speak.

"I'm dying, Oscar. I haven't got much time. It's OK, I'm an old man and I've had a good life, no regrets. But there's something that happened a long time ago, sixty years or more, that I've got to clear up. I want you to be the one to hear it cause I trust you to tell this the way it should be. You've known me for a long time. The things I've tried to do I don't want it all ruined by this. You'll know how to put it in the best light. I want to tell you about a young man I knew a very long time ago. His name was Pickle Mather."

"Pickle?"

"That's right. Like a cucumber. Pickle Mather."

As the old man began talking about the past, his eyes seemed to brighten a little. Oscar's curiosity had been piqued, as he knew the Senator to be a serious individual. Either his condition was bending the normally rational intellect he possessed or Oscar would be hearing something that Dwight Morton considered pretty damned important.

"You know, Oscar, I wasn't born in Columbia. I grew up in Lydia, just a little west of Florence in your neck of the woods."

"I had heard that somewhere before, Dwight. Pretty country."

"It is. Now don't interrupt me; I lose my train of thought too quickly. It was a different world then, one I liked a lot better. I really miss how simple the times were. Not that we didn't have our share of problems. It's just that they were our problems and we could usually work them out. We didn't have fifty different special interest groups dictating how everything was going to be handled. Hell, maybe we should have. Anyway, it was about I guess....1925 or 26. My family lived out in the countryside on the most beautiful farm you ever saw. Over two thousand acres we had. It was as manicured as the White House lawn and I loved every minute I ever spent there."

CHAPTER TWO

"Nineteen twenty-eight was a good year in the South. Just enough rain and sun to bring in a good crop. The war in Europe was over and America was in a good frame of mind. Not that the world situation played any great part in the day-to-day affairs in Lydia. Folks from Florence, which was already a booming city, would ride out to the area around Lydia on weekends to get back to their roots. Time had stood still there since the years after the Civil War. Most of the locals had never even accepted that the war was over and that the South had lost. If it weren't for a few memorials and bronze markers at the courthouse and a goodly number of graves in the local cemetery, the event would have gone largely unnoticed in that sleepy little community. Everyone there liked it that way. Change came about very slowly in that part of the world. "

Dwight Morton was only eighteen years old at that time. As he walked along the dirt road that ran beside a two hundred acre crop of corn, he looked out over the hands working the fields and admitted to himself that he loved the sight and smell of farming His family owned almost all of the land surrounding Lydia. It comprised a large plantation that had been called Fountainside since the Revolutionary War. Under the shrewd eye of the Morton family, it had prospered for the past two hundred years. They were good businessmen and saw the value of land utilization and crop rotation years ahead of their peers. Their interests had grown into the feed and fertilizer business and eventually into almost every profitable area of the mercantile business. As they prospered, they invested in banking and acquired any piece of land that others found too cumbersome to keep. They in turn would cultivate it and turn it around into profitability in a few short years, in an ever-expanding spiral of wealth and influence. Dwight Morton was born into this very privileged setting in 1910.

Dwight walked along the white sand road that connected Fountainside to the main road into Lydia. Though only May, it was already sticky hot. He held his school shoes in his hands as he walked. He loved the feel of the soft grains of sand as they pushed up between his toes. It reminded him of visits to Wrightsville Beach and warm ocean waters. He was a senior at the Lydia School, a compendium of grades one through twelve where every school-age citizen of the community attended. He was excited that this would be his last few weeks of school and soon he would be off to the University of South Carolina. He occasionally accompanied his father on business trips to Columbia and he loved the hustle of the big city. At the time, he didn't realize that the few years he had spent around Lydia as a youth would come back to him as the most wonderful of his life. He was living in a stoic, elegant world that had remained constant for many years. A world of security, warmth, large magnolia and live-oak trees draped in Spanish Moss. Even on his deathbed these scenes would play through his mind. On this day, his thoughts were on his future. He had a rendezvous scheduled for the evening with Dorothy Blair, or "Dot" as he called her. They had been sweethearts since childhood and everyone in the community and both of their families gladly accepted the fact that one day they would marry and continue both of the families' traditions. Though not as wealthy as the Mortons, the Blair family was prosperous by most people's standards and had been prominent in the area for years. Dwight appreciated every aspect of Dot's personality and the warm and nurturing side that she shared so readily with those who knew her. She was tall and thin with dark blonde hair and a radiant smile. She was striking in a natural way and didn't need to dress up to catch the eye of any man in the room. Her preference was to roam the countryside with Dwight in a pair of denim jeans. That was very uncommon for a young woman during that time. Dwight loved her thirst for adventure and felt since early on that he had found the perfect soul-mate for life. She felt the same about him.

    As Dwight entered the main house at Fountainside, he could hear his father talking to an employee beside the verandah of the ancient antebellum home.

    "Damnit Emory, if it turns out to be one of ours, I want him fired and turned over to the authorities. We treat our nigras better than any other farm in the county and if they need something to eat they know they're always able to get a chicken or vegetables right here. I mean it now, if it turns out one of ours took the cow, let me know. You hear me, Emory?"

"Yes sir. You know I will, but I'm sure it wouldn't be one of ours."

Emory, the farm overseer and a decent sort, quickly dismissed himself from his irritated employer. Robert Morton, Dwight's father was upset over the theft of a neighbor's cow. It had been implied that perhaps one of the many Negroes that the Morton's employed had taken it for their own. The Morton's had the same Negro families in their employment since before Robert was born and he had grown up with many of them. He felt certain they were not involved.

"That you, Dwight?"

"Yes sir. What are you fussing about Dad? Can't start that tractor you bought? I told you Emory was right about sticking with the mules."

"Dwight, you have to be willing to spend a little on innovation to stay ahead of everyone else in this business. I'm willing to bet you we'll all be using tractors before it's over with. They don't get tired, no broken legs and they won't kick you. What're you up to today? Where's Dot?"

"We're going out tonight with some friends. We won't be too late. Can I have a buck in case we want to get a drink or something?"

"Sure, you be careful and should you wind up over at White Lake, don't swim after dark by yourself. Got it?"

"Yes sir. Let's eat."

They entered the old home together and joined the others in the large formal dining room. There was always a big meal at supper time and the family often invited visitors or friends over to share it with them. After wolfing down two helpings of virtually everything on the table, Dwight dismissed himself early and ran out to the Model T roadster to go pick up Dot and their friends for the evening. He might make fun of his father's tractor but he would readily admit he loved being behind the wheel of the car as it flew down the dirt lanes at speeds of over twenty miles per hour. It was so fast he could barely make out the faces of people sitting on their porches as he passed.

Dot was waiting in the wooden swing on the front verandah of her home. Dwight pulled up in the T model, the engine popping and spitting as he stopped. Dot yelled to her folks.

"Mom...Dad.....Dwight's here. I'll see you later. Bye!"

Her mother came to the screen door and waved to her as she ran to meet Dwight.

"Y'all be careful. Dwight.....look out for my baby now and don't speed!"

"Yes ma'am. She'll be looked out for just like you were with us."

Dot smiled as she leaned over the door and hugged her man.

"Such a line. They know what you've got on your mind."

"And that is?"

"Why, dancing all night, of course."

"I swear, Dot, you're gonna get them wondering about me if you don't quit that."

"Momma loves you more than I do. I don't think you could make her upset at you."

"Well, that's good to know."

Dwight opened her door and gave her a polite 'your parents are watching' kiss on the cheek and shut the door behind her. The car spun around in the dirt lane and they proceeded down the road, absorbing the remainder of the dust cloud that still remained in the air from Dwight's approach moments earlier. The sun was setting quickly and the lane, covered as it was with live oaks forming a virtual tunnel, became dark enough to need the headlights. The evening was still warm and the breeze from the open top felt good to them.

"We still going to the lake, Dwight?"

"Absolutely! Got your swimsuit with you?"

"What makes you think I'm going to wear a suit?"

"I think that maybe Zeke and Rachel being there might encourage you to be a little discreet."

"Rachel told me that she and Zeke go skinny dipping up there all the time. You aren't chicken are you?"

"I like the word modest. You're not serious are you?"

"I might be."

"Sometimes I worry about you, Dot. You've got some hot blood in you don't you?"

"I'm just a modern woman, Dwight. Don't you approve?"

"I definitely approve of you. I'm just somewhat old fashioned myself. Don't let that stop you though. Be as progressive as you want. Just don't get us in hot water. I like having this car to drive and my folks are definitely old fashioned about most things."

"You might be surprised. Parents don't tell their children much about those things. How do you suppose you got here? Holding hands?"

"OK, OK, I give. You want naked, you got naked."

"You're silly, Dwight. You know I'm just teasing."

"You're wearing me out."

As they rounded a bend in the lane, they both saw the glare from headlights of several vehicles parked in a field to the side of the road. Dwight slowed down to see what was going on.

"That's Bill Moore's truck, I think. I wonder what they're doing out there. Maybe they hit a deer. There's been a lot of them on the road lately crossing over to the river to get away from hunters. Let's go see."

"Be careful, Dwight. They might be moonshining. My dad says Bill Moore runs liquor at night to clubs back in the county."

"You'll be safe with me. I know most of these fellas. Dad sells 'em feed on credit. They won't be out of the way."

They pulled into the middle of three vehicles that all had their headlights shining on an area just in front of the woods at the back edge of the field. They were not prepared for what they saw. In the center of the converging beams of light a young black man sat on his knees. His hands were tied behind his back and a rope was draped around his neck in a hangman's fashion. As Dwight and Dorothy approached, he picked up his head and they both realized immediately who it was.

"It's Pickle! What are you fellas doing to him? He works for us."

Bill Moore became the spokesman for the group of a half dozen of the worst elements of the community.

21

"This here nigger stole one of Ralph Cutter's cows this morning. We tracked him right to his place."

"Did you find the cow there?"

"Naw, he's pretty smart for a darky. He's got it stashed somewhere or he's already slaughtered it."

"So what are you doing with him? You should just take him to the Sheriff and swear out charges against him. He's got a right to a trial."

"We already tried him. He's guilty as shit and now we're going to give him his just punishment."

"Which is? From the looks of this, you're getting ready to hang him."

"Well, that would be just as good, but, actually we're just gonna take him on a ride."

"A ride? To where?"

"Nowhere special, just down this here road a piece....behind my truck. Don't worry, we don't plan on killin' him. No sir, we want him to go back home lookin' real pretty so that the rest of his kind can see how we feel about this sort of thing around here. They won't be stealin' cows anytime again soon."

"Bill, I can't let you do this. He works for us. If he took the cow, we'll pay for it and we'll see that he gets punished."

Pickle, feeling like he had just slipped out of the hangman's noose, spoke to Dwight.

"Thank God Almighty, Mr. Dwight. I never stole no...." His words were quickly stopped by a backhand to the face from one of his captors.

"Shut up, nigger. You're not being spoke to so shut your mouth."

Dwight, beginning to get very upset at the proceedings, realized that these men were a dangerous group and that he would have to be careful what he said. He also knew he was not going to let them hurt Pickle any more than they already had, cow or no cow. Bill Moore was a particularly large and nasty sort. Weighing more than two hundred pounds with a mouth full of chewing tobacco, which dribbled out of his mouth and onto his chin as he spoke, he was a man prone to bring trouble into most any situation. The stream of black ooze which worked out of the corner of his mouth and down his face was more than likely wiped with the back of his hand and then transferred to the front of his bib overalls. The most distressing thing about him was his ability to gather others of his kind; roughnecks who were willing to follow his lead without exercising any rational thought. This night he had an assortment of ne'er-do-wells and other troublemakers looking for some excitement. Dwight knew they would not be stopped easily.

"The way I see it, Mr. Silver Spoon in Your Mouth, this ain't none of your damn business. That's the way I see it. What do you make of that?"

"Bill, there's a young woman present and she doesn't need to hear a bunch of foul mouth and certainly not see somebody half-killed."

"You brought her. And nobody asked either one of you to be here. So why don't you just leave before......well, before it gets unpleasant."

Dwight steeled himself. He wasn't leaving without Pickle who was now bent over to the ground, half sobbing and scared to death. Pickle was already beaten up thoroughly with most of his face bloodied and his eyes swollen.

"Here's how I see it, Bill. We leave now and Pickle comes with us. He'll be at our place if you have any proof he stole the cow and want to call the Sheriff. If you want to stop us you'll have to deal with my father and the Sheriff yourself and I will press charges."

Just as he spoke, a large fist crashed into the side of his face. Moore pulled back and was delighted at his show of courage in front of his cronies.

"I guess you might say I don't give a shit what you or your family think."

Dwight was afraid that it was getting out of control and decided to play his best hand out right then.

"You're going to remember that punch every time you need to buy feed or hay on credit, or groceries, or even cross over a lot of this county. And you fellas, are you willing to stake your livelihood on beating up a young colored boy? Better think about it. I know most of you and I'm willing to let it die right now and forget this happened. Otherwise, this will follow you all a long time."

Even Bill Moore was sobering up at this forecast of what might happen. They all knew the Morton family controlled most of what went on in this part of the state. They were in over their heads.

"Hell, take your nigger and get out of here. He knows we mean business. He won't be stealing no cows for a while. You hear me....BOY?"

Dwight and Dot both reached down and helped Pickle to his feet. He could barely stand without help.

"Thanks Mr. Dwight, Miss Dorothy, I'll be all right. Let's just get out of here."

Without further words, they all went back to Dwight's car. Pickle was helped into the rear seat and they took off for Fountainside. Dwight thought that would be a better choice than the hospital as his father needed to be consulted about the situation before any decisions were made, and Pickle's injuries, as bad as they were, did not seem to be life-threatening. No one said it but they all could not help but think about what might have happened to Pickle if they had not come along at just the right moment. As bad as Pickle was hurting at the time, crowding into the small T-Model and being pressed tight up against Dot was doing wondrous things to his spirits.

As they pulled into the front yard at Fountainside, Robert Morton walked out to greet them.

"Back awfully soon, aren't you, son? Car trouble? Good gracious, Pickle! What on Earth happened to you?"

Dwight answered for him.

"Bill Moore, Ray Browning and few of their drinkin' buddies said Pickle stole one of their cows and they were going to drag him behind a truck for a short while, just till they killed him, I'm sure."

"Those damned idiots. Let's get him inside. Dot, hi darlin', would you go ask Mrs. Morton to call Doc Stevens for us? Come on Pickle, we'll get you fixed up."

"Don't you worry 'bout me Mr. Morton, I'm gonna be jus' fine."

As Dot ran ahead, Dwight and Robert helped Pickle get inside the main house. Mrs. Morton and Dot washed his face and dressed the cuts and bruises. They were relieved to see most of the cuts and scrapes were not serious.

"Pickle, is the alcohol burning bad? These cuts need to have the dirt cleaned out of them. You don't want any of them to get infected."

"I'm jess fine, Mrs. Morton. I'm so glad I'm here instead of back in that field that most anything you do is gonna feel good to me."

After several hours, the doctor had come and gone and Pickle was resting comfortably. As suspected, he had no serious injuries. Feeling greatly relieved about the evening's events, Pickle was left to rest in an upstairs bedroom and his rescuers went into the dining room to have a cup of coffee and settle their nerves.

The Mortons and Dot were seated at the supper table and the conversation became nostalgic recalling when Dwight and Dot were small. Dwight teased Dot about how she had been such a tomboy.

"The reason I didn't ask you out on a date until you were fifteen is that I didn't know you were a girl until then. You stayed covered in dirt and wore bib overalls practically till you finished tenth grade."

"You're playing with fire... Before you start, remember, I know a few things about you too! Don't get me started."

"All right, I know what you're going to say, so I'll change the subject. You   win."

"That's better."

"Dad, do you think Bill Moore and those rednecks will leave Pickle alone?"

"They better had. But just to be safe, I want him to stay close by the house here for a couple weeks. I'm going to put the word out to a few folks that I don't appreciate them tampering with my help and that it better not happen again. Might even have the Sheriff drop by and pay them a visit. I can sympathize with somebody having their cow stolen but we all know Pickle wouldn't do it. You know I don't believe in abusing my darkies."

Dot was uneasy about the whole thing.

"I've known Pickle since he was a little boy and he wouldn't take anything. His momma would tan his hide if he even thought about it. My folks used to let me stay at her house when I was young and Momma Mather told us the best stories. Pickle and I would listen as long as she would tell them. I remember teaching him how to read. He's real bright and I always wished somebody would pay for him to go up north to college. Do you know that they have black doctors and college teachers up there?"

Dwight's father, though a decent, fair-minded person, carried around a lot of the southern stereotypes of blacks that would be with him till he died.

"I'm sure they have a lot of things up north we don't down here. Yankees for one. The North and South are still very different and I hope it stays that way. Never met many folks from up there that I cared a great deal for. And black folks have been working for white people for two hundred years around here and most of 'em like it that way. They couldn't make it on their own. Some of them are real good workers, but learning is not their strong suit. Won't be any black teachers or doctors around here during my lifetime."

Dot was amazed that he would say such things with the black maid and butler within hearing distance. They had worked for the Morton family their entire lives with little chance for any reward other than food and the most modest of possessions. What was even more tragic was the fact that the Mortons were generally considered to be "soft" on blacks by most of the community. Dot was strong in her support.

"I just don't think it's right they don't have a chance for a good education or decent jobs. A lot them are just as smart as we are and it's just not fair. Pickle is a nice young man and we played together the whole time we were growing up. Then I got to high school and my folks said that I should discourage him from coming over. I think my father even told his momma to keep him away. Anyhow, he just quit coming over and every time I see him now he acts embarrassed and won't even look me in the eye."

"Well, Dot, there's a lot of history preceding you that one or two people are not going to change and you might as well not worry yourself sick over something you can't do anything about. Why don't we change the subject? How are your folks doing? I saw your mother a few weeks back and she said your dad's back was bothering him."

"Yes, sir, he hurt it again messing around with one of those old hay balers."

"He needs to back off some of that physical work and let the younger folks have their turn at it. I've been trying to do just that. Besides, I'm real fascinated with the banking business right now. I've bought into that new bank in town and I believe it's going to be one of the best investments I've ever made. Got a good man running it too. The oldest boy of Richard Fulbright. Name's Nathaniel, Nathaniel Fulbright. He's well educated and comes from a fine family. He sees what's happening years down the road and uses investors' money to buy into it. You ought to tell your father about it. Tell him I said to come over one morning and I'll take him right down there to meet him myself. It would be a good thing for him to look at and it might get him away from hay balers. You know what I mean?"

"Yes sir, I'll tell him tonight when I get home. And Dwight, you better let Rachel and Zeke know we're still alive. They're probably wondering what on Earth happened to us tonight."

"I'll see Zeke first thing in the morning but I'll guarantee you we didn't change anything they had planned."

The evening passed into another graceful southern night. The soft light from the parlor drifted out into the dark and tagged the shadows of the magnolias and Spanish moss surrounding Fountainside. Pickle recovered and went back to the small shack that he lived in with his mother. It was only about a quarter of a mile down a dirt road that began at the backyard of Fountainside and continued through a ramshackle neighborhood of sharecropper's cottages. This was where people who made their living in the fields of the great plantation lived. Most were paint bare and sparsely furnished with only the most basic of necessities. Some had large cracks in the siding with rags shoved into them to help hold the heat. There were only a few that had hand pumps on their porches and residents of the others would have to go to a community well to get their water. The roofs were varying shades of brown and red due to the rusted tin used to cover them. Each shack had an old brick chimney that kept a steady stream of smoke pouring through it continuously during the winter months. With no insulation, letting the fire go out could have serious consequences on a cold winter night. Generally, one or more residents of each shack would arise several times a night and make sure the flames had plenty of wood or coal to keep them alive. They also served as ovens in most of the shacks. That meant that even in the summertime a fire remained a necessity at mealtime. This created the ever-present danger of fire. In large homes such as Fountainside, the kitchen was built separately from the main part of the house as a safety precaution for just such an event. A small shack didn't have that luxury and an errant spark had claimed many a life in the tinderbox dwellings.

This small collection of shacks was a world unto itself and this is not to say it was an unhappy place. It was filled with children's laughter and the evenings found it a magical village of great storytellers and musicians. As many white children played there during the daytime as black. They were comrades in arms up until the mandated separation occurred in their early teens. Most would look back with fondness on this time in their life. On this particular afternoon, Pickle was hard at work on the back porch of his family's shack. His mother, who'd been watching him on and off, could contain her curiosity no longer.

"Pickle, what on Earth are you up to? You ain't worked so long in a stretch since I can't remember."

"Makin' a present, Ma."

"A present? For who?"

"For Miss Dorothy. If she hadn't come along with Mr. Dwight, I'd be layin' up there on Potter's Hill 'bout now. She was real good to me while I was getting well too. It was just like when we was little again. I wants to make somethin' for her. It's goin' to be a special thing box where she can keep stuff that's important, like rings or letters and stuff. I'm going to keep sandin' these planks I got from that old tobacco barn that fell. I'm goin' to get it as smooth as a baby's ass, Momma. Pretty, ain't it?"

"You do have a way with your hands, Pickle. But I got's to tell you that a lot of white folks are funny about a black boy givin' things to a white girl. You hear what I'm sayin', don't you?"

"This will be just between Miss Dorothy and me. She ain't like that. While I was up at Mr. Dwight's and she was nursin' me, we was talkin' 'bout all the good times we used to have when we was little. You remember, she 'bout taught me how to read by herself. I learned better with her than both years that I went to school. She takes her time and don't make me nervous. Readin' is hard if'n you get too nervous."

"Well, Pickle, just the same, you make sure there ain't nobody sees you give that to her. You hear me?"

"Yes, Momma. I understand."

Pickle continued sanding until the wood was virtually like satin. Once he was satisfied that he could do no better, he oiled and hand-rubbed it thoroughly to bring out the most shine possible and make it last. As the final step, he carved into the bottom, "For Dorothy, Thanks, Pickle, 1928."

Pickle had learned how to use hand-tools by watching the workmen in the farm workshop as they worked on the machinery that kept the farm going. He had a good feel for working with wood and had made up his mind to follow that course.

Being small framed and thin, he had long ago determined that the fields were not for him. He could remember his daddy telling him many years earlier, "to white folks, field hands is just like the crops they pick, they's only worth what you can get out of em." He had died of consumption when Pickle was only ten, but his advice had remained with him.

"You know somethin' Momma?"

"What's that Pickle?"

"I believe that if Papa were alive today, we'd be livin' in a nice house 'bout now. I can remember him talkin' 'bout buildin' us a new place, not on the row here. You remember that, Momma?"

"That seems like a long time ago, Pickle. You still remember a lot about your daddy, don't you?"

"I think about him a lot. I used to love to go fishin' with him on Sundays after church. I think that was just about the best times I ever had."

"Well, son, maybe one day you'll be takin' your own boy fishin'. That'd be real nice. And maybe you'd let Grandma Mather come with you."

"We wouldn't never go without you."

"That'll be real good' son. But don't be running away from home too quick now. I'd miss you too much jess yet."

"You sure don't have to be worryin' bout that. I'd have to have a gal first and I sure don't have no idea who that'a be."

"Don't you worry, Pickle, the right one'll come down that road outside one day and you'll know her right off."

"You think so?"

"I know so."

Whenever Sunday proved to be warm and hospitable, Dot walked home from church along Brice's creek. This Sunday was no exception. She held her shoes in her hands and waded in and out of the shallow parts of the stream as she walked. It was a clear, swift stream which ran alongside the road for over a quarter of a mile. She loved the sound of the water as it fell over the dark rocks and rushed around the bends in the stream. Every so often there would be a group of turtles on a branch in a section of quiet water, and now and again, she would surprise a deer or a raccoon that had stopped to refresh itself. She had loved Brice's Creek ever since she could remember and she passed many summer days on its banks. Pickle considered it one of his favorite haunts also and determined to take the chance he would find her walking there this Sunday.

The anticipation of presenting Dot with his masterpiece kept Pickle in high spirits the whole week. He got up early and grabbed a cane fishing pole, some worms, and headed for the creek. The day was warm and the sun high in the sky very early.

He picked out a favorite spot and proceeded to pass the time fishing till after church. In short order, he caught a fine mess of bream. Not wanting to deal with them or the accompanying smell, he released them as quickly as he caught them. He knew his momma would be upset with him if she had seen the supper that he had put back in the stream; especially knowing how much she loved the taste of fresh fish.

As the midday heat began to build, he found a shady spot under a live oak tree and dozed off, pole still in hand. He was awakened by a massive pull on his limber fishing pole.

"Caught you, didn't I? You thought I was the granddaddy of all bass."

Pickle looked up and saw Dot holding the end of his fishing pole.

"You sure did, Miss Dorothy. You liked to caused me to jump in the creek."

"From the looks of things I don't need to ask how you're doing. I don't see any fish."

"I've caught a few, I sure have. Been letting 'em go."

"That's one of the oldest fishing lies there is Pickle. I always say show me the fish."

"I thought you might come by this way on your way home from church, Miss Dorothy, so I brung you something."

He reached down and picked up the small present, wrapped as best he could with a brown paper lunch bag.

"This is for you. Kinda a thank you present for what you and Mister Dwight did the other night. I know I woulda been in bad trouble if you hadn't come along like you did."

Dot excitedly opened the package and beamed with approval at the small box.

"It's beautiful, Pickle! It's a jewelry box, isn't it?"

"I calls it a special box where you can put anything special, like a ring or letters you want to keep. It ain't much I know, but I don't have a lot of tools or stuff to work with."

"You made this?"

"Yes ma'am. I hope you likes it."

"I will treasure this, Pickle, and I'll show it to everyone and tell them you made it."

"You better not be telling folks that I made that for you, Miss Dorothy. A lot of 'em wouldn't understand about us being.....friends and all. You know what I'm sayin'."

"I do. I'll just tell them that I asked you to make it for me cause I knew how good you were with your hands. They'll all be wanting one."

"Well, it makes me real pleased to know that you like it."

"I'm going over to the Mortons to meet Dwight and his family for lunch. You want to walk a ways with me to Fountainside?"

"No, ma'am, I'm just going to stay and catch a few bluegills for my momma so she don't mind me coming down here when I wants to. I'll see you later."

"Thanks again, Pickle."

She walked off, shoes still in her hands. In her yellow cotton dress, with her lovely smile and radiant charm, Pickle thought she surely was the most beautiful person he had ever seen. She never acknowledged that she had any awareness he was black and always treated him with the utmost sincerity. He knew he could never tell anyone how he truly felt about her. The South was not a very understanding place for thoughts of that nature. He knew only too well.

As Dot walked down the old dirt lane on her way to Fountainside, she took great delight in the white sand that formed the road. It would be no whiter if it were on the beach. The road was lined on either side by live oaks that expanded across it to the point it gave the feeling of walking through a great cave. On the hottest days it was cool and balmy. With their ancient gnarled and twisted trunks and great sheets of Spanish moss in their crowns, they painted a scene in her mind of how the old South must have looked before her time. Dot found it funny how most southerners felt about the few remaining plantations. Many of them had the peculiar characteristic of being nostalgic for a time that they never actually knew; only what they had seen remnants of. It never dawned on them that during those years, most people, black and white, were dirt poor and that only a few, very privileged families lived in those beautiful homes with servants in abundance. Nonetheless, she loved the South and everything about it. It didn't bother her that she lived in a tiny town with only one schoolhouse, one church, a few stores and a railroad station. It had charm and grace and besides, the things she loved the most about it were not in town anyway, they were in places like she found herself this afternoon.

As she walked, she pulled the box Pickle had given her out from the paper bag. She studied it carefully, appreciating the amount of time it must have taken him to make such a lovely thing. When she was young, she spent a great deal of time with Pickle and his mother. She could picture in her mind those pleasant days at the Mather shack. Mrs. Mather cooked and washed for the Mortons and had been in their employ her entire life. She was large and robust, always singing and praising the Lord. She lent a happy atmosphere to any room she entered and was a favorite of the Mortons. She had been a good mother to Pickle, growing up as he had, without a father. She had practically raised many of the white children from the surrounding farms. Those children loved to spend their summers in her care as she made each of them feel special and would take a great deal of time to talk with them, to hear what they were thinking about. This was something that did not occur very often in their own homes as it was still a time for children to be seen and not heard. Not so with "Momma Mather", as the kids called her. Dot loved her and thought she might go visit her one day soon. Pickle had been a favorite of Dot's and she spent many an hour playing with him, even though he was several years her junior. She taught him to read and had read him many of her favorite childhood stories. She could not imagine a time or situation in which she would not consider him a friend though most of the other white children had discarded their black childhood acquaintances as they got older. Pickle and Dot had covered every inch of the countryside together as kids and even later, with Dwight, they had pursued many adventures down this same country road.

After getting closer to Dwight and a little older, they had not spent many days in those pursuits of childhood. Even though she still thought a lot of Pickle and his mother, she just didn't get by to see either of them as she had in the past. She would make up for it later in the week. She would spend an entire day with

them and even have supper with ho cakes and cane syrup. Her
mouth watered at just the thought of it. Maybe Dwight would
want to go also. She would ask him later during lunch. There
was no way that Dorothy could know just how much Pickle loved
her. She never thought of him that way and she could never understand the dream she represented to someone coming from the
poverty and realities of the situation Pickle had grown up in. It
was ironic that they could have spent so much time in the same
place and not even be in the same world. Ahead, Dot saw the
white columns of Fountainside, framed in the arch of live oaks,
just the way it had appeared for over a hundred years. She could
see Dwight and his father leaning against the black T-model roadster in the drive by the porch. As she came into view, Dwight ran
down the road to meet her.

"You walked? Why didn't you tell me you were going by
the creek so I could have walked home from church with you?"

"I didn't make up my mind 'till after you left, and besides,
I enjoy being by myself sometimes. It doesn't mean you weren't
on my mind. I thought about you most of the way."

"Really? You're teasing, aren't you?"

"Maybe. Just remember that if you want me to be thinking about you when you're not there, you have to be extremely
nice to me when we're together."

"Oh, I see. Bribery."

"Call it what you will. That's just how we women are.
The weaker sex you know."

"What a load of baloney! Come on inside. Momma said
she hadn't spent any time with you the last couple of days and she
wanted you to talk with her when you got here."

"OK, see you in a few minutes."
Dot walked ahead to the dining room where Eileene Morton was
preparing for lunch.
The house was mammoth. Though she had lived there for years,
it always made her feel that she was in a museum. There were
large oil paintings in gilded frames covering many of the walls.
The faces they carried on their canvas represented eight generations of Dwight's family. In the older paintings, the subjects were
clothed as if they were residents of a castle in old Europe, with

their lace and opulent attire. The foyer of the home was immense with a grand stairway that spiraled its way three complete revolutions before landing on an equally impressive setting on the second floor. The furniture was very old and would certainly have qualified as antiques. There were elegant pieces of Victorian furniture that would never fit in a house of normal dimensions. With oriental rugs, bronze and marble statues on pedestals, and even a grand piano, it was a home that would have been extraordinary in the largest of cities. There were many rooms in the mansion but very few were used any more as the family preferred to be in the parlor or the large dining room.

Conversation was the main entertainment for everyone and many spirited debates raged with family and friends after supper each night. Mr. Morton was quite the orator and enjoyed playing the devil's advocate, taking opposing sides on the same issue in successive arguments. He tried to engage Dwight as much as possible but his son was his principal supporter in all he did and said. If his father had said the sky was green, Dwight would agree with the man who he thought could do no wrong.

Sunday lunch was always the largest meal of the week and quite often there would be many guests present to either socialize with the most prominent family in the area or just to visit, as was most often the case with relatives. Dot expected to find a crowd there this afternoon.

"Why, Dot, don't you look lovely in that dress today."

"Thanks, Mrs. Morton. Can I help you do anything?"

"I guess you could set the table since Mildred is busy checking on the turkey in the kitchen. Set enough places for six if you would dear."

"Yes ma'am. Who's coming today?"

"Well, Robert has asked that young banker Nathaniel Fulbright and his wife over. He says it's so we can meet them but I'm willing to bet he just wants to talk business with him. He says he's as smart as a whip. He's got Robert all stirred up over the banking business. I suppose it's a good business but I just like farming. My daddy always said to stick with what you know and that's pretty much how I feel. Besides, I don't like the thought of having all our friends and neighbors looking to us to borrow money when they're having troubles. Can't do anything except cause hard feelings. Imagine if you had to foreclose on someone's farm that you knew. A lot of the small farmers are just hanging on by a thread and one bad year could ruin them. I just don't know if it's something we should be getting involved in."

Robert Morton caught the tail end of the conversation as he entered the room.

"Now dear, don't go bad-mouthing the banking business. People have to have banks and credit in order to run businesses today. None of them have enough cash on hand at any one time to keep a business going. It's actually a very good, needed service and I might just make a lot of money in it."

"Well, don't try and sell me on it. You do what you think you should. I'm quite happy right here on the farm."

"I'm glad. That's right where I want to keep you, down on the farm. Now please don't be putting down the banking business while they're here. I tell you what Dot, she's a strong-minded woman. Makes me toe the line all the time."

A car pulled into the driveway and Robert Morton went to welcome his guests. During the next two hours, Dwight learned several things about Nat Fulbright. First and foremost, he could not stand him. From the moment they were introduced and Fulbright said "nice to meet you son," to Dwight who was only his junior by several years, he knew this was one pompous pretty boy. He was conceited and arrogant and Dwight could only guess that his extensive vocabulary of business terminology must have excited his father. He was overly polished with black hair slicked back with what looked like motor oil to Dwight and Dot. He had enough pearly white teeth for two mouths and he would expose them every time anyone said anything. If his father spoke, he smiled affirmatively on every subject. If his mother spoke, he smiled affectionately. If Dot spoke, he smiled seductively even though his own wife was present and if Dwight spoke, he smiled condescendingly. They would never be friends. Furthermore, he didn't trust him and would try his best to sway his father's business interests at the bank in another direction. Dwight always valued Dot's opinions on matters of character and in his assessment of Nathaniel Fulbright, she was in agreement. After the rather awkward lunch was over, the guests left and Dot and Dwight dismissed themselves to walk through the fields around the house. Dot held on to Dwight's arm as she spoke.

"You know, I wish we spent a little more time walking and visiting with some of the folks we used to see, like Momma Mather. Why don't you go with me to spend an evening with her some time?"

"You pick the time. I'll go have some of her ho cakes any time you say."

"Great! I really do miss her, and just walking down the road together, I really enjoy doing that."

"OK, you're on."

"Did I show you the present that Pickle made for me?"

"No, what did he do?"

"It's the most beautiful little jewelry box. He made it out of an old plank from a tobacco barn. He said it was for us helping him when Bill Moore and his thugs were going to hurt him."

"Boy, I guess that says a lot."

"What do you mean?"

"I get my chops busted, risk getting killed and he makes you a present. It's a man's world all right."

"I guess he realized if you couldn't handle them that I was there to back you up."

"You're probably right. Show it to me when we get back. I'd really like to see it. Now for more serious matters, when are you and I going to tie the knot? You know you can't let a 'catch' like me run around loose, not with all the pretty girls in the county just champing at the bit to get at me."

"My, but you're awfully high on yourself don't you think?"

"Would you settle for less than the best? I rest my case."

"I guess you have a point. Are you sure you're ready to get married?"

Dwight turned and pulled her close up against him. He looked sincerely into her dark eyes as he spoke.

"Since the very first time I saw you. You have always been and always will be the only woman for me. I love you, and I want to spend the rest of our lives together, right here, taking care of Fountainside. It would be a perfect situation, the right man, the right woman and the most beautiful place on Earth."

"You are a charmer. Do you promise to take me fishing and horseback riding whenever I want to go? Even if it means dropping what you're doing?"

"I promise."

"OK, you've got a deal. I'll marry you whenever you say. Spring has already passed. How about a beautiful Christmas wedding? That would really be special, and everyone would come because they would be visiting anyway."

"Sounds wonderful. If you're sure, I'm going to tell our folks."

"I'm sure."

They kissed and embraced. They had no idea of the paths they would be taking or the trials they would encounter during their life together. All they understood was that they were right together. It was not a pact entered into lightly and in this one decision, they had both made the correct choice.

CHAPTER THREE

The months prior to Dwight and Dorothy's wedding were wondrous. They spent the long warm nights walking down the road and talking about their future. Dwight had determined to learn the farming business inside out. Dot decided to pursue what had been a dream of hers for as long as she could remember. She would open a school for young children and its doors would be open to anyone regardless of race or whether they had any means of paying for an education. She enjoyed reading and helping the kids experience the magic of the books that she loved so much.

She had cleaned up an old shop building close by the main house and along with Dwight was anxiously preparing it to serve as her first classroom.

"This is going to be great, Dwight. You know, a lot of the kids back in the row have never been to school. This will mean so much to them. It could change the course of their entire lives. You know that, don't you?"

With sweat pouring off his face and his clothes almost black from removing layers of dirt, he responded with a grin.

"Probably so....I know it's changed the course of mine. I could have been down at the tobacco sale today with my father. Not that I wouldn't rather be with you."

"You better. Won't this be wonderful? I'll be able to have my own class here in a couple of weeks. The books I ordered should get here by the first of the week. I'll go over the lessons for a few days and then...I'm in the school business. Just like we talked about."

"The only problem I see is that a business generally makes money and I can't picture the kids you're wanting to teach being able to pay anything to attend. Am I wrong?"

"You know I'm not going to turn down anybody just because they're poor. They need an education just like anybody else. If I teach for free, so be it. I'll still do it."

Dwight came over and grabbed her around the waist from behind, lifting her feet off the ground and spinning her around the room.

"You are a feisty young thing, Miss Dot, I'll give you

that."

"And you need a bath."

"Hey, the sale would have been clean. This dirt came from obeying the wishes of the woman I love."

"As well they should. Give me just one kiss. Lips only! No dirty hands, thank you."

Time passed quickly and the long hot summer days gave way to fall and the approaching holiday season. Dot took in her first class of delighted kids and Dwight continued helping his father run the farm. Farm communities loved the fall as their crops would be harvested and they generally had a little extra cash to buy the things they'd been putting off all year. And of course the holidays were the perfect excuse to get together with families and friends. Dot saw to it that none of the children in her school attended without a coat or decent shoes. Dwight suggested a new name for her venture; the Christmas School. He said it jokingly but Dot loved it, so that is what it came to be called.

Coupled with the festive Christmas spirit and all the relatives and neighbors dropping by, the time passed quickly. By anyone's standards, Dot and Dwight's wedding would be the most impressive affair ever held in Lydia. No doubt there would be dignitaries and business associates of the Mortons, coming from all over the state. It was the main subject of conversation throughout the tiny community. Fountainside was being groomed for the affair. Fresh paint on the main house and fences was underway. The grounds were being manicured while Eileene Morton and a number of her friends were busy getting the house decorated and prepared for the extensive entertaining that would take place. Dwight and Dot took in every moment with delight. Living as far out of the mainstream as Lydia was, all the excitement and bustle was refreshing, and to be the focus of it all was quite an experience.

Robert Morton had been stressing to Dwight that this was not only his wedding but his own coming of age affair. He would meet the men with whom his father did business. These were men that he would soon need to conduct the affairs of Fountainside as had his ancestors for many years. One day it would all be his and these connections would prove to be very important. His father was wise in the affairs of business. Dwight understood this and always paid close attention when his father explained to him how the family enterprise was run. His father felt that he would one day be leaving it all in capable hands with Dwight. The Mortons were generally liked throughout the county. They had their detractors though most of that vein could be directly attributed to jealousy. One thing for certain, this would be a memorable Christmas in the town of Lydia.

Carlton's Barber Shop was the hub of all tales, both true and false. It was situated in the dead center of Main Street and six days a week, rain or shine, it was packed with the area's well-heeled and shoeless. Everyone knew each other and the family history of everyone who entered. The conversations ranged from politics to sex to religion and the discussions occasionally got heated. The group present this particular morning was witnessing a very exciting debate. Bill Moore was dragging the Mortons over the coals and virtually antagonizing anyone who was willing to speak on their behalf. In his usual dirty bib overalls and railroad cap, with a mouthful of chew, he spewed out venom between discharges of the brown sticky tobacco waste.

"There's nothin' special about 'em. Their granddaddy came here and got all the land for nickels and dimes before it was worth a damn. They's just lucky that they got borned into a family that already had more money and land than it could use. Me or you, that kind of start and no telling how rich we'd be. Why I know I'm a better farmer than old man Morton. I been makin' a living off a measly ninety acres and two mules my whole life. If I ever had a stake, I could've made a killin'. They ain't got nothin' over me but luck, and that's the whole damn truth of it."

From the corner chair, getting a shave, an observer of the proceedings spoke out. It was Nat Fulbright.

"I wouldn't underestimate that family if I was you. I know them quite well and they strike me as extremely intelligent and very aggressive. Perhaps the younger Morton is not as sharp as the old man, but I think they seem to be quite on top of things."

"Well, that's just one opinion mister. I ain't never had no love for none of 'em and I ain't the only one. A lot of the boys and me know 'em for what they are."

"And that is?"

"Troublemakers and nigger lovers. Why, we caught one of their niggers stealin' and was all set to teach him a lesson when that worthless son of his came up and threatened us if we didn't set him free. Told us that we'd never get no more credit at the feed mill if we didn't let him go. So, just what the hell do you have to do with 'em? You work for 'em or something?"

"No, sir, I run the bank that opened this year, just down the street. They're one of our largest customers and also an investor. Without Robert Morton's wise insight, there would not be a bank here."

"Well, that explains why I don't know you. You ain't got no need for somebody that ain't got no money to put in your bank."

"That's just not so, sir. We are in business to lend money also. If you are as good a farmer as you say you are and have a decent track record, I'd certainly talk to you about financing your crop. Do you own your land?"

"My family's owned the land for a hundred years. We own it clean. I sure don't want to borry no money against it."

"Nonetheless, come by and talk to me sometime and I might be able to make you an interesting proposition. You might say I'm quite interested in your opinions."

As the wedding day got closer, the focus of the entire community was squarely placed on Fountainside. On the morning of the wedding, the great house was a cauldron of activity before the sun came up. There were three large striped tents with their sides rolled up erected on the large expanse of lawn adjacent to the main house. In respect to the season, the six mammoth columns on the front of the house had been wrapped in garlands and each had a five foot diameter wreath mounted at head height. The front door had a wreath also as did each window all the way across the front of the home. Inside there were candles on each window sill and the entire interior was a combination of the best of traditional Christmas decorations and a formal southern wedding. To the most callous hum-bugger, the sight instilled a wonderful holiday feeling. A stringed quartet played in the foyer and the Mortons waited just inside where they greeted the arriving

guests with a cup of Robert's special recipe eggnog. He and
Emory Walker had stayed up late making several gallons the previous evening. Robert swore to Eileene that it was mostly milk,
eggs, vanilla extract and the standard makings, but Dwight had
seen enough local brewed liquor go into it to make a funeral a festive affair.

Pickle was elated. He'd been chosen to welcome the
guests at the front door of Fountainside. For the occasion he'd
been fitted with a tuxedo that sported a red cumber bun and
matching bow-tie. With his white gloves and spit polished shoes,
he felt the part and was extending the warmest of greetings to
each guest as they arrived. Momma Mather had been up since
dawn supervising the kitchen along with Eileene Morton. The
smell of frying chicken and fresh coffee was everywhere. Most
everyone in the community was present as either a guest or a vol-
unteer to help in staging the affair. Robert Morton had predicted
as many as a thousand guests would come during the course of
the day. The wedding was to be at 1 p.m. and the reception
would start at 4 p.m. and continue until everyone had enough.
Dwight was the apple of his father's eye and nothing would be
spared. The family's connections and power extended far beyond
the tiny community of Lydia, much more so than most of their
neighbors could even imagine. Today, they would see to what
extent their influence had spread.

Dwight and Dorothy were being sequestered from one another until the ceremony began as was the custom. Though mild
for December, the temperature was in the fifties and the sun was
shining. Even the mild chill could not keep Dwight from sweating.

"How do I look, Dad? I'm sweating like a dog."

"That's normal, son. I couldn't eat for two days before
your mother and I got married. Lost ten pounds. You'll feel better once the wedding's over. Tonight's gonna be real special at
Fountainside. Hasn't been this many people here in a long time.
You and Dot couldn't be a more perfect match if you'd been de-
signed for each other, so quit worrying. I'm the one who should
be worrying; I'm having to pay for all this."

"I know, and I really appreciate it. Dot always wanted a

big wedding. I'd say she's getting it. I'm sorry it's costing so much."

"I'm just joking. Your mother and I have been looking forward to this as much as you two. Let's go meet a few folks, what do you say?"

"Fine with me."

Dot was in the upstairs bedroom that had been set aside for her and Dwight as they would be living there for a while. At least until they decided what direction they wanted to go in. It was an assumed fact that Dwight would eventually be running the family business and his future was right where he had been born. Dot seemed much calmer about the day than Dwight. For her, it was the fulfillment of all her dreams and expectations. She had never considered any other option than this. Dwight had been her first and only love.

"Mom, how much longer?"

"Two hours, sweetheart. Just relax."

"I can't. I'm too excited."

"You know you can't see folks until after the ceremony; it's tradition. You look so pretty."

"Thanks, Mom. Are there a lot of people here already?"

Margaret Blair walked over to the window and surveyed the constantly growing crowd.

"I'd say there's several hundred in the yard and the house sounds like it's about to burst with people. You aren't getting nervous, are you?"

"No, I'm just ready for the ceremony, and then I want to dance all night with Dwight."

Dot's mother sat down on the large canopied bed and patted next to her indicating that Dot should sit down also.

"What, Mom? You've got that 'serious talk' look on your face. What's on your mind?"

"I just feel that I need to tell you a couple of things and now seems like a good time, since we're basically stuck in here until the wedding starts. Dwight is a fine young man and your father and I could not be happier about the two of you getting married. We always hoped you two would remain close. You're so much alike. I guess what I wanted to say was that even though you get along good and for the most part won't have a lot of the financial problems that most young couples do, you shouldn't think that it's going to be all downhill. Marriage is tough. It's a lot of compromise and patience. You have to love someone enough to let them do things their way sometimes, even when you know they're wrong. And, a family like the Mortons has a lot of friends, but they also have a lot of people who don't like them."

"Why is that? I've never heard anything bad about them. Not ever!"

"It's mostly jealousy I'm sure, dear, but nonetheless, you can't have as large an influence as their family does without having some hard feelings. You're going to be a Morton soon and I just don't want you to think it's all going to be easy. Nothing ever is. But, you and Dwight think of each other first, always, and that's what will make the difficult times workable. That's what your father and I have always tried to do and I'm convinced that is what it takes to make a marriage work. I'm sure you and Dwight will have a wonderful life and I hope that you'll do one thing for me."

"Sure mom, what do you want?"

"Grandbabies, and soon."

The two women embraced with tears of joy flowing. This was a special moment and they both knew it.

Robert Morton and Dwight made the rounds, shaking everyone's hand and paying their respects to the many guests, some of whom had traveled a very long distance to be there. An invitation to this wedding indicated a certain prominence in the business affairs of the entire state, and there were virtually none who did not come if they were invited.

"Dwight, this old timer here goes back with me a long time."

Robert extended his hand warmly to a distinguished looking, gray haired gentleman who looked to Dwight to be someone of importance. He had great bearing. He smiled broadly and threw his arm around Dwight.

"I haven't seen you since you were a puppy. A fine young man you are now. John Richards, Dwight."

"Governor Richards?"

"At your service. Now tell me, son, are you going to stay out here in the sticks running this farm or do you have a taste for a little larger arena, say for example Columbia?"

"I've seen the capital and I love the city, but I would miss Fountainside too much to ever go away for long."

"I don't blame you, son. I miss the times your father and I had back here when we were young. Those were some fine times, weren't they, Bob?"

"They certainly were, John. Things were a lot simpler then. I think about how it was back then a lot."

"Well, if you ever get interested in a political career, you just give me a call, Dwight. I could use a smart young man like you on my staff."

"You're serious?"

"I'm real serious about my staff. You want to try it, just let me know. I don't promise things like this unless I'm serious. Except of course to constituents every few years and nobody ever expects a politician to keep election year promises. That reminds me Bob, elections coming up next year. I'm counting on your support if you know what I mean."

"I do. I just need to wait till the crops are in..."

They all laughed and continued to make their rounds meeting all of the guests, with special attention given to some. Dwight could see that his father was somewhat of a politician himself. This was a side he hadn't seen before but he always assumed his father knew how to handle these sort of relationships since the family businesses required it.

By all accounts, the wedding was beautiful. Dot was radiant and she and Dwight looked as though they'd been removed from the top of a classic wedding cake. After exchanging their vows and what some thought was a pretty lengthy kiss, they fled under a shower of rice to the grand staircase and upstairs. After a while the orchestra began to play and as the first shards of darkness fell across the county, the old house filled with music, soft lights and laughter. Dwight and Dot danced until they could not stand without holding on to one another. It was a grand day both would remember as long as they lived. Neither had any forewarning of the horrendous times that lay immediately ahead - for them and for the entire country.   They were closing the final page of a beautiful story. This day would be a fitting epitaph for a time and setting that would never be again.

CHAPTER FOUR

Nineteen twenty-nine brought the prosperity and optimism of the twenties to an abrupt end. Across the country, businesses were closing and people were being thrown on the streets in numbers unheard of since the post Civil War era. No section of the country went untouched. In Lydia, small farmers were being evicted in record numbers. Because the previous years had been so bountiful, most had borrowed against their crops or mortgaged their land to expand. The banks that had so easily extended credit during the good times were now foreclosing on farmers in an effort to stay afloat themselves. Hard cash was disappearing from their everyday life. Never had a dollar been so hard to come by. Even at Fountainside, where Dwight was now working side by side with his father, times were becoming difficult. Fortunately they were not in debt. In fact, with his father's large investment in the Lydia Bank, the Mortons were in the uncomfortable position of being a major owner of the bank that was putting many of the families they had known all their life off their own land. More than one neighbor had come by, hat in hand to ask Robert Morton to speak with Nat Fulbright on their behalf, to try and buy them a little time; to see if maybe they could make it to the next season. Having closely monitored the bank's financial condition and certainly knowing what was happening to many banks across the country, the elder Morton knew there was very little he could do to help them. The bank was in a precarious situation itself and he didn't feel he could ask Nat Fulbright to take any unnecessary risks that could possibly involve his own family losing a substantial amount of their cash. Their money was needed to see Fountainside and all the families dependent on her solvent. It bothered Dwight considerably to see these impoverished farmers all but crying as they asked for help. Robert would always agree to see what he could do and he always added;

"Don't let your family go hungry. You can get corn and vegetables or even a pig right here any time you really need it."

It was mid-December, almost one year since the festive wedding at Fountainside. Dwight and his father were up early as usual, lining up work schedules for the reduced crew that was operating the farm. Frost was still on the ground and their breath was punctuated by smoke-like bursts from their mouths as they spoke. Dwight felt invigorated by the chill. His father would complain about the cold bothering his bursitis as usual and mumble a curse word every time he had to bend over. Out of the early morning fog, the easily recognizable sound of a T-model could be heard on the dirt lane. A dirty black pickup truck with the cab full and several men in the bed came to a stop in front of the farm office. They all hopped out and approached the building looking for Robert Morton. Robert recognized all of the men; most were friends and neighboring farmers. Wearing worn overalls and patched jackets that showed the hard nature of their occupation, their lined faces displayed the strain that was becoming the main force in their lives. Irving Brown, who Robert knew the best of the men in the group, spoke up.

"Morning Mr. Morton....Dwight."

"Good morning, Irving; gentlemen. What can I do for you this morning? Looking for some feed? I've got a load coming from Florence in the morning that I could let you have a little of."

"No, Robert, that's not why we're here. We've come to speak to you about the bank. About that damn Fulbright. We want you to speak to him on behalf of all the farmers here. Others would have come with us if they thought it would help."

"Well, I've already made my case for several of you men and I guess you see my hands are somewhat tied. I'm an investor, a sizable one as you all know, but banking laws and foreclosures and things of that nature are regulated by the State and I can't just interfere with what they're doing at the bank, even if I wanted to. You know I've tried to help you as much as I could."

"You have, Robert. You've been a good friend to all of us and we appreciate it. Our problem is not with you. That son-of-a-bitch Fulbright has gone too far. He's lied to several of us about getting extensions on our loans and told us that if we missed a payment, he would tack it on the end of the loan. So, we skip a payment, just like he said we could, and the next thing you know the Sheriff and that asshole hired by Fulbright show up with a foreclosure notice giving us twenty days to vacate the property. Take a look at this. They just come to my place last night."

He handed the legal notice to Robert, who examined it and returned it to him.

"It looks legal, Irving but I'm shocked that he would lie to you. He's done this to more than one of you?"

"Every one of us here is losing our farms, our homes. It's a damn shame; that son-of-a-bitch is going to own the whole county the way it's going. A couple of us let it get around that he better not get too far away from his office and next thing you know, his thugs show up and rough us up. Broke old Medlin Taylor's nose. Medlin's almost seventy. Damn, I wish I'd been there. I'da showed that Bill Moore a thing or two. That's for damn sure."

"Bill Moore? He's working for Fulbright?"

"He's his main strong-arm. Him and a couple of other rednecks have caused trouble for anybody that questioned what he was doing. We're either going to get fair treatment or we're going to find a tall tree and a short rope and entertain Mr. Fulbright and Bill Moore one evening.....soon!"

"You can't go taking the law into your own hands, men. I'll go see Fulbright in the morning and see if I can reason with him. He'll have to listen to me, that's for certain. Promise that you won't do anything of that sort until I've had a chance to get all this straightened out. OK, Irving?"

"We respect you, Robert. That's why we're here. If you say you'll try and help, that's good enough for us. Let us know after you talk with him, what was said. I want him to know that we're not gonna just walk away from farms we've lived on all our lives and let him have them. That's not going to happen."

"All right fellas, you'll hear from me within a couple of days. That's a promise."

The men all nodded in agreement. They shook Dwight and Robert's hands and left. Dwight could see the growing concern on his father's face. He was normally unshakable and reserved, but the problems on the farm and in the community were beginning to show on him. He was in his fifties and Dwight knew that he was not feeling up to all the agitation that was filling his days. Dwight determined to take as much of the load off his father as he possibly could. If this was to be his farm and his life, he would start taking a stronger stand in its affairs. He had disliked Nathaniel Fulbright since he first met him and he never trusted him. Dwight decided that he would go with his father and confront Fulbright with the accusations of these men. It was time to let this pompous oily headed upstart understand his ranking in the community.

Dwight and Robert Morton were up by dawn and off to town. Robert Morton always addressed a problem head on and at the first possible moment. The Lydia Bank was the most if not the only imposing building in town. It was a new building and its architecture contained detailing and trim that was normally found only in the more prosperous cities. This gave it an air of affluence and solidity that a bank requires to attract investors. It seemed that the reasoning was, "if we're making so much money that we can afford to piss it away, then why not let us handle your money for you; then you'll have money to waste also." The bank had been funded by a few large investors, and their prominence and influence in the region convinced the not-so-prosperous to put what money they had in the bank or to borrow there. It was certainly more convenient than driving all the way to Florence and making loan arrangements with people they didn't know. The idea made sense and the bank had grown in the short time since it was founded. Besides, a home town bank made everyone feel the town was growing and there was a future there.

None of the illusion impressed Dwight. Nathaniel Fulbright rubbed him the wrong way. He had been against his father investing so heavily in the Lydia Bank from the start, mostly because of his distrust for its President. Had he been a little older and more involved in the family's affairs at the time, he surely would have protested vigorously against it.

As they parked between several pickup trucks and a couple of mule drawn wagons full of hay, they both saw something that lent credence to the testimony of the farmers who told them what Fulbright was up to. Though it was a full fifteen minutes before the bank would open at 9 a.m., the front door opened and from it exited Bill Moore and two other men, all of whom Dwight knew were present the night Pickle was harassed. This convinced them what they heard was probably true. Fulbright was using investors' money, strong-arm tactics and the economic realities of the depression to make a land grab from area farmers. Dwight could see his father's face redden and the veins in his neck grow large as he set his jaw. Very seldom had Dwight seen him this angry. Together they walked up to the front door and pounded at the locked entrance to the bank.

A teller came over and peered through the blinds to see who was there. After recognizing the Mortons, she went to Fulbright and got permission to let them in. She came back and unlocked the door for them.

"Good morning, Mr. Morton. Is this your son? My goodness, I haven't seen him for several years. You're certainly grown up now, aren't you?"

"Yes ma'am, he is. Tell Mr. Fulbright I need to talk with him right now."

The woman immediately responded to the unpleasantness in his voice and went to Fulbright's office. She quickly returned.

"Come with me, Mr. Morton. He'll be right with you."

They followed without speaking. The Mortons wanted no pretense of being glad to be there in anyone's mind. Fulbright, dressed like the peacock he was, rushed over to meet them, hand extended and the snake oil salesman's grin wide as usual.

"Good morning, good morning, Robert, and you young man, how is married life setting with you?"

Dwight did not respond. Robert Morton replied instead.

"This is not a social call, Fulbright. I need to speak with you in your office."

Fulbright's fake smile quickly left his face and he motioned for them to follow him. They entered his overly done office and much to the pompous banker's dismay, Robert seated himself behind Fulbright's desk in his tufted and pleated red leather chair, not in the much less ostentatious chairs that were reserved for customers in front of his desk.

"Excuse my arrogance in sitting here, Fulbright, but I want to make it perfectly clear to you whose money bought this chair. Grab a seat and listen."

Feigning total ignorance of why they could possibly find any fault in him, Fulbright casually sat down.

"Why, Robert, you seem upset. What's the problem? What can I do to help?"

"You can shut up and listen, Fulbright. I've got a lot of money tied up in this bank. I know your family and trusted you largely for that reason. That, and I felt the city needed a bank if it was going to grow and its citizens, our neighbors, were going to have a chance at a decent future. Whether you believe it or not, it was as much for the city as it was for us. Not to say that I didn't expect for it to be profitable; that's what business is all about. But from what I've been hearing, you've been using the bank as your personal gun to rob these same people of their land."

Still flashing an occasional smile, Fulbright tried to speak.

"Robert, you don't believe for a moment that I would....."

"I thought I told you to shut up and listen, Fulbright. I'm here to talk, not to listen to you deny that you know what this is all about. I'll make this real short so you can understand what I expect from you. First, I want a board of directors meeting called, and I want to see the mortgages and notes on any property that you've foreclosed on in the last twelve months. That includes any that are behind or in danger of being foreclosed on. I also want to see any notes that were behind that changed title-holders to prevent foreclosure. What I'm saying is, I want to know who got the property if it changed hands and the notes were paid up. You understand this, Fulbright?"

"Yes. I believe I do."

"That's good. Call the directors today and set up a meeting for the end of this week. And by the way Fulbright, if it turns out that any of this property wound up with your name on it, you're going to be doing some very interesting explaining in Columbia before the State Banking Commission. Don't bother to show us the way out."

Dwight and Robert Morton hastily exited. Dwight could not remember being more proud of his father. He always felt his father believed in fair play and treating others right. He just wished that the rest of the town could have seen how he had stood up for them. And was it ever great to see Fulbright sweat! As they headed back to Fountainside, Dwight could contain himself no longer.

"You handled that real well, Dad. Fulbright almost crapped in his pants."

"I wanted to make him nervous and see what his eyes did when I confronted him. I can always tell if a man's lying by looking him right in the eye. I guarantee you that most of those farms have his name on the deed now. I really feel for his parents; he does come from a fine family. His father and I had a lot of dealings over the years and I would have trusted him completely. The son is not half the man his father is."

"Well, I just wanted you to know that I was real proud of you. One day I'm going to tell your grandchildren about it."

"Hey, let me tell them. By the way, there aren't any headed this way, are there?"

"You'll be the first to know. Well, at least the third one."

CHAPTER FIVE

Momma Mather stoked the fire until the flames filled the center of the old brick hearth. Her cabin was small and drafty. On a bright day, light could be seen filtering in between the cracks of the old lap-strake siding and mud that formed its walls. It had been built originally to house slaves and could only be described as Spartan. It had been home to many generations of Momma's family and now she and Pickle called it theirs. She maintained it as best she could and it was quite comfortable for the two of them. One thing that stood out in the minds of the many children, both black and white that she had cared for there, was the continual smell of fresh baked bread that filled it. Most just guessed that so much fine baking had taken place there that the very walls had become permeated with the wonderful aroma. It was more likely that she kept fresh baked bread and biscuits there for the better part of her fifty odd years. There was no doubt that the lady could cook.

As paint-bare and dilapidated as the exterior was, the inside was as warm and inviting as Momma could make it. There were pictures of family members on the walls and shelves and lots of interesting cutouts from the magazines she got from the Mortons. She had hung several of her homemade, patchwork quilts on the walls and they not only added a wonderful mix of color and atmosphere they also served as excellent insulation. She made many such quilts over the years and very few homes in the area did not have at least one to show for her efforts. During the warm months she kept the outside porch covered with flowering plants and when the colder days came, she spent her free time crocheting and knitting. All this was of course sandwiched between caring for the many children entrusted to her hands.

This particularly cold winter evening found her readying a meal for two people who had practically grown up there alongside Pickle and the others she had cared for. Dwight was keeping his promise to Dot and trying to have supper with Momma and Pickle at least once or twice each month. It was not as if he was doing her a favor, since no one loved her cooking more than Dwight. As they arrived, Momma hugged them both as she would her own children and welcomed them to her humble home.

"Lord bless me, you chilin' has all grow'd up now. I miss havin' you around here. I'm so glad you've been comin' to have supper with me and Pickle."

Pickle sheepishly shook Dwight's hand and Dot gave him a warm hug.

"Hi, Pickle, we couldn't wait to come have some of your Momma's chicken and see both of you. Remember when we used to do this every night? I loved it then and I miss it more than I ever thought I would."

Momma, though very plain spoken, could perceive the truth in all matters of the heart.

"When you gets older, your mind jess' discards the things it don't want to remember and it kinda' paints the good memories with real bright colors, and that's a fact. I had sure missed you two. Pickle and me talks about you all the time."

Dot pulled out a small package from her bag and handed it to Momma Mather.

"This is for you, Momma."

"Lord, child, you didn't have to bring me nothin' but your-selves."

She quickly unwrapped the package to find a gold embossed King James Bible with her name on it.

"We knew you'd love this Momma. I'll come and read it to you real often and Pickle can read it for you when I'm not here."

Even though she could not read, Momma recognized the names of each chapter and with only the first words of a verse, she could finish almost all of them by heart. The gift touched her.

"Well, Miss Dorothy and Mister Dwight, this is as fine a gift as a person can get. I'm gonna keep it in a special place I has, right by my bed. Now you two come on over and sit down. I'll get you a plate and we'll just try some of this fresh bird that Pickle brought home for us."

After a while, the conversation turned to Pickle. He was seventeen now and Dot was concerned that he not become just another hired hand or a sharecropper.

"Pickle, what are you planning on doing? You know you

should be going to school."

"That sounds real fine, Miss Dorothy, but I need to stay and help Momma, and I really don't mind workin' in the wood-shop. Dwight's daddy has been letting me build all of the shipping crates and I've 'bout learned how to use all the tools in the shop. One of these days I'm gonna start building things like tobacco barns on my own."

"I know you're very good with your hands, Pickle, but you've got too good a mind to not go on with your education. There's a school in Virginia called the Hampton Institute. It's a black college, and lots of teachers and even black doctors and lawyers went there. You could do it if you wanted to."

"That would surely be nice, Miss Dorothy, but we don't have no money for school."

"That's not going to hold water here, Pickle. Dwight and I will pay for you to go if you'll agree to it. Won't we, Dwight?"

"If Dot says we'll do it, we'll do it."

"Well, let me think about it a while. It sounds real temptin' but I would have to think a lot about leaving home and all. I've never been out of the county. Did you know that?"

"Well then, that's just more reason why you should go there. Momma, you make him do it....OK?"

"Pickle's a lot like his father, bless his heart. He's got a stubborn streak a mile long. If he makes up his mind to do some-thin', he'll do it come Hell or high water. Been that way all his life. But they's right Pickle, you can't never 'mount to nothin' without schoolin'. You think about what Miss Dorothy be sayin' here, you hear me?"

"I will, Momma. Course I don't know why anybody'd want to be a black lawyer round here. Black man gets into trouble here, they jess hangs him. No trial, no lawyers needed. You don't need to tell me, I been there, ain't that so, Mr. Dwight?"

"Pickle, there's some truth in what you're saying but I think things are going to be changing in the next few years. There's an awful lot of white people that are unhappy about the ways things are, too. They just need something to make them take some initiative. It'll happen. You can count on it, sooner or later. Then, if anyone needed an attorney, black or white, you'd be here ready."

"If I did go to school, it wouldn't be to become no lawyer. I'd be a teacher and teach kids how to read, just like Miss Dorothy did me. That'd be something good I think."

"You're right there, Pickle. You think about it now. You decide to go and we'll help you. That's a promise."

As night fell across the warmly lighted shack, their laughter rang out across the rows of similar huts that dotted the dirt lane behind Fountainside. Familiar sights and sounds had reverberated here for many, many years. When it was quite late, Dwight and Dorothy said their goodbyes to Pickle and Momma, promising to repeat the evening again sometime soon. Dwight had to rise early to help his father get the farm's workmen about their tasks. Into the cold winter evening, the young couple began walking back towards Fountainside.

"You know, Dwight, I love it when it's cold like this. It's invigorating."

"It makes me anxious to get home and stir up the fireplace in our room and then....."

"Yes...go on, and then....."

"Maybe stir up a few fires of our own."

"Now you're talking like the man I married."

Dwight put his arm around Dot as they walked. It was cold and dark but neither of them minded. They were together in the best of all worlds.

As they approached the last bend before they reached Fountainside, they both noticed an orange glow in the sky ahead. It only took a moment to realize there was a fire lighting the entire horizon.

"Oh God, I hope the tobacco curing barn hasn't caught fire again. As late as it is, it'll be burned to the ground before we could get enough help to put it out. All our tobacco is in the big curing barn. Let's hurry."

They both quickened their pace and half-walked, half-ran towards the lighted sky. As they got to the final straight section of road leading up to the house, what they both saw sickened them. There, framed in the center of the tunnel formed by the large live oaks bordering the lane, they could see Fountainside totally engulfed in flames. Dwight began racing towards his home with his heartbeat outpacing his legs. He was growing weak in the knees just seeing the magnitude of the fire. He could see several dark shadows running around the house trying to fight the flames but it was obviously too late. He just hoped everyone was all right. Dwight ran up to Emory Walker, his father's foreman.

"Where are my parents? They're OK aren't they?"

"I'm sorry, Dwight. I don't think they got out. I was the first one here and the house was already a fireball. I'm real sorry. I don't know what to say."

Emory's words tailed off as Dwight's mind began to reel. He could not believe this was happening. His mother and father and his whole world gone in just a few moments. He ran around the house looking for any possible way in or out, hoping that at any second his parents would come up and tell him that they had been outside when the inferno erupted. Helplessly, he and the others watched as the siding disappeared and the large rafters and sills began to appear like the skeleton of a great ship left abandoned on some distant beach. Before too long, these great bones fell onto the foundation also, leaving only a few of the massive columns pointed skyward to remember what had stood there for so long. He sat down on the cold ground and placed his head into his hands and wept like a small child. Dot came up quickly and kneeled beside him. She said nothing.

By now there were dozens of people trying to help put out the fire. Emory showed the men how to hook up a large hose to the water tank that supplied water to the animals during the dry months. By the time the flames were brought under control, Fountainside was only a smoldering ruin. Dot tried to comfort Dwight but in this situation, no words seemed sufficient. Dawn came and confirmed what they already knew. Robert and Eileene Morton had perished in their bed, apparently being overcome by the smoke while they slept. Dwight was grateful they were not awake to realize their fate. For hours he walked around the ruins in a dazed state of mind. There were now many questions beginning to nag at him. How did this happen? Did a fireplace malfunction; did sparks from a tobacco barn or nearby tenant's cottage land on the roof? With so many questions to be answered, Dwight gave instructions that once his parents had been removed, no one should enter the ruins until a Fire Marshal from Columbia could examine the home and determine the cause of the fire. While they waited, Dwight spent most of the day walking the grounds with Dot close by his side.

"What are you thinking, Dwight? I know how upset you are. Please talk to me."

"I'm sorry, Dot. My mind won't shut down. There are too many unpleasant thoughts running through it right now. I don't mean to be ignoring you. I appreciate your being here with me. I don't know what I would have done if you had been in the house too. If we hadn't gone to Momma's, we'd have all been in there. You know, one thing in particular keeps bothering me."

"What's that, Dwight?"

"Tomorrow morning, we were supposed to go to the Bank for the Board of Directors meeting where Fulbright was going to explain all of the crap he'd been pulling at the bank. That seems like an awful big coincidence to me. I never trusted that jerk and if it turns out that this was no accident, I'm going to be paying him a visit."

"Don't even think like that, Dwight. No one could possibly do anything this horrible on purpose."

"I wish I were as sure of that as you are."

Dwight pulled his wife over close to him and kissed her lightly on the forehead. Dot looked up at him and reassured him.

"Remember, no matter what happens, I'm always here for you. For better or for worse just like we promised."

"I would never doubt that."

Aware of the status of the Morton name throughout South Carolina, the Fire Marshal showed up later that day. With him were an expert from the State Bureau of Investigation and an explosives expert. They roped off the entire foundation and stationed a local police officer on each side with the simple order to let no one cross the line. For almost three hours they examined the charred remains, overturning destroyed furnishings and sifting through the ashes. Just before dark they emerged and Dwight, who had not left the area the entire day, went to speak with them.

He approached the Fire Marshal.

"Sir, I'm Dwight Morton. Can you tell me anything? What do you think happened?"

"I'm real sorry about your folks, Dwight. I met your father several times when we investigated tobacco barns that had burned, for the insurance companies. He was a fine gentleman."

"Thank you, sir. What can you tell me about the fire?"

"Well, there's nothing conclusive at this point. The three of us are going to meet over supper tonight and compare our notes. There is a smell of kerosene throughout the house, but with as many kerosene lights as there were inside, we can't say that someone set fire to it. There's one thing that always gives us concern on a house this size is if we can't determine exactly where the fire broke out. If foul play were involved, an arsonist would usually ignite more than one spot to be sure that it went up quickly and didn't burn out. And invariably they would start it on the first floor which I can say with certainty was the case here. So to answer your question, I'm not going to rule out arson yet, even though there's no concrete proof that it occurred here. Do you follow me?"

"I believe you're saying that you think someone probably set it, but they were good enough to not leave any evidence behind. Is that right?"

"I didn't say that and I couldn't without any proof, Dwight, but if it had been my parents in there, I'd be thinking about motives or enemies. You may never have any proof to go after anyone but like I say, I'd be looking for places to ask questions. Were there any people that you might have suspected of doing this?"

Dwight almost blurted out his thoughts and then swallowed his words at the last second.

"No, no sir, I couldn't imagine anyone doing this. But I'll definitely be thinking about it. I'll get up with you if anything comes to mind. And you'll be in touch with me if you uncover something?"

"I'll contact Sheriff Hatcher when we're ready to file a report. It'll probably be in a couple of days. Well, we're headed into town now. Again, I'm real sorry about your folks."

"Thank you."

Even though Robert Morton's business dealings were extensive and involved a lot of people, only one name came into Dwight's head. He hated to think that Fulbright might have set fire to Fountainside to kill his father but the thought was there. The realization that he was now in charge of the affairs of Fountainside came rushing in also and offset some of the turmoil that filled him. He had always dreamed of the day he would step into his father's shoes but this was not what he had envisioned. He hoped to retire his parents to a well-deserved rest at Fountainside with lots of grandchildren to fill their days. This was no longer the case.

The first order of business was to secure the paperwork related to the business and farm. There would be the deeds and accounts at the bank. He knew most of the working capital would be at Lydia Bank. He would use that as not only a good reason to visit the bank right away but also to look Nat Fulbright in the eyes. He felt he would be able to tell with just one look if he had killed his parents. He would take that opportunity the minute the bank opened. As many and varied thoughts and emotions filled him, a comforting voice and soft hand fell on his shoulder.

"Baby, Lord I'm so..so sorry. You has to be strong for your momma and daddy. Momma Mather's gonna help you through this. You gonna be jess' fine. I know you is." She gave Dwight a hug that comforted him like no other could have.

"Thank you, Momma. I know you will. I promise you one thing, if someone did this on purpose, they're going to pay. I won't rest till I know what happened."

"I know you means it, child. But don't let bitterness ruin your heart. It can sure enough do it and there's a lot of folks gonna' be dependin' on you, now that you is running the farm. You and Miss Dorothy come on down to my place and spend the night. I know you ain't eat all day and Miss Dorothy is real upset. You come on and spend some time with her now and we kin talk 'bout what you think you might be doin' 'bout all this."

"OK, Momma, I am worn out. And I need you to help arrange the funeral for my folks if you would."

"You know I will, child. You know I will. Come on now,

let's go home."

They walked slowly down the dirt lane away from the still smoldering ruins. No matter what, Dwight knew a wonderful time and place in his life was gone, never to be replaced.

Dwight slept fitfully, waking up many times during the night. It was reassuring to find Dot always there beside him. Before sunrise, he was dressed and outside trying to start the cantankerous T-Model. They never liked cold weather. After finally getting it going, he left the throttle out enough to keep it running and went inside to find that Momma Mather and Pickle were both up, her fixing coffee and Pickle stoking the fireplace to warm up the drafty shack.

"Morning, Momma Mather, Pickle. Hope I didn't wake you. Pretty inconsiderate starting that thing this early I know. I just want to be at the bank when it opens to try and start sorting out what I'm going to do."

"You ain't foolin' me none, Dwight Morton. You wants to look in the face of that Fulbright scoundrel that you hates so much. You best walk a quiet mile before you start running at him. You hear me? You tips your hat too soon and he'll jess sweep all the trash clean before you can get the goods on him."

"Pickle's been readin' you too many dime novels, Momma Mather. I get your point, though. I'll be careful when I talk with him."

"Be sure you do. Now come eat some breakfast fo' you gets going. Pickle, come on over here and talk with Dwight while he eats."

"I'm coming. How are you this morning, Mr. Dwight?"

"Not too good, Pickle, but I intend to feel better pretty soon."

"If you want me to go with you to town, I'll be glad to. I guess it's going to be a good while fo' they needs me back at the farm, you reckon?"

"Don't you worry, Pickle, you and your Momma will work if anybody gets to. We're all family here. I'd appreciate it, though, if you would stay and help Dot and Momma get ready for my folk's funeral. Momma, I don't feel up to having to see and talk with everybody they knew. I want to have just a small ceremony at the family cemetery and then put an announcement in the paper. I was never much for funerals and this one is going to be particularly rough. Tell Dot to just let her folks know and together you can get up with our friends if there are any who haven't heard about the fire yet. I'll be back around noon."

"I think that's a good idea, Mr. Dwight. Folks will understand."

Still not able to think about food, Dwight finished toying with his breakfast, then followed it with a cup of black coffee. Looking at the old wall clock, he threw on his jacket and headed for the door. Dot caught him before he made it to the car. She was still in her nightgown and bare feet. Just seeing her concern and remembering how caring she had been throughout the night made him feel more determined than ever to keep the family strong and together. If he had anything to say about it, Fountainside would continue to prosper.

"You're not leaving without kissing me goodbye, are you?"

"I just didn't want to wake you. I must have kept you up all night."

"I wanted to be there for you. You weren't sleeping very well."

Dwight hugged her tight and kissed her. He noticed the steam of his breath in the frosty air, and realized how cold it was.

"You need to get inside now. You'll catch your death of a cold out here and I need you well and in good spirits. I'll be back in a few hours."

"OK, baby, please be careful. You sure you don't want Pickle to go with you?"

"I'll be fine. Now go on back inside. Momma Mather will get you some breakfast."

"I love you."

"You too."

CHAPTER SIX

The streets of Lydia were empty except for a farm truck or two when Dwight got to town. Fog was still rising off the frozen ground as he walked the three blocks of sidewalk, waiting for the bank to open. An occasional merchant, unlocking his doors and moving display items out onto the sidewalk greeted him as he passed. Their comments were all basically the same.

"Morning, Dwight. Sure sorry about your folks. A terrible thing that was. Let me know if I can do anything to help you."

Dwight knew they meant well, but he could see the doubt in their eyes. They knew he was young and not nearly as familiar with his father's affairs as he needed to be under these circumstances. They wondered if he could hold it all together. He knew they had just cause to doubt his experience, but if they doubted his mettle then they didn't know him as well as they soon would. The fabric of his whole being was first and foremost a Morton. His family created this part of the state and he was not about to be a weak link in the family chain. As he turned at the end of Broad Street to head back in the other direction, he saw Nat Fulbright pull up in front of the bank and unlock the door. He quickly entered and locked the door behind him. Dwight checked his watch. Eight thirty. Another half hour. His pulse was racing at the sight of the man. He would wait till the bank opened and handle this in the same manner his father would have.

The door to the bank was unlocked to begin the business day, and no sooner had the lock turned than Dwight entered. There was a new expression on his face. The shadow of Robert Morton could be seen crossing his brow. Unannounced he marched straight to Fulbright's office. The banker was inside, back to the door, staring out his window at the Marshburn Coal and Ice plant that ran along the road behind Broad Street. Dwight walked over and startled him by placing a hand on Fulbright's shoulder, rather firmly. Every fiber in his body wanted to strangle Fulbright, but he knew it was important to keep his head until he had secured all of his father's bank accounts and whatever he had locked in his safe deposit box. All of Fountainside's papers and his father's business records had been burned.

"You startled me, what can I do for you young Morton?"

"First off, since my father is dead, in case you hadn't heard, I would say that I'm no longer a young Morton. You can call me Mr. Morton."

"Certainly, Mr. Morton. What can I help you with? I was completely devastated when I heard about the fire at Fountainside. Anything I can help you with, I would be honored to do."

"I'm glad you feel that way. I imagine I would be safe in saying the Board of Director's meeting my father asked you to call never occurred. Would that be a correct assumption?"

"Of course. It would have been in very poor taste to continue on with a business meeting in light of such a tragedy occurring to one of our directors. I'll be happy to convene one in the very near future."

"Fine. Within the next two days will be perfect. Now I would appreciate it if you would get me a key to my father's safe deposit box and all the information on his accounts. His copies were burned and we couldn't find his key. I will be in charge of his affairs and the family businesses from here on and I'll want to change the accounts over to my name."

"Certainly. Follow me."

Fulbright very calmly walked back out to the main lobby of the bank and over to a teller at the first window.

"Mrs. Tanner, would you please assist Mr. Morton here in every way possible to straighten out his family's accounts. He is the late Robert Morton's son and will be taking over his business. Also, open his safe deposit box and get him any copies of account summaries and deeds that he might require. Mr. Morton... Mrs. Tanner here will be glad to help you. I'll be in my office if you need me."

"Morning, Mrs. Tanner. Can you open the safe deposit box first and let me see what records are in there? I'm hoping that copies of our deeds are in it. If not, I'll have to get an attorney to research the records at the courthouse in Florence and make copies."

"Of course, Mr. Morton. Follow me please."

The elderly woman, quite bent over at the waist, walked

slowly to the rear of the bank, and after opening a barred steel door, directed Dwight over to a row of boxes built into the dark plastered wall.

"Here you are, sir. I'll be just outside if you need me. Take your time."

Dwight unlocked the box with the key she had given him and began going through the stack of documents inside. As he examined each document, he placed it on the small oak table in the center of the room. There were deeds to many pieces of property, but much to his disbelief, they were deeds of trust, not outright deeds. Attached to each was a promissory note bearing his father's signature using the property as collateral for loans at the Bank of Lydia. His heart pounding and his mind flooded with rage, he scanned each document, finding that every piece of property had been mortgaged to the hilt, all within the past thirty days! There were bank books for a number of accounts that were in the Lydia bank. Upon opening them, he was not surprised to find that they had also been purged within the past month. This ruthless asshole, Fulbright had put fake loans against the property and shown the proceeds being put in his father's accounts and then quickly being withdrawn. Leaving the stack of papers on the table, his face as red as stoked embers, he stormed back into Fulbright's office. He stopped in front of the ornate desk where Fulbright was calmly reading documents relating to the day's business. He looked up and smiled as he said.

"Mr. Morton, you look flustered. Is there a problem?"

"You smug son-of-a-bitch. You steal from everybody in the county and then when you were confronted by my father, you burned his house down, killing both of my parents. Now I see you also plan to steal what you haven't set fire to. My first instinct is to kill you where you sit...and don't think I can't break your skinny pampered ass in two. No, I'm going to ruin you and watch you die in jail. You're not as smart as you think."

"I don't have a clue what you're talking about, Mr. Morton, but I can assure you that any dealings your father had with the bank were all above board and quite legitimate."

"My father borrowed hundreds of thousands of dollars two weeks before he died? And then just happened to withdraw all the money the next week?"

"A lot of businesses are failing. There's a depression on. Your father had apparently accumulated a lot of debts and paid a good deal of them off with the money. Or maybe it just burned up in the fire. I wouldn't know about that, but I do know that as his heir, you will have to make good on our loans or we will be forced to sell off your father's assets to settle them. I would hate to see it come to that."

"Oh, I'm sure you would. The best thing you can do is get right with the Lord because you're heading for a quick exit to Hell as sure as I'm standing here."

"Are you threatening me?"

"You're damn right. You need to be real scared of me. This has only just begun."

Dwight stormed out of the room and slammed the door behind him so hard that pictures fell off the wall in Fulbright's office.

Several of the tellers looked up in response to the commotion as Dwight raced through the lobby of the bank to the lock box room. He picked up all the papers and left. Fulbright, alone in his office, stood up and walked back over to his window, staring blankly outside as he was when Dwight first entered. He folded his arms and stood motionless, but there was an aura of concern settling around him.

The full realization of what had been done was now clear to Dwight. If Fulbright succeeded in his scheme, not only would he control the Board of Directors at the bank so he could have a free reign on the county's other farmers, but he picked up Fountainside and all of the Mortons' assets to boot. Dwight boiled inside as he pushed the T-Model to its limits on the dirt roads back to Momma Mather's shack. He was so captured by his thoughts of revenge that he drove off the edge of the road several times. Shortly, he ended up back at Momma's where he brought the car to an abrupt halt almost on top of the steps to the ramshackle dwelling. Those inside, including Momma, Pickle and Dot all knew instantly that Dwight had run into serious problems at the bank. Dwight threw off his coat and paced the room as he spoke. He tried to remain calm but his blood pressure had become the throttle on his voice.

"It's worse than I even thought. He did it. He killed them both, or at least had it done. Probably Bill Moore and his cronies. Fulbright is trying to, or already has, stolen everything. He's got phony mortgages signed by Mom and Dad on all our land and our bank accounts have been emptied except for a few thousand dollars. It looks like their signatures but I know it's not. He literally said they would be foreclosing on us. This from the bank we financed. I can't believe Dad couldn't see through this guy. He was too sharp for this."

Momma Mather walked over to the mantle of the old brick fireplace and picked up the Bible they had given to her.

"Everything works out fo' a purpose, Mister Dwight. Jess 'cause you don't understand what's happening right now, don't think the good Lord ain't watchin'. No sir! He's got somethin' in mind sure as you is standin' here. Don't you be forgettin' that. Now come on over here and sit down a while. I'm gonna fix you and Miss Dorothy a plate of food and some coffee. We'll talk about this and I'm sure it'll come to you, what to do and all. Pickle, hang the coffee pot in the fire there, son."

"Yes, ma'am. Mister Dwight, you let me know what you want to do and I'll help you. This here's our home too and my Momma's got no place else to go."

"Hush up now, Pickle. Our problems is small compared to Mister Dwight's. Half the people in the county gonna' be out of work if he loses Fountainside, or workin' for that worthless scoundrel down at the bank. I sure ain't gonna' do no cookin' for that man. No sir, I ain't!"

"Well, jess the same, I ain't afraid of him or nobody, Mr. Dwight. You jess let me know what you want me to do."

Dorothy had seated herself at the table beside Dwight, silent till now.

"He will, Pickle. Thank you. Thank you both. We'll think of something. Your father had a lot of powerful friends, Dwight. Why don't you get hold of that Senator in Columbia that offered to help you get a job? He might know how to go after Fulbright."

"John Richards. He's the Governor. That's a good idea,

Dot. I'm going to visit him tomorrow. I'll take all the papers with me and show him just what Fulbright has done. He'll know exactly how to handle this. Great idea!"

Momma set a hot plate of pork and collards in front of them and they began to eat and make plans for the next day. After an hour or more, Dwight finally settled down. He was feeling better about having a plan to pursue that might help straighten out the nightmare they were caught up in.

The funeral was very somber. The family cemetery was located on the corner of the yard in front of Fountainside. The ruins of the home were still smoldering in the background. There were two closed caskets, and even though there had been little notice to anyone of the funeral, both caskets were covered in flowers sent and brought over in person by distraught friends and neighbors. While a light rain fell, Pastor Whitman read from the Bible and committed Robert and Eileene Mortons' souls to their creator. An informal choir made up of members of the church and friends from the large gathering of black mourners who lived and worked at Fountainside sang a highly spiritual version of In The Garden. Most of the verses could not cover the shouts of Amen or the occasional cry from one of those gathered for the tearful service. As their voices filled the air, Dwight looked across the grounds and tried to remember the day not too long before, that this same area had been filled with laughter and rejoicing for his wedding. The pleasant thoughts helped him fight back the tears which were so close to the surface.

After the service, friends came by and paid their respects. Many just left quietly knowing how difficult this was for Dwight and Dot. The remainder of the day passed slowly as each went about meaningless chores to pass the time. Without Fountainside, all of their lives would be drastically altered. This very real prospect was seated in the forefront of their minds. As evening began to swallow the small row of dark paint-bare shacks, a quivering pair of headlights came bouncing up the road. After stopping at the first shack for a moment, most likely to ask directions, the driver continued to the front door of Momma Mather's shack. Out of the car and into a light, freezing rain, the occupant, dressed heavily against the cold night air, walked up to the door and banged as if trying to escape some unknown presence that had been following.

"Is anyone here? Hello?"

"Jess one minute, I'm coming," called Momma Mather. She grabbed a kerosene light off the kitchen table and shone it on the dripping face of an old woman standing on her porch.

"Is Dwight Morton here? I need to speak with him for just a moment."

"Well, jess one minute. I'll get him. Why don't you come inside? It's miserable out there."

"If you don't mind, I will. I'll wait right here just inside the door."

"Well, you is welcome to come on inside and warm yourself up by the fire."

"No, thank you. I can't stay."

Dwight came to where the women were standing. Momma Mather, Pickle and Dot stood quietly in the dimly lit room as Dwight spoke to the woman.

"I'm Dwight Morton. What can I do for you?"

"It's more like what can I do for you Mr. Morton."

"What do you mean?"

"I'm Eloise Tanner....from the bank."

"Right! I recognize you now. What do you need? You know your boss has taken, or at least is trying to take, everything we have."

"I know. I'm not happy about it either. About thirty years ago, when I was first married to Everett, my deceased husband, we wanted to get us a piece of good land and get started farming. We couldn't borrow money nowhere and was about to give up and move back to a city where Everett could find a job. Mr. Robert Morton, he come to us and offered us fifty acres with no money down. It's down on the southern end of the county. My son and his wife farm it to this day. I rent it to them since my husband died and I went to work at the bank. Well sir, we was happy there for twenty five years and now my kids are. We owe Mr. Morton something. He trusted us when nobody else did and made it possible for us to get our place. It just makes me sick to see what Fulbright is doing to the farmers and working people in this area. Why even that young wife of his had enough. She up and left him a couple of weeks back. Seems like he's throwing away everything for money. I need the work and hated to say anything, but he's just gone too far."

"Do you know anything about what he's doing? How we might be able to prove what a crook he is?"

"I don't see any of the paperwork and I'm sure it would all be in order as slick as he is. But, I can tell you that the day the withdrawal slips were made out on your folks' account, he handed them to me himself and later that evening...."

"Yes..later...?"

"Well, Mr. Morton, he left work with two black leather bags that he just about struggled to carry to the car. I can't help but feel that if you could get your hands on those bags, you'd not only get a big hunk of your money back, but a lot of paperwork that would help you clear up what he done to you. That's about all I know. Find them bags."

"Do you think he took them home with him?"

"Could be. He's bought that big old house that Dr. Otis Smith built for his young bride back before she took the fever, bless her soul. He's got it fixed up like a mansion. Please, don't mention to anyone that I've been here. I need my job. I just couldn't see Mr. Morton's family being mistreated like this, not as good as he was to us. Well, I best be going now. Please, remember; don't mention this...I..."

"You were never here. And thank you, Mrs. Tanner. You did the right thing."

"I hope so."

The elderly woman turned and went back into the drenching rain, driving slowly out of the row of shacks, both back tires spitting mud on the way. It was all she could manage to keep the narrow tired T-Model on a straight course. Dwight watched her taillights disappear. His mind was now in high gear, trying to plot a course of action in light of this revelation. He walked back over to Dot, Pickle and Momma at the table. They heard most of the conversation, straining their hearing as much as possible without being offensive. The look on Dwight's face said it all. Now there was a glimmer of hope, a crack in the granite face of deceit.

Pickle broke the silence.

"That Fulbright is the sorriest poor white trash I ever heard tell of. He ought to be strung up and beat like a dog. I believe he....."

Momma stopped his tirade.

"Pickle! You hush up now. Don't be gettin' Mr. Dwight no more upset than he already is. You remember who vengeance belongs to, don't you?"

"Yes, Ma'am. It jess makes me real mad. I hates to see somebody done this way."

"Well, all the same, Dwight will handle this jess the way it needs to be handled."

Dwight spoke up.

"I might Momma, but right now I feel just about like Pickle does. I need to find those bags and that's the truth of it. I'd be willing to bet they're somewhere at his house. He wouldn't chance leaving them at work knowing what a stir all this was going to cause. He'd a seen that coming. They're at his place, I'd bet on it."

Dot could see the wheels turning in his head.

"Dwight, you can't just drive over to his house and say 'hi, I'm here for the bags of money.' What can you do? Tell the Sheriff?"

"I don't think so. Fulbright's bound to have them hidden somewhere and that would just tip him off that I know. Let me think on this a little while. There has to be some way I can look into the house without him knowing. Momma, you have any more coffee ready?"

"I sure do, baby. Pickle, pour Mr. Dwight another cup of coffee. Get me and Miss Dorothy another one, too. Lordy, it's sure gettin' cold outside tonight. This rain keeps up, we might have snow fo' morning. I sho' do hate cold weather. Makes my bones chatter. You know, that was a fine funeral today. Sho' was a lot of folks there, too. Don't know how so many knew to come. Jess shows how well loved your folks was."

For the next two hours, Dwight said very little. He only occasionally responded to questions from Dot or Momma. He was very deep in thought. Having never been in Fulbright's home, he had no clue as to where to look or what to do if he got inside. One thing was a certainty in his mind. Time was important. He needed to get inside and find those bags soon. Fulbright knew that Dwight's family was well-connected, and if he sensed that he was being undone, he might run out with the money. Dwight would check it out that night. He would give him as little opportunity to run as possible. When the old eight day banjo clock on the wall struck eleven, Momma said she was ready to turn in. Dot tried to get Dwight to go to bed also and sleep on the problem one night. He would have a clearer head after a night's rest.

"You go on, Dot. I couldn't sleep just yet anyway. I'll stay up and stoke the fire a while. Cold as it is, it'll take a lot to keep this place warm tonight."

Pickle turned to Dot.

"You go on to bed, Miss Dorothy. I'll stay up and keep Mr. Dwight company. We'll jess talk about what he's gonna do 'bout Fulbright tomorrow. Ain't that right, Mr. Dwight?"

"That's right, Pickle. I'll come to bed shortly. 'Night, Momma."

Pickle stirred the flames until the fire raged and the warm yellow light filled the cabin. After an hour of watching the flames, Dwight turned to Pickle.

"I'm going out for a short while, Pickle. You don't tell Momma or Dot that I've left, OK?"

"You sure 'bout this, Mr. Dwight? It's awful cold and startin' to sleet outside. You know you shouldn't be goin' up to Fulbright's place tonight. You might oughta' wait a while; go tomorrow while he's at work."

"Pickle, don't you worry about me. I'll be fine. I just want to see the place, look it over. I can't sleep now anyway. Promise me you won't wake them up?"

"If that's what you want."

"Good. Now, help me push the car a little ways from the house so we don't wake them up and make 'em worry."

The two men went out into the freezing night and pushed the T-Model about a hundred yards down the road. Pickle ran back into the house and Dwight started the cantankerous vehicle, steering in the same ruts that Mrs. Tanner made earlier in the evening.

The roads were dangerous and visibility was less than fifty feet. About every tenth drop of sleet was turning into snow. This was no night to be out doing anything. The narrow tired car literally crept along for a half hour till Dwight saw the faint kerosene light in the window of Fulbright's elaborate house. Dwight parked down the road far enough that he would not be heard and slowly made his way to the front yard of the house. He thought it fortunate there was not enough snow yet to leave footprints in the yard. The sleet on the tin roof would make enough noise that his steps would not be heard in the house. It was just about one a.m. when he reached the back steps of the house. Quietly, he twisted the door knob. It was locked tight. He crossed the back porch to a bay window that he knew must be in the dining room. Finding all of the windows securely fastened, he pulled out his pocket-knife and jammed it between the upper and lower sections of the lock, moving it back and forth against the turning section of the lock. After half a dozen passes, the latch started to move. Several more and the window was free to open. The weighted counter balance started to pull the window up on its own. With the slightest of assistance, it rose completely and Dwight, without hesitation, entered the room, shutting the window behind him. The only light inside was from the dimly lit kerosene night lamp. After a few moments, his eyes began to adjust and he could see the reflection of the flame on many pieces of glass and polished brass. Fulbright had been quick to furnish the place as befitted the wealthy man he was becoming. It didn't impress Dwight. Compared to the home that this weasel had destroyed, it was a beggar's camp. He strained his eyes into every corner and hallway, looking for a possible place for a man to hide his ill-gotten horde of cash.

The thought entered his mind that if he were caught here prior to finding proof of a crime, this seemingly irrational behavior would add strength to Fulbright's case against him in a spitting contest. As it stood at this point, the Mortons were just another prominent family being decimated by the depression. He would not be the first person led to criminal actions by these hard times.

With that possibility in mind, he moved as quietly as possible, not even knowing what his prize looked like. Just a couple of large black leather bags. It seemed that the quieter he tried to step, the more the floor creaked. Even the pounding of his heart felt loud enough to be audible. The sleet was increasing in strength and as it cascaded onto the tin roof, he hoped it masked his presence. After thirty minutes and a pound of nerve-induced sweat, nothing had been uncovered that remotely resembled his target. By this time Dwight's pulse was racing and he felt that he was pushing his luck to remain. Still, he hated the thought of leaving no better off than he came. If he could only find a....

Dwight opened his eyes, realizing that he was on the floor. He was prone and his head felt like a rotten pumpkin. What had happened? Had he tripped? He could feel a warm wet stream running down his face. And then the familiar hated voice came out of a dark recess behind him.

"Ah, young Morton. And now you're reduced to common robbery. Remove your silver spoon and out comes a common criminal. I'm sorry, but you just don't have the grit of your father. He was a tough old bird, I have to admit."

Fulbright was holding a fire stoker in his hand, the end of it covered with Dwight's blood. It was clear he was not disappointed with this turn of events.

"This is almost too good. I was wondering how much trouble you would cause me and now, you solve my problems without even a word of input from me. How thoughtful!"

"You bastard. You've got our money here, don't you? You set fire to my home and killed my parents. Go ahead, say it! You did it, didn't you?"

"I would never stoop to such a low act.....personally. I merely arrange things. The rest is done by people a little less civilized than myself. I really don't like blood, truly I don't. I will however, make an exception here in your case. It does give one a sense of power, I have to admit. And now, I'm afraid that I have to finish what you started by coming here. Goodbye, young Morton."

As he raised the stoker in the air to continue the beating on Dwight, Dwight rolled swiftly towards him, causing him to miss as he swung the iron club. Trying not to think about the pain in his scalp, the blood flowing down his face, he continued rolling until he slammed into Fulbright, taking his legs out from under him. From that point on it was not much of a battle. Dwight, after years of working on the farm easily out muscled the soft, weak-boned banker. He pulled him to the floor and removed the weapon from his hand. Feeling no sympathy for the man who had ruined his life to satisfy his own avarice, he stood over him, poker in hand, with his foot placed firmly on the throat of the filthy predator.

"I'm not real good at fancy small talk like you, Fulbright, so I'm telling you flat out, you've got ten seconds left to live if I don't get my family's money back and you go with me to the Sheriff's office. You're going tell him exactly what you've done. Everything...You understand?"

Silently he nodded affirmatively as best he could under the weight of Dwight's hard-soled boot.

"Get up! Don't even think about trying to get away. I'm in no mood to put up with anything else from you. Smashing you with this poker would be a real treat for me. Now, where is the money?'

"It's....it's over there." He pointed towards a Victrola in the corner. It was dark but Dwight could clearly see him as he proceeded to the cabinet and opened the front door. There, just as he had been told, were two black bags.

"Here, here's the money. It's all there."

Fulbright grabbed the bags and threw them towards Dwight's feet. Dwight took his foot and pushed one bag back to Fulbright.

"Open it! Show me the contents. I don't trust you for a moment."

Carefully, in the darkened room, Fulbright opened the first bag. Reaching in, he retrieved several large stacks of bills and laid them out on the floor. He then reached back inside for another handful but instead, held it to his chest.

"Set it on the floor with the rest!"

"Sorry, but I can't do that."

Dwight heard the unmistakable cocking of the hammer on

a pistol. Fulbright had left a gun in the bag and Dwight had fallen right back into his hands.

"You won't be quite so lucky this time, my silly young friend. I'm sorry, but now I have to kill an intruder. A common thief. Dwight saw the flash and felt the impact in his upper right shoulder. There was the sound of the hammer cocking again. Dwight blindly grabbed at the gun. It fired again. Not giving Fulbright a chance to cock the weapon a third time, he smashed the banker's face with the poker as hard as he could swing it. It hit him squarely and Dwight could feel the man's skull give substantially to the impact. The dazed Fulbright still tried to fire the weapon. Dwight grabbed the gun this time as it exploded. It erupted into Fulbrights's chest. It was a mortal wound. Without so much as a groan, he fell to the floor, blood circling his body and quickly forming a dark glistening shadow off the glow of the kerosene lantern.

This was not what Dwight had anticipated but he felt no remorse. He knew only that he needed to get out of there quickly and take the money with him back to Fountainside. There were many people counting on him and he would not let them down. No one would ever suspect him of such an offense. As he left the room, he remembered the fire at Fountainside. This monster lying on the floor had killed his parents. This was almost too good for him. As he passed the kerosene lantern he almost instinctively picked it up and tossed it back on Fulbright. Quickly it burst into expanding flames that danced off the polished brass and crystal in the room.

"Your fortune started and ended with a fire. Burn, you worthless bastard!"

Dwight ran back out through the sleet and down the street. He was glad he had parked so far away. As he turned the car around in the road to leave, he could see fire filling the inside of the house. He had killed but he felt no guilt. What was done just had to be. There were no choices.

CHAPTER SEVEN

Dwight Morton's aged face reddened and he grimaced in pain. He grasped Oscar's hand and squeezed tightly as if trying to counter some unseen force pulling him into unconsciousness. In a matter of seconds he slackened his grip and his eyes rolled up in their sockets. The alarm on one of his monitors began to scream for help. In a few seconds, the nurse in charge of the critical care ward ran to his side. She quickly took in the situation and pressed a speaker button over the bed.

"Code Blue STAT! Fourteen."

She turned to Oscar.

"I'm sorry sir but you'll have to leave now."

Oscar could see that Dwight was in trouble and he doubted he would ever hear the end of the fantastic tale the Senator had been telling him. As more emergency hospital staff and doctors poured into the room, Oscar stepped out of the door, looking back just as the team was preparing to jolt Dwight's heart with electric charges to try and re-establish a heartbeat. He could hear the first discharge as he walked out into the critical care waiting area. The door shut behind him. Oscar was hungry and tired but he was too keyed up to leave the waiting room until he knew if Dwight had died. As he sat down, he noticed that the two young boys, Marcus and Cody, were still in the waiting room. Cody was curled up in his brother's lap. Both were in a very sound sleep. He wondered why there was no adult with them and if they had been waiting by themselves all this time. He walked over to a nurses' station down the hall and inquired of the nurse,

"Excuse me, I'm here with Senator Morton and I wonder if you could answer a question for me."

"You're not with the press, are you?"

A little stung by the intimation that there might be something unhealthy about his profession, he replied,

"I'm just a friend of the Senator's. But I was curious about the two young boys in the waiting room. They've been there an awfully long time. Is their mother all right?"

"She came through surgery just fine but she's still out and they probably won't get to see her till morning."

"Has anyone told them how she's doing? I know the little one is quite scared about this whole thing."

"Well, I'm sure someone has spoken to them."

"But you don't know for certain if they've heard anything?"

"I'll check on it right now."

"I suggest you do. You should be glad they're not your kids waiting there all this time."

"I said I would check on it, sir. I know that Social Services has been called about them."

"What for?"

"They certainly can't stay here until their mother is ready to leave the hospital. That could be next week and I'm sure they need to be in school or at least where someone can watch them."

"I'm going to go tell them you said their mother is fine and sleeping. I want to know what happens here with these young boys. If a social worker shows up while I'm not here, get the name and number of whoever they send."

"It will be here on this desk."

"Make sure it is."

As Oscar turned to walk back over to the boys, a familiar face came towards him.   As he looked his way, the man smiled and held out his hand.

"Robert Meecham. And you must be Oscar Phipps."

"I am. How did you know? I recognize you now; you're Bob Meecham. You work on the President's staff. What are you doing here?"

"To answer your questions, I'm obliged to keep up with anything of importance in this town and a serious stroke to one of our best-loved senators is a matter of great concern to me and, of course, to the President. Dwight Morton is one of the few men in this town that is respected by everyone who has had the opportunity to know him. As a black man I can tell you that he has been of particular importance to me and the causes that I fight for. When he passes, the civil rights movement will lose one of the people who supported it before it was socially acceptable. He's a man of great conscience. And you are Oscar Phipps. Anyone who has heard the news today knows that you're here with him.

All the networks have their trucks set up outside as well as many who are standing vigil for him. Take a look out that window over there."

Oscar walked to a large window that looked out over the parking lot in front of the hospital. There, on the lawn, and all over the grounds were numerous candles lighting the area like a collection of lightning bugs on a summer night. To see such an outpouring of emotion in a time and place when most politicians were being looked at with disdain was truly inspiring.

"They're keeping a vigil? Dwight has that kind of following here?"

"He does and deservedly so. Have you eaten today, Mr. Phipps?"

"No, why?"

"Let me take you to a place I know just down the street and buy you supper. It won't take long and I'm sure you need it. We'll come back in an hour. I'll have one of the Marine guards page us if anything happens while we're there. I'd like to speak with you a while. What do you say?"

"OK, certainly. Let me say something to these young fellows over here and I'll join you."

Meecham watched as Oscar went over to the boys and knelt down in front of them. He awakened the older boy.

"Marcus. Have you heard about your mother?"

"No sir. Nobody's told us shit. Have you heard anything?"

"She came through the operation fine and is sleeping right now. The nurse says it might be morning before you can go in and see her. Where are you staying?"

"We ain't goin' nowhere's till I know she's OK. I want her to tell me she's all right. We'll be fine right here."

"I understand. You want me to bring you some burgers or something to eat? I'm going out right now and would be glad to pick you up some."

"I don't have my money with me right now. We can wait."

"No, I'm going to bring you some and you can eat them when you want. You can pay me back later."

"You would do that?"

"You'd do it for me, wouldn't you?"

"Sure, I guess so."

"OK. That's it, then. I'll be back shortly. Let Cody sleep and maybe I'll be back before he wakes up."

"Yes sir. And.....Oscar.....Thanks a lot, man."

Oscar was pleased that the iron curtain was falling a little. He walked back over to where Bob Meecham was waiting.

"I'm ready. Don't let me forget to pick up some food for these youngsters."

"I won't. Grab your coat; it's cold outside."

The two men walked down the hall and to the front of the hospital where a car was waiting. As they approached, reporters and camera crews rushed them.

"How is the Senator, Bob? Was he able to speak to you, Mr. Phipps? Is he going to make it? ....Is he in great pain? What does this mean to the black initiative, Mr. Meecham? ....Can we have a comment please?..."

The questions continued unanswered as the car pulled off and left the cameras still running, taping their departure. Meecham instructed the driver to evade anyone following them and drop them at the service entrance to the restaurant. A few moments later, they arrived at the back street behind the small eating establishment. With the staff alerted to their arrival, they were greeted at the car by the Maitre'D with an umbrella to shield them from the light snow that was falling. They entered the restaurant unnoticed, and were seated at a private table in a dark corner.

"The Reuben here is damn good, Oscar. May I call you Oscar?"

"Of course, I don't respond very well to Mr. Phipps. I always feel like someone is talking to my father."

"I know what you mean. Seems like we're kids one day and old men the next. It's hard for me to believe that Dwight Morton is in his eighties. He's been here as long as I can remember. If it weren't for him, I'd probably still be picking cotton in Georgia."

"How's that?"

"No money, no scholarships for minorities when I was growing up. We're talking the late forties. Brown versus Board of Education hadn't been heard of at that time. I was a good student and in love with world history. My folks thought I was just wasting my time and tried to get me to learn a trade where I could earn a living, but I was very determined and had some help. There was a teacher at my school who liked me. I guess he admired my ignorance of the odds I was facing. Anyway, he gave me the name of a man to call and plead my case. I did just that and told him my story. He said very little to me and I wondered after I hung up if he even knew what the Hell I'd been talking about. Two weeks later, I got a letter from New York University telling me that I had not only been accepted to the school based on a highly regarded referral but that my tuition and books were already paid for."

Meecham paused, breathed a sigh and wiped his eyes. Then a smile showed through as he continued.

"I'm sorry; I still get pretty emotional thinking about it. Dwight Morton paid for me to go all the way through college. Hell, I had never even met the man. I wrote him a thank you note and that began a series of letter writing that continued for many years. He bought my clothes, sent an occasional check for spending money and even came to my graduation. I was expecting George Washington or Alexander the Great or Hell, I don't know, some kind of bigger than life character. And then, this tall, slender white-haired man with a soft voice and big smile came up and hugged me. I swear, walked right over to me and hugged me! I'd hardly even touched a white man before and here was this guy hugging me in front of everyone. His wife Dorothy was with him then. She kissed me on the cheek and told me how proud they were of me. And when I thought I was just going to explode with gratitude, my parents, my dad in a new suit, came up behind them. This man, who I'd never seen before, had even paid for my parents to come up and see me graduate. After the ceremony, he told me he wanted me to keep going to school, maybe even an Ivy League school. He was going to pay for me to go as high as I could. He was a smart old rascal. He was grooming me for a job that I never even contemplated in my wildest dreams."

"What job was that?"

"He wanted an educated, well-spoken black man from the South to help him push his interests in this town. He knew that Washington insiders would never give an ear to a sharecropper or field hand. He groomed me to become what I am today. I owe him as do many others of all races, a debt that most will never even know. That's why I wanted to talk to you. Dwight deserves a special epithet. His life and his passing need to be exemplified. There's too much negativity today. The press ruins all our heroes. Dwight would be a hard man to impugn. You see what I'm talking about, don't you?"

"I believe I do. I'm considering doing a story on the Senator and following up on some of what he was talking to me about earlier today. He was telling me a pretty amazing tale and then he had another attack before he finished. So, I'd be very interested in hearing anything you had to tell me about him."

"That's wonderful. I'll tell you what. Let's call the hospital and see how he is and then, if he's stable, we'll stay a while longer. What do you say?"

"It's fine with me."

Bob Meecham went over to the manager and borrowed a phone. Oscar watched him as he walked off. He was quite distinguished looking. He had close cropped silver hair and strong prominent features. He carried himself with an air of confidence and pride that bespoke highly of a man who had come up from the cotton fields of Georgia to a position of such prominence in the White House. He was eloquent in his speech and it was apparent that he knew that he was a role model of sorts and conducted himself as such. He would be a hard man to overlook.

After a few minutes he returned with the welcome news that Dwight was alive and still fighting to hang on. No visitors would be allowed to see him until his condition improved somewhat. There was no need to go to the hospital at the moment. They would stay and talk.

Bob took his seat back at the table and they ordered a fresh pot of coffee. The service Meecham received at the restaurant was indicative of the fact that the owner was quite aware of exactly who Bob was. It was the treatment reserved for power brokers and movers in a town sensitive to such things.

"You know Oscar, Dwight could probably have been President if he wanted to. He had the support of both houses and even the media loved him."

"He wasn't interested?"

"Nope. He didn't even like politics. Left up to his own vices, he would have been content to just live out his days on his family's place in South Carolina. You ever been there? You're from South Carolina, aren't you?"

"I'm from Florence, and I know the area where Dwight was from but I never actually saw his home. I heard it was special."

"I only know from the things he told me about it. He loved it there and when he does pass on, he wants to be buried there. So, I guess I'll be seeing it before too much longer. He talked of dirt roads, great oak trees and quiet streams where he loved to fish. He could almost take you there just talking about it. But, he felt a calling to pursue the best interests of other people."

"What do you think his motivation was?"

"The best way I could describe it was that he took a personal offense at the injustices in our society. You know, most of the white men who could be called sponsors or forefathers of the civil rights movement in this country had a peculiar attitude towards black people."

"How's that?"

"They believed that black people should have equal rights, but they never believed that they were actually equal. They had a conscience but couldn't overcome an inborn feeling of superiority. But Dwight, he was different. He truly believed that everyone was just alike. He believed in what he always called 'equality of the spirit'."

"That's very interesting. He was very much a humanitarian, wasn't he?"

"It would be hard to put him in any category. I've never met anyone else quite like Dwight. Have you ever heard of the Dorothy Morton Education Foundation?"

"No. I certainly know who Dorothy was though. She's been gone for a number of years now, but there was a time that

Dot Morton was just as well known as Dwight."

"Exactly. Her foundation is based out of Atlanta and believe it or not, sends over a hundred disadvantaged young people to college every year. Has for many years. Over the years, Dwight funneled most of his business gains into the Foundation. He and Dot, up till she died in '73 I believe, lived very modestly even though they were easily one of the wealthiest families in the South. It seemed the more he gave away, the more successful his businesses became. He put very little time in them and in fact, most of them are run by men and women that he had sent through college with grants from the Foundation. Funny how it all comes back to you, isn't it? I know it sounds pretty corny but he was proof that we truly reap what we sow. There have many other donations over the years, more than I could even remember but what he gave the most of was his time and energy. He marched with Martin Luther King. He bankrolled many a march and participated himself. Did you ever wonder how poor unemployed men and women could afford to charter buses and spend a week at the capital? Or where the money came from to start up a civil rights organization? Most people never did. I can tell you where a lot of it came from. Dwight Morton. He helped find work and education for every group of immigrants that hit the country. The immigrants from Cuba, right on up to refugees from Vietnam, have all benefited from his caring. And the amazing thing is that he never wanted his name on anything and no credit. Damnest thing I ever heard of. I still don't know what makes a man that way."

"You make him sound like Mother Theresa. I'm sure he had detractors, every politician does. What about skeletons in his closet? There's bound to have been a lot of people who didn't like what he stood for."

"There were. But it's hard to find any dirt on a man whose family fortune was as old as the country and who never seemed to want anything for himself. The biggest problem in ever finding fault with someone is just what you were talking about earlier."

"What's that?"

"Motives. His only motivation seemed to be, as unusual as it was, helping people who couldn't help themselves. I think it will be a long while before we find another like him. All this seem a little too hard to believe?"

"I have to admit, as a newsman, I tend to question it when someone seems unselfish but, from what I've seen of Dwight, I can't find a lot to question."

"Well, it's getting pretty late. You're heading back to the hospital, right?"

"First, I've got to pick up some food for those boys. My bag is still there too. If you can take me to some sort of fast food place and then to the hospital, I'll catch a cab and go find a motel."

"You'll do no such thing. We'll pick up your bags and you'll spend the night at my house if that's suitable to you."

"I'd be honored."

"That's great. Waiter! Check please and have my driver pull the car around."

"Certainly, sir."

By the time they arrived back at the hospital parking lot, the number of those keeping a candlelight vigil for the Senator had swelled dramatically. The entire parking lot, now void of visitors' cars due to the late hour, was almost full of well wishers solemnly holding their candles. From the sky it must have looked like an entire galaxy of stars had settled there. The sight took Oscar's breath away.

"All this for one man. It's a most unforgettable scene, isn't it?"

"It truly is, Oscar. This is a time that I imagine we'll all remember for a very long while."

Oscar pressed quickly through the news crews and their barrage of generic questions and made his way back to the waiting room to keep his promise to Marcus. He had overbought cheeseburgers, fries and shakes for the boys and was anxious to give it to them. The waiting room was dark and he could see the silhouette of Marcus in the same chair where he had left him. Cody was not with him. Marcus saw him coming.

"Oscar. You got to help me get Cody."

"Where did he go?"

"Some lady came and took him. Didn't ask me shit. Just

showed me some papers and told me that we was both supposed to go with her. I told her I wasn't leavin' till I could talk with my mother. She said she'd send somebody else back to get me but Cody was going with her and she would bring him back tomorrow. Can she do that?"

"I'm sure that she works with Social Services and she will take good care of Cody until the morning. If you're still determined to stay here, I'm going to leave you a phone number and if anybody tries to do anything that you don't like or tries to make you leave, you call me. I'll talk to them. This is an 800 number. It doesn't take any money to call. Somebody will answer it around the clock where I work. They'll know how to get up with me. Tomorrow, I'll speak to Social Services with you and we'll work it out. That OK with you?"

"I guess. I know I ain't leavin'."

"Here's some food I brought for you. Just eat what you want and throw the rest away. I know there's too much there. Look, here's twenty bucks. You can eat in the cafeteria downstairs in the morning and I'll be here early. You sure you'll be all right here?"

"I ain't leavin'."

"OK. See you first thing in the morning."

Feeling a little better about the boys, Oscar grabbed his bag and sped off with Bob Meecham. He would try and catch a small amount of much needed sleep so he could be back at the hospital early. Maybe then he could help Marcus and Cody, and Dwight could continue their conversation.

By six a.m., Oscar was back in the waiting room. There were the ever- present Marine Guards still at attention on either side of the door to Dwight's room. Doctors and nurses were making their early rounds. After thoroughly inspecting the hospital floor it was apparent that Marcus was not there. Dwight approached one of the guards.

"Sergeant, I'm Oscar Phipps. I was here visiting with the Senator yesterday."

"Yes sir. I know who you are. What can I help you with, sir?"

"The young man, about sixteen years old, who was in the

waiting room. Do you know where he went?"

"Late last night, a man from I believe the Social Services and a city policeman came up to see him and he took off. He ran straight down the hall and disappeared. They couldn't come close to catching him. They left and another police officer has been by a couple of times looking for him. He's not been back."

"Thank you, Sergeant. Look, do me a favor."

"Yes sir."

"I'm going to be back in with the Senator for a while this morning. If anyone comes looking for the boy or if he should come back, come and get me. Don't try and get his attention. You'll just scare him off."

"Yes sir. But I don't think he'll be back, not the way he ran out of here."

"He'll be back. His mother is hospitalized a few doors down, and he won't go far away as long as she's here. If he shows up, just let me know first. He's having a tough go of it now and I think I could help him. OK?"

"Yes sir."

Oscar opened the door and took a quick glimpse into Dwight's room. He could see that Dwight was still asleep but the heart monitor by the bed seemed to be indicating stability again. Maybe he would be able to finish the unusual account he had been relating to Oscar the previous day. The ward nurse came up behind Oscar and asked him to wait outside a while so Dwight's doctor could give permission for him to have company.

"It'll be just a few minutes, Mr. Phipps. He's examining a patient a couple of rooms away and will be coming here next. I'll call you when it's OK to come back in."

Dwight went back to the small waiting room and sat down. He was feeling fairly rested after staying at Bob Meecham's for the night. Having the chance to talk with him about Dwight made for a very insightful evening. Meecham's knowledge of Dwight's career and personal life made the Senator's recounting all the more meaningful. As Oscar was waiting, he spotted a young woman walking up the hall holding Cody by the hand. Cody saw Oscar and waved to him.

"Hi, Oscar. Have you seen my brother? He's run off."

"No, Cody. I heard about it and I've been keeping an eye out for him. And who have you got with you?"

"This is Miss Robinson. She's letting me stay with her till my momma is better."

The young woman smiled and walked over to meet Oscar.

"Good morning. I'm Betsy Robinson. I work for the Department of Social Services and I'm looking out for Cody. Are you a friend of the family?"

"You might say that. I've been visiting with Senator Morton and met Cody and his brother here yesterday. Oscar Phipps is my name. What's the problem with Marcus?"

"He's just afraid that he and his brother will be placed in a foster home until Mrs. Frye is well enough to look after them again. Her doctors tell us that she needs several weeks rest before she should do anything and that she might never be able to work like she has in the past. Like a lot of others, she takes care of the boys by herself and has been working two jobs to make ends meet. She's a short order cook during the day and a hotel maid in the evenings. They were living in a city project until she got too sick to work and then they went to a shelter. I'm afraid that unless some relatives or friends offer to help look out for the boys, they might well need to be in foster care. In actuality, it would be the best for them."

"Well, they obviously don't agree with you, at least Marcus."

"There are thousands of boys like Marcus in this city and it gets worse every day. He needs to be in a stable home and in school. Otherwise, he'll be in trouble in pretty short order and none of us want that. Cody will do fine with us but you're right; Marcus is going to be a hard case, I'm afraid. Anyway, I've brought Cody to see his mother and please, if Marcus shows up, call me. Here's my card and I'll write my home number on it for you. Call no matter what the time is."

Betsy turned to see that Cody was back in the waiting room chair looking at the book that Oscar had told him to keep.

"Come on, Cody. Let's go see your mother. Nice meeting you, Oscar."

Cody went up to Oscar and grabbed his leg in a hug.

"Can I stay with Oscar? He likes to read to me. Can I, Oscar?"

"I wish you could Cody, but I don't live near here and I won't be staying long. I'm sure you'll be happy with Betsy. I'll give her my phone number, though, and you can call me if you need somebody to talk to."

The young boy's head fell silently and he relinquished his grip on Oscar. It was sad to see someone so young have such horrendous problems to deal with. Oscar was no stranger to the plight of large cities. He had seen most of the country and realized fully the extent of the nation's social ills. However, this one instance did hit him harder than just reading about the problem or seeing the projects from a cab window.

"I hope your mother's doing well, Cody. I'll see you soon."

Betsy took the young boy by the hand and entered his mother's room. The door closed behind them and Oscar went back to the chair in the waiting room. A few moments later, the nurse called for him.

"Mr. Phipps, you can come in now."

As he approached the doorway to Dwight's room, the nurse came up close beside him and whispered,

"He's weak and the Doctor says he could go any time. He asked for you as soon as he woke up and several times since then. Hit the call button if he starts to have any breathing problems. There'll be a doctor at the floor station all day, so just call if you need anything."

"Thank you. I'll watch him closely."

Oscar entered and went over to the side of Dwight's bed and pulled up a chair. Dwight recognized him right away and spoke with a very faint voice full of anxiety.

"Good. Oscar, it's you. Listen to me. I'm Dwight Morton. I'm eighty-five years old. I was born in South Carolina in nineteen hundred and eight. My wife's name was Dorothy. I served two terms in Congress and six in the Senate. I'm dying. I'm at Washington Metropolitan Hospital on the third floor. There are two young Marines right outside the door and you've been here with me since yesterday. Am I right?"

"Yes, Dwight, on all counts. Why are you telling me these things? I know who you are and where you came from."

"I want you to know that I still have my senses about me and that I'm not out of my head or anything. Can you tell that I know what I'm saying?"

"Of course, Dwight. I never thought you didn't."

"Then I want to tell you something. Come a little closer."

Oscar bent down and the old man said in almost a whisper,

"They were here. They were all here last night. Even just a little while ago."

"Who, Dwight? Who was here?"

"Dot, Momma and even Pickle. Right here in the room with me. I swear to God I wasn't dreaming. They didn't speak but they smiled and stayed right by me for a long while. It was so good to see them. You believe me, Oscar? You do, don't you? You know I wouldn't lie about it."

Oscar was taken aback by what Dwight said because he could see that he was so lucid. He looked around but seeing nothing, still replied,

"I'm sure they were, Dwight. They're looking out for you. They loved you. Just like many other people who have been out in the parking lot all night. You've touched the lives of a lot of people and have been a very special person. I do believe you."

"They came to take me with them. I know I haven't got much longer and I have to finish telling you about Pickle and what happened back then. All this here today is happening because of what happened back then. I would never have even left Lydia if it hadn't been for Pickle. The fight with Fulbright was only the start of it. Now, when I look back at it all, it seems like it was supposed to be that way. I have to believe it was."

CHAPTER EIGHT

Down the rain-soaked roads, Dwight hurried as fast as the dim headlights allowed. The rain was now half sleet and the dirt road had become a slippery treacherous path. His shoulder still oozing blood, the pain increased with each jerk of the steering wheel. He was concerned but not nearly so much as before. The problem now was just his. There was money to save the family and if he was found to be Fulbright's assassin, so be it. He would only have to worry about himself then. The bank records would show that his father had withdrawn the money, so there was no explaining to be done there. And why would he have killed the polished banker? After all, his father had put him in business. He had been an honored guest at Dwight's wedding only a year earlier. There was no motive and no connection. Only Mrs. Tanner might suspect and it was not likely that she would say anything about any suspicions that she might have. It would probably be determined that Fulbright had found an intruder in his home and been shot by his own gun after a struggle. Why would they suspect anything more? They wouldn't.

Outside of Momma's shack, the old T-Model came to a quiet stop. Dwight had killed the motor a little ways back so as not to wake anyone. It was now the middle of the night. Dwight took off his shirt and looked at his shoulder. It had stopped bleeding and even though it hurt tremendously, it did not look as bad as he had expected. There was a small hole on both sides of his shoulder. The bullet had gone through him. He took the shirt and stuck it out the window of the truck until it was soaked and then pressed the freezing cold material against the wounds, washing off the blood at the same time. Convincing himself that he would be OK, he opened the car door and ran through the frozen mud to the house. He opened the door quietly and entered. Once again, the sound of sleet against a tin roof concealed the small sounds of his entrance.

He went over to the dying fire and stoked it till it began to pour out a wonderful drying heat. When the flames were at maximum height, he tossed his bloody shirt into the fire. There was no blood on his pants and unless he volunteered to show someone his wound, he was home free. He didn't want anyone else to know what occurred. Their ignorance in the matter would not only keep them from worrying but from having to help him cover up his actions. Not knowing would be their protection.

The fire felt good on his sore body. He quietly lifted up Momma Mather's old cane-laced rocker and placed it directly in front of the flames. He pulled another shirt out of some clothes that Dot had washed earlier for him. Her parents had brought them a few things to wear after the fire. He slipped it on and then covered up with a homemade quilt in the rocker. The adrenaline had long since passed through him and not even the turmoil that had made up this day could keep him awake. Quickly he passed into a deep, welcome sleep.

The smell of fresh coffee filled the small room and Momma Mather, slightly bent at the middle as she was most mornings due to her arthritis, stirred the fire again. In the cold months of winter, the making and tending of a fire was a never-ending chore.

"Don't you be getting up yet, child. You done slept in my old rocker all night and I can tell you that ain't no good for your back. Besides, you needs to be keeping Miss Dorothy warm. That's what men folk are the best at. I hates cold feet. I sho' do miss my man on these here cold nights."

"I guess I just fell asleep in the rocker. It's the first time I haven't slept in the same bed with Dot since we were married. You're right. It's not nearly as comfortable."

His shoulder felt like he had been kicked by a mule but he would not let on that it bothered him.

"We'll be real quiet and let Miss Dorothy and Pickle sleep a little longer. At least till I can get the heat up in here and some biscuits and bacon fixed."

"That sounds real good. Put me down for some and some of that coffee too. I'm starved."

"It'll be just a minute. Got some fine fig preserves here too. Jess like your daddy liked so much. Fixed it for him jess a few weeks back. I'm sure gonna' miss him and Mrs. Morton. Some of the finest folks there ever was. Yes sir, jess like family they was. Treated me jess like family."

"You are family, Momma. You don't need to worry about anything. I think I have everything figured out now and we're all going to be just fine. No need to worry."

"What about that banker Fulbright? How you going to handle him?"

"I think I can persuade him to come to terms with me. I'll handle him just like my father would have. He'll come around."

"I sho' hope you is right. I'm too old to do wash for a living. And I wants Pickle to go to that school Miss Dorothy's been tellin' him all about. I think he's bout made up his mind to go. I'd sure miss him, but it's something that he needs to be doin'. I don't want him endin' up no broken old field hand. No sir! Not my Pickle. Well, go ahead and wake him up. Let Miss Dorothy sleep as long as she wants, but I need Pickle to go out and get a little firewood."

"I can get it, Momma. Let him sleep."

"No sir. That's his job and he 'spects me to get him to do it. Go ahead and wake him. Don't need to be wastin' no more time in the bed."

No sooner had she spoken than the stillness of the morning was broken by the sound of a car coming up the road. Dwight went over to window and looked out. He felt his pulse accelerate and he literally froze at the sight through the window.

"Who is it comin' here so early, Dwight?"

"It...it's Sheriff Hatcher and a deputy."

"What in the world are they doin' here this early in the day? Maybe they's found somethin' out about your folks, you reckon?"

"Maybe so, Momma. I hope that's the case."

Dwight looked down at his shoulder to see if there were any stains showing through the shirt he was wearing. Satisfied there weren't, he watched through the window as the Sheriff approached the door, followed by his deputy. They did not seem to be in an aggressive mood and knocked on the door calmly. Perhaps there could be some other reason they were here. Dwight's heart continued to work overtime but he determined to stay reserved and not give himself away through any unnecessary show of nerves. Momma walked over to the door. The law was no stranger to tenant shacks but it usually was on Sunday morning bringing home someone after a night in the drunk lockup. However, they had never come to Momma Mather's home before.

"What can I do for you, Sheriff? You lookin' somebody?"

"No, Mrs. Mather. I'm not looking for anyone. I've come to talk to you if I can come in."

"Well, sho' you can. Here, come on in."

As he entered, he saw Dwight standing by the window.

"Oh, good morning, Dwight. I didn't know you were here."

"Yes, Sheriff. Since our home burned, Dot and I have been staying here with Momma Mather. It's just till I can get a place of our own again. Probably start building something in the spring. Nothing like Fountainside, but a nice house."

"Yeah, that was a terrible loss. I was real upset about it myself. Did you ever hear from Columbia about what caused it?"

"I was hoping that you were here with some news about it now."

"No. That's not why I've come out here. I came to tell Mrs. Mather that her boy's in jail. Got him locked up downtown."

Momma placed her hand on her heart.

"Not Pickle! Not my Pickle. He's still in bed right here. Pickle! Wake up, son. Pickle, get up!"

There was no answer and Dwight pulled back the old curtain that separated Pickle's bed from the room.

"He's not here, Momma. What's this all about, Sheriff?"

Momma half sat and half fell into her rocking chair. Dwight came up beside her and put his hand on her shoulder as he talked.

"What's he charged with?"

"I hate to tell you this but the boy tried to rob the banker, Nathaniel Fulbright, last night and he apparently made some noise and woke him up."

"And...?"

"Well, as best we tell, there was a fight and Fulbright got killed. Killed with his own gun. That probably means second degree murder since your boy didn't bring a gun with him. Right now I'm more concerned about keeping him safe from the townsfolk till I can get him moved over to Florence. Folks around here got some pretty strong feelings about a black man breakin' into somebody's home in the middle of the night and killin' them. There's already some of 'em, rednecks mostly, Bill Moore and such, talkin' about a lynchin'. Now I ain't gonna let that happen, but right now, I just came to tell Mrs. Mather what was going on."

"My Pickle would never do nothin' like that. He ain't never took nothin' in his whole life. He's a good boy!"

"I understand how you feel, ma'am but there's a few around that says they already caught him once before stealin' a cow and that Dwight here saved his neck then. Ain't that so, Walter?"

The Sheriff looked towards his deputy who nodded affirmatively. Dwight looked into the officer's stubbled face. His hit-or-miss shaving technique made the brown tobacco juice dribbling out the corner of his mouth take a circuitous course to the bottom of his chin where his left hand stood at the ready to wipe it dry. He was right-handed but reserved that appendage to stand guard over the butt of his revolver in case someone in the shack decided to get tough with him.

Momma was weak with shock.

"I don't care what nobody says. Pickle wouldn't never hurt nobody. It ain't in him."

"He might not have intended to, Mrs. Mather, but it happened just like I told you."

Dwight, trying to fathom what was going on and still not panic, asked the Sheriff.

"What makes you so sure it was Pickle? I agree with Momma Mather. I've known him his entire life and I don't believe he could possibly do something like this."

"Hell, he confessed."

"He confessed? I don't believe it."

"Well, it's a fact, happened just like I'm sayin'. He set fire to the house to cover up what happened. When we responded to the fire, we found his tracks still fresh in the mud out in front of the house. We got some hounds and followed him to about a half mile from here. We took him down to the station and he just flat out said he done it. Why would he lie? Couple of minutes sooner and we'd probably have caught him running out the door of the house. If you think it would help any, get him a lawyer and come talk with him. I'd wait till tomorrow, though, he's a little under the weather right now."

"Under the weather? Did anyone hurt him? I swear if anybody's touched him, there's going to be trouble."

"Hell, Dwight, he killed one of the town's most prominent citizens. You can't expect folks to feel very kindly towards him. He ain't hurt bad. They just roughed him up some. A split lip and some bruises, maybe a cracked rib. He'll be fine. He's lucky me and my deputy here showed up when they found him or they'd have hung him for sure, right on the spot. Pretty damned lucky if you asked me."

Momma was in shock by this time. Dot had awakened from all the noise and came to her side as Dwight finished speaking.

"Sheriff. I'll be in town in a short while and I suggest you get back there and watch over your prisoner. If he gets hurt, I'm holding you personally responsible and I promise you I can cause you problems you never dreamed of. My family has a lot of friends in this state and Pickle is a friend of mine. A good friend! Do I make myself clear?"

"I see exactly where you're coming from, Dwight, and I'm sorry to say I never believed what people always said about you, but now I see there was truth in it."

"And what do 'folks' say about me?"

"You don't know what side of the fence to be on. I ain't going to get in no war with you, Dwight, but your friend done it. He's confessed and it's a pretty open and shut case as far as I'm concerned. You do what you think you have to. I'll be in my office and your boy will be in the jail until they come and take him to Florence. Other than that, send your lawyer if you want to talk to me about it. That's all I'm sayin' about the whole damned thing."

"I'll be down there shortly. He better be all right."

The Sheriff shook his head disgustedly as he walked back out through the door. Not quite out of earshot, Dwight heard one of them say to the other,

"Damn nigger lover."

Dot heard almost all that had been said and was in as much a state of disbelief as Momma. .

"He couldn't have done it. Pickle is one of the most gentle people I know. I don't think you could even make him mad enough to fight somebody. I know you couldn't. Dwight, what's going on?"

Dwight now found himself in the situation of either revealing what he'd done or trying to find a way out of the mess. He couldn't bring himself to say what he knew he should to his wife or Momma Mather. This was a moment he would never be able to forget. His decision would put the remainder of his life on a course beyond his control. At the time, he felt he could find some workable solution. He'd get a lawyer for Pickle. Since he wasn't guilty, it should be simple to prove someone else did it. He'd try this approach without anyone taking the blame. Pickle was just in the wrong place at the wrong time. But what was he doing out there in the freezing rain in the middle of the night? He hoped above all that Dot and Momma Mather couldn't see the hurt and guilt he felt was taking over every breath leaving his body. There had to be a solution. Momma Mather was still sitting in the rocker crying and Dot was standing behind her hugging her neck. As the police car turned and drove off Dot began to voice her own concerns to Dwight.

"You know how this whole community is about black people who get in trouble, Dwight. We need to get a lawyer for Pickle right away. How can we pay for one? Look, how about calling that Mr. Richards your dad knew so well from Columbia and get him to send someone good here? We can sell some livestock and pay him. Let's do that. Go ahead and call him now, Dwight. I don't want Pickle staying with those horrible people another minute. I know they won't treat him right and we need to get him out of there."

"I know, Dot. We'll get him out. You stay here with Momma and I'll go to the jail and check on him. I'll send a wire to Governor Richards while I'm in town. Look, don't you worry. You either, Momma. We'll get this straightened out today. I promise you Pickle will be fine. He'll be out by tomorrow morning."

Dwight knew he had one foolproof way to get Pickle out. He would confess if necessary. He knew his chances would be better than Pickle's. He wouldn't let Pickle suffer for something he'd done. He wished now he'd told Dot and Momma Mather the truth immediately. But that would have hurt them, too. There was no easy way out of this mess. Thank God he had gotten back the family's money. He could at least pay for a good lawyer and take care of everyone. He quickly dressed behind Pickle's curtain so that his wound wouldn't be seen. In a few moments he kissed both of the women and left, assuring them as he went all would be fine.

"I'll be back shortly. Don't you worry, Momma."

"Thank you, baby. Thank you so much. Please bring my boy home."

"I will."

Dwight went outside, started the car and in a few minutes was headed into town. As he drove, he kept wondering why Pickle would've confessed. Surely they'd beaten it out of him. As small and frail as he was, it wouldn't take much to scare him into saying what they wanted. But, what was he doing out that late in the first place? Before long, Lydia and the town hall came into view. There were a lot more cars and people gathered around the jail than usual. There was a crowd out front and it didn't take Dwight long to figure out what was going on. There was Bill Moore and his assortment of goons, right in front of the building. Bill was running his mouth as usual. Dwight knew what Moore was saying even before he parked the car. He had to park half-way down the block to get a space. He walked up the street and into the group he had just seen. Of course Bill Moore was the first to speak.

"Well, look who's come to visit his nigger. It's his old friend Dwight Morton. It's too bad your father didn't live long enough to see this, Morton. His only son... the biggest nigger lover in the county!"

Dwight knew they were in a foul mood, looking for trouble. The smell of alcohol was strong and it wouldn't serve his purpose to engage himself with the loudmouth just yet. The time would come. He passed through them, taking a few sharp elbows in the side as he entered the jail. Sheriff Hatcher was not there but the Deputy who had been at Momma Mather's earlier was and he scowled at Dwight as he entered.

"The Sheriff ain't here. You'll have to come back later."

"You can let me see Pickle. I just want to talk to him and make sure he's all right. I won't be but a few minutes."

"The Sheriff wouldn't want me to do that, I don't believe. It ain't my decision."

"You know, Walter, my father staked your family for I don't know how many years and forgave the loans when your daddy didn't have the money to pay for what he had gotten. And this is how you repay us?"

"Well, it ain't me, Dwight. I'm just doing what I was told."

The deputy looked embarrassed, wringing his hands and wiping his brow. Dwight looked him right in the face. He would make him as awkward as needed to get in to see Pickle.

"I don't suppose it would hurt to see him for just a minute," the deputy said, "but if you hear me callin' you, you better get up real quick so's I don't lose my job. You understand?"

"That's more than fair."

"OK, follow me. He's back here."

The deputy led him down a narrow, dark hallway with cinder block walls and no windows. The jail was intended only as a holding area to be used until authorities from Florence could arrive and transport a prisoner to a more secure jail. At the end of the hall, he unlocked a thick wooden door. A few feet more and there was a cell door. In the back of the cell on a small cot, he saw Pickle lying on his side. The deputy let him in and shut the cell door behind him.

"Now listen out for me. I'll be watchin' for the Sheriff."

He walked back down the hall and left Dwight alone with Pickle.

"Pickle, you OK? It's me, Dwight."

Slowly, Pickle tried to sit up, groaning as he did. He turned his head to face Dwight and the extent of the beating he had taken became apparent. His face was swollen double and even his nose was twisted severely enough that on first glance Dwight could tell it was broken. One eye was completely shut and his swollen lips were still dripping blood. He was holding his stomach as he tried to sit up and the pathetic sight literally made Dwight sick. Knowing how innocent he was only made it harder to bear.

"Pickle, here, let me help you. How bad are you hurt? Is it hard for you to breathe?"

Pickle spoke slowly and lisped as he spoke with his swollen tongue and mouth.

"Not too good, Mr. Dwight. I'm beat up pretty good. They done a job on me. I thought they was gonna' kill me fo' sho'. I guess I'm mostly just hurtin' now. I ain't dying or nothin' like that. I'm jess beat up."

"How did you get here? The Sheriff swears you confessed to killing Fulbright the banker. You didn't, did you?"

"You mean I didn't tell them that I kilt him or that I didn't do it?"

"I know you didn't kill him, Pickle. Did you tell them that you did?"

"Yes suh, I guess I did."

"Did they beat you to get you to say that?"

"No suh. They didn't seem to need to hear nothin' from me fo' they started to whippin' me."

"Pickle, why on earth did you tell them you did it?"

Pickle sat for a moment and then slowly, picking his words, he explained his actions.

"You remember when you was so upset last night when you come home from the bank and told us about what that poor white trash at the bank had done to us. I knowed you was real mad. I could see it in your eyes. I knew you weren't gonna' jess sit back and let him steal everythin' your family had. I figured he must have had somethin' to do with the house burnin' and all too. Anyhow, after Momma and Miss Dorothy had gone to sleep and I helped you to push the car down the road a ways, I was lookin' out the window and was thinkin' bout it all. Anyways, I seen you way off down the road, drivin' with the headlights off till you reached the bend. Nobody had to tell me where you was goin'.

Any man would'a done the same. I got to thinkin' though that you might be needin' some help and put on my heavy coat and a pair of your boots cause it was sleetin' like the dickens. I bundled up real good and took off to town."

"You followed me? In that freezing rain? On foot? What in the world did you think you could do?"

"Don't be mad with me, Mr. Dwight. I jess thought that I was helpin' out, so to speak. I didn't have no idea 'bout what was goin' to happen, like it did and all."

"Were you at Fulbright's house when I came out?"

"I was jess behind you leavin'. I seen your car turn in the middle of the road and then I seen the fire inside the house. It was spreadin' real fast and I seen you was leavin' so I lit out too. I run as fast as I could. Weren't too long, I heard dogs behind me. They caught up with me real fast and I had to climb up a little shrub oak to get away from 'em. I believe them dogs woulda' jess eat me up right there if I hadn't got up that tree. Anyhow, weren't too long that Bill Moore and that bunch that don't like me come up and started laughin' at me and sayin' how they'd tree'd 'em a 'coon.' I was mighty scared but I figured they was still better than gettin' eaten by a bunch of dogs. Well, I come down out of the tree on my own and they didn't ask me nothin'. They jess started beatin' on me and cussin' at me and even after they knocked me to the ground they kept on kickin' me in the gut. They's kicked out some of my teeth. Momma's gonna be real mad about me loosin' my teeth. She's always sayin' how much she misses hers and that I should take care of my teeth. And, look at me now."

Pickle opened his mouth, and just barely, through his swollen lips, the empty holes where teeth had been were visible. The sight was sickening to Dwight.

"After they'd beat on me a pretty good while, the Sheriff come up and told them they better quit for' they kilt me. I never thought I'd be so happy to see the law come lookin' for me. Anyhow, they told him that if he took me to town they wouldn't never have to spend no money tryin' me cause they was gonna' lynch me jess as soon as they could find them a rope. Yes suh, they said that. 'Bout scared me to death. I can still hear them cussin' me and screamin' jess outside the jail here. I don't reckon they can get me in here, but it sho' do make me nervous, all that talkin' about hangin'."

Dwight wiped Pickle's forehead and even untucked his shirt and cleaned the blood off his mouth. The more he'd tried to find a way to straighten out their lives, the worse everything became. He was so upset with himself he was having trouble keeping his thoughts straight. One thing he knew for sure. He was not going to let Pickle take the blame. He was going to get all of this straight as soon as the Sheriff got back. He would tell him the truth and clear Pickle.

"Look, Pickle, everything's going to be all right. I'm going to tell the Sheriff you didn't do this and clear you. It's going to be OK. We'll get you to a doctor and get you fixed up and back home in no time."

"How you gonna' do that without tellin' bout you and Fulbright? Looks to me that you'd be settin' yourself up if'n you do that, Mr. Dwight."

"Don't you worry about me. I've got some ideas on how to get all this straight. We've got to get you home to Momma. She's worried to death about......."

The Deputy shouted from the office and interrupted them.

"Let's go; the Sheriff's back. Get up! Let's move!"

"I'm ready; just open the cell door."

His face red with worry that his actions might be discovered, the deputy quickly opened and shut the cell door, shoving Dwight ahead of him.

"You're pretty scared of the Sheriff, aren't you, deputy?"

"You don't know him like I do. He can get right nasty when you cross him. I don't want him to know any part of what I let you do. Just remember that I did you a favor."

"I don't forget favors."

Just as they both sat down, the Sheriff, with a scowl on his face, entered the small office and hung his hat on the coat rack, ignoring both of the men inside until he chose to acknowledge their presence. He casually crossed the room, lit a smelly cigar, and sat at his desk. He propped his boots up on the desk with his feet crossed and addressed the deputy first, apparently showing Dwight of how little concern he was to him.

"Crowd under control while I was gone to supper? Nobody trying anything, is there?"

"No, sir. I can hear 'em fussin and carryin' on but it's been just talk. But if they keep on drinkin', Bill Moore might get 'em riled up enough to try somethin'."

"And you, Morton. You come to see your nigger, did you?"

"I came to see Pickle, Sheriff."

"Whatever. Well, he ain't acceptin' no visitors here. Security reasons. If a lawyer shows up, all official and everything, that's a different situation. Far as I'm concerned, you're obviously not a blood relative and friends ain't got no grounds to visit. Once they get him over in Florence, the Sheriff there can do as he pleases. Here, this is how I please. Got me?"

"Oh, I understand, Sheriff. Now I want to make a statement. For the record."

"What, that he was with you last night at his Mammy's shack? Won't hold water. We tracked him and caught him on the way there. No, sir. He's guilty. Guilty as sin!"

"No, Sheriff. He wasn't with me. And I know he didn't kill Fulbright, because I killed Fulbright. I went to his place late to ask him about money that he stole from my family and he pulled a gun on me. He hit me with a poker and even shot me in the shoulder. Then, while we were fighting over the pistol, it went off and he got shot. It was self-defense. Whether you believe me or not, that's how it happened and you can rest assured I'll have the best lawyers in the state on my side. Now let Pickle go. You can lock me up right now. I'm ready."

"I thought I told you back at your Mammy's place that the only talkin' I wanted from you about this case was from a lawyer. So, if you want to confess, that's your business. Ain't nobody here going to take you serious. You go get yourself a hot-shot lawyer and do whatever you want. 'Till a judge tells me I got to let this nigger go, he stays right here in the Lydia lockup. Understand?"

"You're making a big mistake, Sheriff."

"Won't be the first, sonny boy. Now get out of my jail before I lock you up with the darky."

Furious, Dwight walked over to the Sheriff and pointed his finger in his face.

"I want you to remember this day. It's going to be a real important one in your future. There's some big changes coming here, real soon. And I'll be back with my 'hot shot' lawyer...soon. And Sheriff, you better pray there's not another scratch on Pickle when I come back. I'm still holding you responsible."

"So, you've seen him already. Walter, you let him back there to see the nigger? I thought I told you..."

The deputy, sweating from every pore, interrupted out of fear.

"He made me, Sheriff. He threatened me. His family's real powerful...you know what..."

"Shut the hell up, you idiot....Serves me right for hiring a moron..."

Dwight stomped to the door and swung it open. As he walked out he shouted back at Hatcher,

"Remember. I'm holding you accountable. I'll be back."

"You do that, sonny boy! You do that. You don't scare me none."

Dwight walked through the center of the mob outside the jail. The elbows were thrown again. He was too enraged to even feel them. One of the group purposely stepped in front of him. In a burst of furor Dwight grabbed him by the lapels of his wool jacket and lifted him completely off the ground and threw him onto the hood of one of the trucks parked against the sidewalk. Without so much as a turn of his head he continued down the street to his car. Several in the mob wanted to go after him but were held back by Bill Moore.

"Let him go. We got more important things to worry about than him. He's just upset cause we're going to hang his nigger."

At those words the crowd roared in drunken approval. It was a nasty group, growing more drunken and dangerous by the minute. Dwight could see what was happening. He drove immediately to Emory Walker's house, the foreman who worked so long for his family. Emory heard the car coming and stepped out onto the porch of his neatly kept farmhouse to greet Dwight.

"Afternoon, Dwight. What brings you this way? Haven't seen you since the funeral. You and Dot getting along OK? I was hopin' to help you start rebuilding the..."

Dwight, fully realizing that he was racing the sentiments of a mob, hungry for a hanging, interrupted.

"Emory, listen. I need you to go down to the train station and send a telegram for me. If we can't get Governor Richards to send some help over here immediately, I'm afraid a mob down at the jail is going to hang Pickle."

"You mean Momma Mather's boy? What on earth for?"

"They think he killed Nat Fulbright while he was robbing his house. He's innocent, though, and they won't listen to reason. Give me a pencil and I'll write the message for you."

Emory quickly found a pencil and piece of paper and Dwight wrote a short message to the Governor which read:

"TO GOVERNOR JOHN RICHARDS.
COLUMBIA ,S.C.
EMERGENCY. I AM DWIGHT MORTON, SON OF ROBERT MORTON OF LYDIA, S.C. MOB TRYING TO KILL INNOCENT MAN IN LYDIA JAIL. SEND HELP IMMEDIATELY. I WILL BE THERE. PLEASE DO NOT WAIT. HELP ME. DWIGHT MORTON, LYDIA."

Dwight folded the note and handed it back to Emory.

"Emory, this means an innocent man's life and he's a friend of mine. Please hurry. I'm going to stop off at Momma's and then I'll meet you back at the jail. Thirty minutes, Emory! Will you meet me there?"

"You know I will. Half an hour. I'll be there."

Both men got in their vehicles and raced off in different directions. Dwight drove as fast as the old T-Model would go. As he pulled in, Momma and Dot were both standing in the doorway looking every bit as distraught as they did when he left them.

"What's happening, Dwight? Momma's been worried sick. Is Pickle all right?"

"He is now, but Bill Moore's got a crowd all fired up just

outside the jail. Go down the row houses here and see if you can get some of the hands to take the grain truck and meet me down at the jail. Emory Walker is wiring the Governor to get some real law over here. Till then, I'm going to stay at the jail and make sure nobody gets to him. You both stay here and don't worry if I'm gone all night. I'm going to camp there till I know he's going to be set free. Dot, take care of Momma."

"I will. Dwight, please...be careful. I love you."

"I love you too, Dot. I'll be fine. I'm just worried about Pickle. It's going to be OK. Now try and get some men down to the jail."

Dwight drove off again heading back to Lydia. Dot sat Momma down by the fire in her shack and went down the row of tenant shacks trying to find help. Even though she could see the concern in the eyes of each family, she could find none willing to face a lynch mob of bigots. There were only a few men left in the row houses since the fire. Most had gone to other cities looking for work as there was none to be found in a depression-riddled farming community. When Fountainside burned, so did their livelihood. Those who remained were either too old or young to venture into the dangerous situation waiting on the streets of Lydia. Heartsick, Dot returned to Momma and had to lie to her about the response she had gotten.

"Did you get some men, Miss Dorothy?"

She didn't want to lie but Dot could not let her know the truth.

"A few Momma. They're going to go down in just a little while. Pickle's going to be fine. Dwight and Emory will be there by the time they arrive and even the Governor will be sending some help. It's going to be all right. I know it is."

As Dwight approached Lydia, the last rays of daylight were disappearing. The temperature was falling fast and he hoped bad weather wouldn't keep responsible law enforcement from getting there quickly. He wished Dot knew the whole story before he told the authorities but there just wasn't enough time to get into it. He couldn't let Pickle sit in the jail with no one there to look out for him. It had only been a little over an hour since he left him alone and he hoped everything was OK. He felt that he'd thrown enough fear into Sheriff Hatcher that he wouldn't allow anything to happen he could be called to task for. Dwight felt relieved when he turned the last corner and saw Emory's truck just down the street from the jail. He was a large man, not easily intimidated, who would not be frightened off by the likes of Bill Moore or the crowd which had gathered.

Dwight got out of the truck and walked quickly to the jail. The wind was picking up and the cold air stung his face and ears. The mob had almost entirely disappeared. He figured the cold had also helped to reduce their enthusiasm. He pushed open the heavy wooden door to the jail and was glad to see Emory sitting on a bench just inside the door. Sheriff Hatcher practically fell all over himself to greet Dwight at the door.

"Dwight. Glad you made it back all right. Weather sure has been nasty lately. Emory and me have been just talking about how much we liked your folks and how we missed them and all."

Dwight looked over at Emory to see if had any idea as to why Hatcher had suddenly become so chummy.

"Yes sir. I knew Robert was well thought of over in Columbia. I hope you aren't still upset over the disagreement we had a little earlier. There ain't been a murder here before this and I guess I just overreacted a little. No hard feelin's, huh, Dwight?"

"I guess not. As long as Pickle is treated well and you help me get this all straightened out."

Dwight walked over close to Emory and whispered.

"What's going on here?"

Emory smiled and answered.

"John Richards sent a wire back to the Sheriff within fifteen minutes. I brought it over when I came. He was explicit about how you and Pickle were to be treated. He said a Marshal from Florence would be here tonight to pick up Pickle and place him in protective custody until this was settled. I would say it made a real impression on old Hatcher. No doubt the only correspondence he's had from the Governor."

Dwight and Emory smiled at each other. Dwight felt a huge sense of relief. He would stay here and then go with him to Florence to make sure he was all right. When he returned, he'd tell Dot and Momma the whole story and then get a good attorney to help him handle the case. Everything was starting to work out.

"You want me to stay with you, Dwight?" Emory asked. "It's fine with me."

"No Emory. You've already saved the day as far as I'm concerned. I can't thank you enough. Hopefully I'll have the farm up and running by spring and all this will be just an unpleasant memory. You go on home to your family. With the Sheriff's assistance, I'm sure everything will be fine. Isn't that so, Sheriff?"

"Absolutely, Dwight! I feel much better about the whole thing now. I was beginning to get concerned we had arrested the wrong man before you ever come in Dwight. Just had a hunch based on years of experience. He didn't look like no killer to me. I could buy the robbery but not a killin'. Just ain't the type."

"Good night, Emory. Thanks again. If you could go by Momma's on the way home and tell her and Dot that Pickle's fine. Tell them I'm going with him to Florence to get this taken care of. I would sure appreciate it. Tell Dot I'll be home tomorrow and hopefully have Pickle with me."

"Will do, Dwight. Let me know if there's anything else I can do. Night."

Emory walked back into the cold night air leaving Dwight, Sheriff Hatcher and Pickle alone in the quiet jail. None of the crowd remained outside.

"Yeah, they've all left," Hatcher said. "I pretty much run 'em off after I got that wire from the Governor. Oh yeah, I got a wire from Governor Richards askin' me to kinda work with you. Addressed it to me by name. Kinda surprised me that he would know my name and all. That's one of the good things about this sorta work; you get to meet a lot of really fine people. I sure am pleased that........"

Dwight could surmise the rest of the Sheriff's speech. He interrupted.

"Sheriff, could I please see Pickle?"

"Of course, son. Of course you can. Let me get my keys. Come on and follow me back there."

Hatcher led Dwight back down the long hall to Pickle's cell and opened it.

"Hey boy! You got company. Mr. Morton has come back

to help you out. You go on in, Dwight. I'll be in the front office
if you need me. Just give me a shout when you're done."

"Thank you, Sheriff. I'll just stay here in the cell until the
Marshal arrives from Florence."

"Suit yourself, son. That's fine with me." Hatcher walked
back down the hall leaving Dwight and Pickle alone in the small
dark cell.

"Pickle, I think everything's going to work out now.
There's a Marshal from Florence headed here. You and I will ride
back to Florence with him and then I'm going to make a statement
to the authorities that will clear you. With a little luck, you'll be
home by noon tomorrow."

"Thank you, Mr. Dwight. I appreciates what all you have
done cause I was mighty scared to start with. Now I got some
other things that are startin' to worry me."

"What's that, Pickle?"

"You say you're gonna' tell 'em you done it? That you
killed him?"

"That's right. It was self-defense. I'm going to prove he
was stealing from me and I went to confront him and he tried to
kill me. It was even his gun. I'll get a good lawyer from Columbia and I'll be OK."

"Didn't you say that Fulbright come from rich folks too?
What's his folks gonna' be sayin' 'bout all this? Ain't no man
takes somebody killin' his son very good. Not even a bad one like
Fulbright. It might not be so easy. What if they say's you gotta
go to jail, I mean just maybe. What would happen to Miss Dorothy and Momma? They got nowhere else to go. Most of the field
hands has moved on lookin' for some work and I don't know
nothin' bout farmin'. The farm would jess go to seed without you
there."

"Look, Pickle. You didn't have anything to do with Fulbright. These problems are mine and I'm prepared to deal with
them. You need to worry about what you're going to be doing
with your life and taking care of your momma. She's getting
along in years and needs to know you're all right. That's what you
need to be concerned about."

"That's all true...everything you're sayin' and all but I jess don't think it's all that simple, Mr. Dwight."

"How's that, Pickle?"

"Well, let's say you do hafta' go to jail, even for just a couple years. What will happen to the farm? Why, half the people in the town worked for you. They's all countin' on you to take care of 'em. And Momma's too old to do washin'. Besides, I don't want her doin' wash for other folks. And then there's Miss Dorothy. You know how.....well...I ...swear, she's been awfully good to me and Momma and I don't want to see her worryin herself to death over you. I jess can't do it, Mr. Dwight. I told 'em I done it. They all believed me and that's what I'm goin' to keep sayin'."

"That's crazy, Pickle! They wouldn't treat a ....well..."

Pickle knew what he was getting at.

"A nigger?"

"No! A black man like you. I don't like it but it's a fact. You know they wouldn't care as much about what happened to you. And besides, I did it! You're completely innocent. I'm not even thinking about letting you say that you did it. And I don't want to hear any more about it. You understand?"

"I hear you but you got to listen to me, too."

"About what?"

"I'm a grown man. I'm old enough to make up my own mind about things and I'm right and you're all wrong 'bout this."

"How do you figure that?"

"Listen, Mr. Dwight. Jess like you know, I'm black. My granddaddy was a slave and ain't nobody in my family ever been nothin' but field hands. I don't want that. You know I don't. I ain't never even been out of the county. I ain't even seen the end of Brice's Creek. They say there's a waterfall down there. Anyhow, I ain't goin' nowhere and we both know it. Hell, the white folks is goin' broke all 'round here and the black folks all work for them! The facts is, I ain't got a whole lot workin' for me. But you do. You got the whole world lined up and the brains to go somewhere. You ain't black like me. You and Miss Dorothy could do things, some good things.   The way I see it."

"No, Pickle! Absolutely not. Just shut up about it. You hear me?"

"Mr. Dwight, I'm a grown man and expects you to hear

me out when I talk, jess like I does you. Now, here's what I can see happenin' 'bout this. I tell 'em I did it. They'll all be happier than if a white man done it, 'specially a well-known one like you. They'll do whatever they wants with me. It don't matter to no-body, not hardly even me. And you, you'll put the farm back together. You'll look after Momma till she passes on and you'll take special good care of Miss Dorothy. The people in town and all the other black families back home will have a place to work and somebody who'll look out for 'em. You're the only white man in the county that most of 'em would look to for anythin'. They know you're a good man, Mr. Dwight. You can do all of the things I want to do and can't. Black folks would have some-body lookin' out for 'em around here. This way, it would be kinda like I helped do it. You understand what I'm sayin', Mr. Dwight? That ain't such a bad thing to want, is it?"

"No, Pickle. It really is a beautiful thought and I'm proud to know that you are a friend of mine."

Dwight bent over and hugged Pickle.

"All of that will happen anyway and you'll be there to see it. Now, let's talk about something else. How are you feeling? Are your ribs hurting still?"

"Jess a little. I'm gettin' along better now. Few days I'll be fine. I been hurt worse by that old cow I took. He kicked me one in the ass so bad. Did I ever tell you 'bout that, Mr. Dwight? That sure is a funny story. Well suh, I got up real early one mornin' and went out to feed him. It was cold as blue blazes and my feet, well suh, they was......"

"You mean you did steal their cow?" Dwight laughed out loud at the revelation.

"Yeah, Momma was wantin' some milk for her ulcer and I jess noticed that old heifer. She was just standin' by the road, mind you. She was almost sayin' "come get me, boy."

Sheriff Hatcher called out from the front office.

"Dwight, you need to come with me a minute."

Dwight stood as Hatcher came to the cell door. He opened the door and let Dwight out, locking it behind him. Pickle felt better now about the whole situation. Half-joking, he said to Dwight.

"I'll be right here if'n you fellas needs me, Mr. Dwight."

Dwight had a new admiration for Pickle and how strong he had been through all of this. He would make certain that Momma knew just how calm and purposeful he had been when they returned. As Dwight entered the front office of the jail behind Hatcher, his worst nightmare slammed him in the face with the butt of a 30-30 rifle. Immediately unconscious, he fell to the rough wooden floor of the jail. And there, standing over him, dressed in the white robes of the Klan, stood a familiar figure. Bill Moore and his assorted rednecks had returned in the regal attire of the bigots they were.

"You asked for this, you nigger lovin' asshole. And I'd say you got it. How 'bout a couple of you boys grabbin' him and totin' him back to the nigger's cell. Hatcher, you stay the hell out of the way. That way, you was only tryin' to save your own skin. Can't nobody say you had nothin' to do with this."

The group went down the hallway following Moore, one of them carrying a lit torch that cast an eerie hue on the surrealistic scene. As they opened the cell door, Pickle, in a state of shock, could only think to ask...

"Where's Mr. Dwight? You ain't hurt Mr. Dwight, has you?"

"No, we sure ain't hurt a hair on his head. He's just gonna' take a little nap here in your cell since you won't be needin' it no more."

"What do you think y'all are doin', you worthless troublemaker?"

"Me a trouble maker? I ain't never stole no cow. I ain't never robbed decent white folks and I sure as shit ain't killed nobody. That is unless they was askin' for it. Just like you did, nigger. Now get the hell up, boy. You're comin' for a ride with us."

Several of the mob grabbed Pickle by his arms and manhandled him in front of them as they pushed him down the hall to the front office. When Pickle passed Dwight, he saw the blood running down his face as they carried him into the cell, threw him on the cot and locked the cell behind him. It encouraged Pickle that they locked the door. It must mean that Dwight was still alive. Once in the front office, the group bound Pickle's hands behind him and shackled his feet together with leg irons that hung on the wall of the jail. Finally, they placed a dark gray flour sack over his terrified face and pulled the draw string around his neck. Terror overcame Pickle. He knew his tormentor and the extent he was willing to go. Without a miracle, his time was going to be short and violent. The last face he saw before the sack was pulled over his head was Sheriff Hatcher, smiling as he watched the proceedings from a corner of the room. None of this was any surprise to him. He recognized the Sheriff's voice as he was pushed out of the office door into the cold night.

"You boys hurry up and get out of town now. They'll be here from Florence any minute and they don't need to see what's happening just yet."

Pickle was forced into the bed of a pickup where two of his captors joined him. They pushed him down on his face and stomped his head onto the frozen metal surface.

"Kiss the floor, boy. You move any and we'll split your head wide open."

As an afterthought, just as the truck started to pull away, Bill Moore got out and walked back over to Hatcher who was watching from the open door of the jail.

"Step back inside a minute, would you, Sheriff? I want to tell you somethin' that just come to me."

The two men went back inside. No sooner had the door closed behind them than Moore took his rifle and smacked Hatcher upside the head with it. Not as hard as Dwight had been struck, but enough to bring a bright red stream pouring from Hatcher's nose and mouth. "What the hell was that for?"

Hatcher, in dismay, spoke through his bloody lips.

"You don't want those folks from Florence thinkin' you let us have the nigger without a fight, do you? You look real convincin' now."

Smiling sadistically, he returned to the truck and the mob disappeared into the night with their prisoner.

The awareness of cold water on his face brought Dwight around. At first he could not gather his thoughts, only stare blankly at the police officer who knelt before him with a wet rag in his hand.

"Mr. Morton. Can you hear me, Mr. Morton?"

Dwight responded to the question and became quickly aware of the pain on the right side of his head.

"Where am I? What happened?"

"You're in the Lydia jail, Mr. Morton. Your friend has been taken by a mob. Do you remember anything?"

"Yes! Pickle, they took Pickle! We have to go after them before they hurt him."

"You're not up to going anywhere, Mr. Morton. You've got a real bad looking knot on your head. Looks like you could use a few stitches. Do you have any idea where they might have taken him?"

"I've got more than a good idea. I guarantee you they've taken him back to the same spot that Bill Moore took him before when I stopped them from killing him. I'm going with you...ah...Damn...this hurts like hell...I'm going just the same. Let's hurry."

"I really don't think you should try to make it, Mr. Morton. Just tell me where it is."

"You'll never find it this late by yourself. How long have they been gone?"

"Sheriff Hatcher says they left with him about a half hour ago."

"Hatcher? He's not with them?"

"No. They busted him up pretty good, too. He tried to stop them and they hit him with a rifle butt. His head looks about like yours."

"I'm shocked. Let's go! If they took him where I think they did, they've already been there for ten minutes. God, I hope we're not too late."

There were three officers from Florence who made the trip. They were armed with shotguns and had been told to expect a rowdy crowd but this was more than they had anticipated. Dwight jumped in the car with them and began to direct them through the night down muddy dirt roads. The rutted paths were quickly freezing over and becoming an oily slick quagmire. The trip was taking longer than usual due to the conditions and for Dwight each moment seemed like an hour. His head was killing him, but his concern over Pickle was an overriding factor to any thoughts of his own pain. He knew what Moore and his gang had in mind and he realized they thought they had a debt to settle with Pickle anyway.

"Please drive as fast you can. If we don't get there quickly, I'm afraid of what they will do."

"Any faster and we'll be in the ditch for the night, Mr. Morton. Just don't let me make any wrong turns."

"You're headed in the right direction. Just make it as fast as we can."

After thirty minutes of sliding around dangerous curves and nearly getting stuck each time they had to slow down, they arrived at the clearing. It was dark. No truck lights or torches were visible. Dwight jumped out while the car was still coming to a stop and ran up the gentle slope to the far end of the field. His boots felt like they were being pulled through cement with each step. His heart was taking ten steps for each one his feet managed. Mentally and physically depleted, he reached the familiar setting. Near the back edge of the field, silhouetted against the angry moon, which disappeared with each passing cloud, Dwight could see the pathetic lifeless body suspended by a noose around its contorted neck. Hanging from a low, large branch of a white oak tree right where he had been rescued from before, Pickle's life had come to a violent end. Spent, Dwight fell into the snow under Pickle's bare feet. As he sat there dumbfounded by the senseless viciousness of the tragedy, the officers cut Pickle down from the rope.

"I'm sorry, Mr. Morton. No way we could have gotten here any faster. I don't believe ten minutes would even have made a difference. Why don't you come on back to the car? We'll get you to a doctor. Don't you worry about your friend. We'll see he's brought back to town. Come on now, you need to get back where it's warm."

"Will you go after them?"

"In the morning, we'll get enough help here to get this handled properly. Don't you worry. The Governor made it real clear about his feelings. He will be more than interested in what went on here. No stone will be left unturned."

"You don't have to turn any stones. That bastard Bill Moore did it. I'll swear to it and even help you find him. I want to see him on the end of a rope, just like Pickle."

Dwight's expression went blank at the thought of another ordeal that lay just ahead, perhaps even harder than this. How would he tell Momma what had happened to Pickle? She would never forgive him. He'd promised that Pickle would be home by morning. Guilt began to fill him like a waterfall dumping into a small pond. What could he possibly do to make any of this better?

The trip back to town, statements to the police and stitches at the doctor's all went by in a fog of mental anguish which had grabbed hold of his mind. Rational thoughts were almost impossible. He felt an overpowering urge to just sleep. Maybe when he was awake and rested, he'd find everything had worked out without him. Maybe he would wake up from a horrible dream and everything would be like before. Nothing had happened except in his own tormented mind.

The first rays of morning brought a red glow far away where the edge of seemingly endless fields turned into sky. There was such a strong layering of frost that it appeared on first glance that the fields might be covered with snow. In a few moments, as the welcome streams of warmth began to cover them, steam would rise up and cover every small recess in the terrain with its own cloud. The car stopped in front of Momma Mather's shack. The Marshal from Florence woke Dwight up from the coma-like sleep he had passed into on the drive back to Fountainside.

"Mr. Morton....Dwight....I believe we're here, sir. You awake, Mr. Morton?"

"What? Oh...we're here."

Dwight straightened up his back which he had contorted in an effort to sleep between the two officers he shared the seat with.

"We'll be back out later in the day to talk with you some more, Mr. Morton. We'll get to the bottom of this. You can count on it. You need some rest, son. Go on in and get some sleep. You need a hand to the door?"

"No, sir. I'll be fine."

He knew he would not be fine. Not now, not ever. He dreaded facing Momma and Dot and having to relate to them what had occurred. He stood up, shut the car door behind him and quietly walked to the door. The Marshal's car turned in the dirt yard and left, quickly disappearing into the morning fog. As he opened the door, Dot, with a look of great anguish on her face, greeted him. She was wearing a housecoat and looked as if she hadn't slept since Dwight's hasty departure. Her first concern was for Dwight. She walked over to him and gave him a comforting hug as she asked the question he knew was coming.

"Are you OK? Where's Pickle? What happened? That was a US Marshal's car wasn't it?"

Dwight breathed in deeply and steeled himself for the task at hand.

"I'm fine. Where's Momma?"

"She's still asleep. She stayed up till almost four and finally passed out on the couch from pure exhaustion. She was worried sick about you and Pickle. Where is Pickle? He's all right isn't he?"

"No. He's not all right."

Dwight reached up and unconsciously rubbed at the stitches on his forehead which the dimly lit cabin had not afforded Dot enough light to notice yet. The gesture brought it to her attention.

"Your head! Why, you're hurt. What happened? What do you mean Pickle's not OK? What's going on?"

"Dot, I don't want to have to go through all of this twice. Go wake up Momma and I'll tell you both together what has happened."

As she turned to wake up Momma Mather, Dot could already tell from Dwight's tone of voice and his appearance that whatever had occurred was not going to be pleasant to hear.

"Momma. Wake up, Momma. Dwight's back."

The old lady slowly sat up on the couch.

"Mornin', Mr. Dwight. Is Pickle here with you?"

"No, Momma. He's not."

Dwight went over to her and knelt in front of her with his knees down on the cold planks of the rough-hewn pine floor. He took both of her hands in his and held them firmly as he slowly and painfully described every detail of what had occurred that evening. He told her every word of Pickle's magnificent gesture to gather all of the burdens to himself to save those he loved from any pain. How his final thoughts and actions only emphasized the gentle and loving spirit that had been his since his first breath at Fountainside. The loud and mournful cry that filled the small shack surely was heard by every creature in the forest nearby and would have pulled at the soul of anyone who heard it. It was a sound that had been heard repeatedly since the first frost filled morning on this lovely blue orbiting sphere. For Dwight Morton, it was the trumpet of resolve.

CHAPTER NINE

Bill Moore was never convicted for the abduction and murder of Pickle Mather. For that matter, no one was ever charged with any offense related to the crime. Certainly all of those even remotely suspected of involvement were questioned, but no hard evidence ever surfaced and the only two witnesses to the event had different stories. Dwight was certain of the identity of the leader and of many of the group. However, Sheriff Hatcher said that he just didn't remember things quite the same as Dwight and since both had been struck severely in the head during the incident, perhaps their recollections weren't all that accurate. No one ever came forward with additional information and those who took part in Pickle's lynching never broke ranks. That is not to say that there was no punishment ever handed out.

Bill Moore appeared to be a cursed man from that time forward. Like many others, the Depression claimed his farm and family. It seemed that no one would hire him for even the smallest of jobs. Occasionally a new business in the area might give him a shot but after only a day or so, they would invariably have a change of heart. Such a poverty-stricken and desperate existence eventually brought him into a much closer relationship with the bottle. This downward slide continued for a number of years, and local farmers who remembered his days as a collection officer for Fulbright would not give him so much as a plate of food, even when they had overflowing crops. Many nights he spent in the Lydia jail, as much to keep the citizens of town from having to listen to his incessant ranting of a conspiracy to ruin him, as from just his public drunkenness. His plagued life under such circumstances would continue for many years.

Sheriff Hatcher continued to act in that capacity for several years after the hanging of Pickle Mather. This came abruptly to an end when a virtual legion of improperly handled matters came anonymously to the attention of higher authorities. His involvement in collection malpractice, foreclosures and unethical handling of criminal cases for personal gain had been well-documented and extensive records of his paper trail eventually found their way to the desk of South Carolina's Attorney General.

Oddly enough, Hatcher also spent a great amount of the remaining years of his life complaining of a vendetta. Again, such complaining fell on deaf ears. He would spend a many years in the company of former clients of the county jail.

Similar tales of despair were told by a number of those who had been party to Pickle's lynching. But, through all of these matters, Dwight, Dorothy and Momma Mather never spoke a word out of bitterness or of a desire for retribution to anyone. The authorities accepted that Fulbright had been killed by Pickle Mather. Even though Dwight insisted he wanted to take responsibility and clear Pickle's name, he accepted the wishes of Momma Mather who believed Pickle would rest better knowing his actions saved his family from any more suffering. Also, it would allow them to push for the things that had become paramount in their lives. Their actions and pursuits bonded into a common goal and in those endeavors they would be constantly absorbed for the remainder of their lives.

Dwight first turned his efforts into saving Fountainside. That spring he offered to furnish land, seeds, fertilizer and tools to anyone in the county who had no money but the willingness to work to support their families. In return, he would take only a fourth of the income from the crop. That was half the usual amount a tenant farmer had to pay to rent farm land. In short order, he was managing the most productive farm lands in the state. Many previously unemployed families, both black and white, were able to carve a future out of the rich black soil around Fountainside. It seemed the more he gave, the more he received to the point it almost became humorous to him that so many business people he knew argued over every penny and never made enough to feel satisfied.

Dwight helped numerous families open small businesses around the area and those who were willing to work but not able always found an answer of some sort by consulting with Dwight about their problems. Though he still had detractors who did not appreciate the apparent ease with which he made no distinction of race or class, he became a well-liked and very prosperous man. Momma Mather and Dorothy were by his side continuously, adding effort as well as counsel to all his dealings.

Dot reopened her school with a renewed vitality. No student was ever turned down for a lack of funds and many of them found their way to colleges throughout the country, courtesy of scholarships provided by Dot and Dwight Morton. Momma Mather made it a point to walk by the school at least once or twice a week to look at the front of the small framed building with the lovely sign just over the door reading "The Mather School of Lydia". Dot wanted to call it the Pickle Mather School but there was still too much controversy surrounding the death of Nathaniel Fulbright and they thought it best for the school to not open the wound.

With Dwight's increasing popularity with the citizens of South Carolina, it was only natural that many of his associates tried to convince him to get involved in politics. After some soul searching on the matter, he gave in and was elected to several state offices. He eventually succumbed to the pressure to run for a seat in the United States Congress. He had no desire to venture out of his beloved home state but nonetheless saw a need for a social conscience to help the nation get a better grip on its heart.

Around nineteen forty, Momma Mather passed on, a much loved woman, happy with her life and contributions. In her last days she would talk for hours of her son and how she longed to hold him and tell him of all the good things she had seen come from his life. True to Pickle's wishes, Dwight saw to it that Momma lacked for nothing till her dying day. On a beautiful spring afternoon, with Azaleas and Dogwoods in full bloom, she was laid to rest beside Pickle in the Morton family cemetery, alongside Dwight's parents and many generations of the most distinguished names in South Carolina's history. When questioned about family servants being buried in such a place of prominence, Dwight would always reply....

"They are there to add dignity and love."

Needless to say, there were many who did not understand the answer, but the numbers of those who did were growing. Dwight had become the leader of an expanding group of prominent people who wanted an end to the injustice that plagued the country. He labored on for years after his body had quit contributing strength to the effort. Even the loss of his beloved Dot did not reduce his commitment. Through his efforts a nation was changed, and a promise was kept. No one could possibly accuse Dwight of not living up to all that Pickle wanted of him, but Dwight still felt the need to clear Pickle's name and set the record straight.

CHAPTER TEN

"And so, that's why I brought you here, Oscar. You know the truth of it all and I trust you to do what's right with it."

"You know I will, Dwight. I want to promise you that."

The old man smiled and cut him short.

"You don't even have to say it, Oscar. I know you. You have no choice now. Just like I didn't. And don't be afraid of doing the right thing. The more I gave, the more I had. And the weaker I've gotten, the stronger I am. Give me your hand, Oscar."

Oscar leaned over close and clasped the frail, bony hand noticing how cold and weak it was. Dwight's other hand rested on top of his and he held them as tightly as he could.

"Your turn now Oscar."

"My turn at what, Dwight?"

"To do what's right. Now, Oscar, there's a few folks outside waiting to tell me goodbye and I want to speak to them a minute or two while I can. Thank you for coming to see me."

"Senator, it has been an honor to know you. Thank you from all of us."

Oscar felt the grip on his hands ease as Dwight's hands slid back down to the bed. He knew the time was short as he walked away. He turned one last time and heard the weak voice of Dwight Morton say to him.

"I'll tell him for all of you."

As Oscar walked through the door and back out into the waiting room he was shocked at the number of people who were waiting to have a word with Dwight. There were a great many, both well-known and obscure, from every walk of life. He knew that only a few would be allowed to see him.

The nurse called for them as Dwight requested. It was no surprise that the first name called was a familiar one.

"Mr. Meecham? Bob Meecham?"

"Right here, nurse. Can I go in now?"

"Yes Sir, he asked for you."

As Meecham passed he reached out his hand to Oscar.

"How is he, Oscar?"

"I don't think he has very long, Bob. You should go in."

"I would certainly like to see you before you leave for home, Oscar. You'll be here a while longer, won't you?"

"I can wait here for you if you want me to."

"That would be fine, Oscar. I won't be too long; there's obviously a lot of folks wanting to speak with him."

"I'll be right here in the waiting room."

Bob Meecham walked into the small room to pay his final respects to the man who changed the course of his entire life. Oscar looked around the room at the many familiar faces that surrounded him. Many of them he knew from following their careers in his efforts to cover the news. It was humbling to see such a gathering, all waiting patiently in hope of one final moment with such a simple man as Dwight Morton.

The impact of Dwight's death bed revelations was just beginning to register. One question kept coming back to him. Why did Dwight choose him over all the well-known journalists that filled the nation's capital, any of whom would have written it verbatim to Dwight's wishes? Why him? As he pondered the question he began to realize how much his back was aching from the solitary position he had occupied for the better part of a day. As he stretched to relive the tight muscles, he saw one face in the corner of the room that he did not expect to see. Looking nervously at him, Marcus motioned for Oscar to come over to him. Shocked to see him there, he walked over to where the young man was standing.

"Marcus, are you all right? How's your mother doing?"

"I was hopin' you'd find out for me, mister. They still got the cops tryin' to haul me down to that youth jail and I can't see her from here. Would you check for me? Tell her I'm OK and that I'm stayin' with a friend. Not to worry 'bout me. Would you do that?"

"I'll do it right now, Marcus. You wait right here."

He could see in Marcus' face that the boy didn't know if he could fully trust him to not tell the police he was there.

"Marcus. It's OK. I won't tell anybody you're here. Just stay put and out of sight. I'll be right back. You're going to wait for me, aren't you?"

"Yeah. I'll wait."

"What's her name?"

"Mary. Mary Frye."

Oscar slipped into the room without knocking. There was only a small night light on and there were three patients' beds in a room the same size Dwight had to himself. The first bed had a small, elderly white woman in it. He looked behind the curtain at the next bed.

"Mrs. Frye?"

Dwight repeated the name very quietly again.

"Mrs. Frye? Is that you?"

"Yes, sir. I'm Mary. Are you a doctor?"

"No, ma'am, I'm Oscar Phipps. I'm a friend of your son, Marcus. He wanted me to check on you. How are you doing?"

"Lord, I'm so worried about my boys. How is Marcus? Are you with the Social Services people that have been lookin' for him?"

"No ma'am. He and I just met here at the hospital while I was visiting with someone else and we just kind of hit it off, you might say. He said to tell you he's staying with a friend and to not worry about him. He wanted to find out how you were doing and he's somewhat afraid that if he came in someone on the staff might turn him over to Social Services."

"Lord. I'm so worried about him. I told him he shouldn't be afraid of them people but he just won't listen. A lot of his friends have been in trouble and they just bad mouth all the folks who run things like that. I need to get out of here to take care of them."

Oscar looked around the room and could tell by the number of monitors and tubes still connected to her that she would not be leaving the room any time soon. More than likely it would be a week or more and she would need to be the one being taken care of even then.

"Mister, do you think you could get him in here for just a minute so's I can hug him? It would sure mean an awful lot to me. Maybe I could convince him to let those folks help him till I'm back on my feet."

"Well, I'll try, but I don't know if I can convince him. He

doesn't seem to want to trust anybody right now. I'll go see what I can do though. I'll be right back."

Oscar walked back out into the room and found Marcus still squeezed up against a wall trying to blend in with the furniture.

"Your mother wants to see you. She wants you to come in with her for just a moment."

"Somebody'll turn me in if I do. I can't."

"Hey. I'll make you a deal. You stay with me and I promise you I'll cover for you. Nobody will say a word."

"How can you do that? I ain't no fool, mister."

"Watch."

Oscar walked over to one of the young Marine guards and whispered something to him and returned to Marcus.

"It's safe. We're covered."

He put his hand behind Marcus' back and gently pushed him toward the door.

"What'd you say to the soldier?"

"Told him you were my kid."

"You lie."

"I swear."

"No shit?"

"Why would I lie about it?"

The thought amused Oscar and he snickered to himself as they entered the room. Marcus went straight to his mother's side.

"Momma. It's me, Marcus."

"Oh, baby. Hug your momma. I been missin' you so bad. You know you like to scared me to death runnin' away like that."

"I know, Momma. But I don't want to go with those people to some kinda kids' jail."

"It's no jail, honey. Cody says it's real nice like a big house with good furniture and a big TV. He likes it there."

"Yeah, but they wouldn't send the older kids like me there. Ernie told me that they just keep the small kids there and guys my age go to some detention center. I ain't goin' to no detention place."

"I don't think this Ernie knows what he's talkin' 'bout, baby. Those people seem real nice to me."

"They just know you're sick, Momma. Why are they havin' cops look for me if they're so nice?"

"I think those police are here all the time, Marcus. They just told 'em to let them know if they saw you. Ain't none of 'em going to hurt you none."

"I'm fine, Momma. How are you feelin'? Are you still hurtin' bad and all?"

"Not like I was, baby. I'm goin' to be better'n ever soon. I just have to rest for a while. Soon I'll be out of here, get my jobs back and we'll all be back together again. I promise you it won't be long. Now won't you let this man help you see if you can stay with Cody? Please baby, for Momma."

Marcus bent over and hugged his mother as tightly as all the apparatus she was hooked to would allow. His voice cracked as he spoke and for the first time Oscar could plainly see the fear in the young man.

"I love you, Momma. I hope you're gonna be all right. I'm so worried about us. I want us to be together. I miss Cody, too. Those people better be treatin' him right."

"They are, baby. Just hush and hug your momma. Everything's' gonna' be just fine. Just fine."

For nearly a minute Marcus just stood there, laying over the railing of the bed hugging his mother. Nothing else was said until Marcus finally straightened up, wiped his eyes quickly and told her goodbye.

"Don't you worry about nothin', Momma. I won't be far away and I'll try and sneak in and see you some. And when you're feelin' better, you can walk over to the window and I'll be out there. You just tell me the time and I'll be out there everyday so you can see I'm OK. I better go now, Momma. I love you."

"Please let this man take you to Cody, baby...Please!"

"I can't, Momma."

Marcus left the room. Oscar walked over beside Mary.

"I'll try to get him to let me help him, Mrs. Frye. I'll see what I can do."

"Thank you so much, sir. Thank you."

Oscar followed Marcus back to his spot in the waiting room. As Oscar turned the corner, he saw that the boy was not waiting for him. He was walking quickly down the hall trying to make good an escape. Oscar followed after him as fast as he could without making a scene.

He could just recognize the back of Marcus's jacket leaving through a small side exit door and sprinted to the parking lot to catch him. The snap of bitter cold and his breath coming out in small clouds of steam quickly reminded him that he was not wearing a coat.

"Marcus! Wait, Marcus. It's just me...Oscar."

At first Marcus didn't acknowledge the voice calling him and continued walking. It was not until Oscar suggested he had a message from his mother that Marcus reluctantly stopped, still not turning around to greet Oscar. He merely shrugged his shoulders in resignation that he would listen for a moment under the chance this was not some ploy, but a real message from his mother.

"This better be for real or I'm really gonna' pissed at you, mister."

"Oscar. Remember? Oscar Phipps. Listen, Marcus. Your mother is sicker from worrying about you than she is from the operation. She would sure get well a lot sooner if she knew you were OK. Why don't you go with me to just take a look at where Cody is staying? If you don't like it, you can go back to your friends. I won't bother you any further."

For a moment, Marcus stood silent in thought as if weighing the possible choices and their potential consequences. After a long stretch of silence he simply replied.

"I don't think so. You've been pretty straight with me and all and I appreciate it. I wish you'd check back on my mother when you're there and make sure she's OK but I'm gonna' stay with Ernie. Tell her I'm fine. I'll be OK till she can get back out."

Shaking his head in frustration with the clouded rationale of youth, Oscar gave him one last chance.

"I'm concerned about you too, Marcus. This is a pretty dangerous city and it's cold as the devil out here. I'm freezing right now. You sure you won't let me take you to a motel or somewhere I can tell her that I know you're not on the streets?"

"I told you, I'm not on the street. I'm stayin' with Ernie and his folks. I'm fine."

Not knowing what else he could do, Oscar pulled out his wallet and emptied what cash he had into Marcus' hand.

"Marcus, here's a hundred bucks. You use this to eat and get a place to stay if you get cold or scared or whatever and here...take my card."

"What'll I do with this?"

"Put it in your pocket and call me if you need anything, anything at all. The number with 800 in front is free around the clock. You tell whoever answers who you are and to get hold of me. I wear a beeper. They'll get up with me and I'll call you back within an hour, night or day."

"All right! A beeper, just like a dealer."

"You'll call me?"

"Yeah, I guess. If it's somethin' important."

Oscar held out his hand and the two shook on their agreement. Marcus turned and walked off into the recesses of the dark parking lot. As Oscar, cold to the bone, hustled back to the hospital, he could not help but feel that he had reacted somewhat differently than he might have earlier in the week. The story of Pickle was lying heavily in the front of his mind, actually increasing its burden with each passing hour. He went to the hospital coffee shop and poured himself a steamy cup of straight black coffee. Warming slightly, he sat on one of the vinyl and chrome chairs and stared at the white tiled wall. Deep in thought, he jumped when Bob Meecham laid his hand on his shoulder.

"It's over, Oscar. He's gone."

"I know. I tried to stop him."

"What are you talking about? I mean Dwight has died. He passed away about fifteen minutes ago."

"I'm sorry. My mind was elsewhere, Bob. I figured Dwight didn't have long. Another stroke?"

"No, it was almost like he just fell asleep for good. Not even a groan or anything. I hope I go out as easily. I'm going to give an announcement to the press in just a minute. You want to come with me?"

"Yes, I believe I will. I want to see this through to the end."

The men stood up and Dwight followed Meecham towards the main lobby of the hospital where a large contingency of the press was gathering. As they approached the crowd, Meecham turned to Oscar and smiled as he spoke.

"None of us will live to see this end. Dwight didn't and we won't either. Nothing really changes very fast. But, once in a while, someone like him comes along, and I guess you could say that they just make things a little better."

Oscar stood in the rear as Meecham walked to the podium. As he arrived, the floodlights illuminating him for the cameras just about obscured him to those in the room.

"At six fourteen p.m. this evening, the Senior Senator and distinguished statesman from South Carolina, Dwight Morton, died in his sleep. I can tell you that I was there at the end and that he passed on peacefully in the company of friends. To those of us who knew him personally and for the countless people whose lives he touched, this is a sad moment. He was a humanitarian above most and a statesman beyond compare. He was a friend to the friendless and a voice for those who otherwise would not have been heard. We will miss him. It was his wish that any gifts of sympathy be given to the Coalition for the Homeless. Once again, thank you."

Oscar fielded a few questions from the reporters and then while crews retrained their cameras on the reporters who were summarizing the summary they had just covered, Meecham made his way back to where Oscar was standing.

"Can you handle another coffee, Oscar?"

"I believe it's going to take gasoline to warm me up tonight. I went outside with my coat off for a while and I swear I'm still shaking."

"When are you out of here?"

"I had planned on leaving today but I guess I'll leave in the morning now. I never liked landing in one of those big jets at night, anyway. I don't see how they hit that little strip of pavement in the daytime and the night is even scarier."

"Come on, Oscar. As much as you've been around?"

"I was nervous every minute. That's the truth."

"What do you say we go back to my favorite little cafe again? That OK with you?"

"That's fine with me."

The two men left together for a waiting car and slowly made their way back to the restaurant where they had dined together the night before. It seemed a lot longer to both of them. It had been a long day. The car dropped them off at the back entrance again and they were greeted by the owner and seated at Meecham's usual table. They ordered a late breakfast of eggs and toast and both started with a shot of coffee to take off the persistent bitter chill. Meecham felt a kinship to Oscar probably due to their southern roots and the relationship both had with Dwight Morton.

"I'll tell you what, Oscar. I've been up here for a long time now and I still haven't gotten used to the winters. I doubt I ever will. Seems to bother me more now than it did when I first got here. I guess the older I get, the thinner my blood gets. Stay cold all winter."

"Don't look at me. Florence, South Carolina is too cold for me in December. I need sunshine and palm trees. Let me ask you a question. How many kids are there here living totally on their own? No parents. I'm talking about kids who are still school age that ought to be at home."

"Thousands. Every big city in the country is full of them. Mostly poor, kids of the illiterate, the drug addicts, fathers in jail, mothers on the streets."

"Isn't there anywhere they can go? So they can stay in school? If they don't, they're going to be the next generation in jail and on the streets having homeless kids. What's the answer?"

"You tell me, Oscar. The prisons are full. The shelters are full. The social safety net is unraveling because the people who pay for it are sick of the taxes and they're putting an end to what little bit of help there was. Chances are if your parents went to college and got an education, they're doing all right and their kids will get to go. If they didn't, you're probably not going to get an education either and the distance between the groups is getting wider every day. And the scary part is, there are a lot more in the down group and it's getting larger every year. When they can't get food and the very minimum basics, there's going to be problems the likes of which this country has never seen. The jails are exploding now. I don't know what the answers are. I guess Dwight's approach was the only one that seemed to make sense to me."

"And that was?"

"Don't wait until there's a clear cut path to start the trip. Just do what you can do every day and maybe those you help will be able then to help somebody else. It's like a domino effect. He just kept on doing what he did like it was all going to work out just fine. What brings all this to your mind?"

"There were these two young boys I met in the hospital. Their mother was there for a pretty serious operation and I guess they're going to be on welfare."

"The young boys you took the food back to?"

"Right. Social Services came and took the younger one, about five years old and tried to get the older boy, about fifteen, to go with them. I tried to convince him to go too, but he would rather just stay on the streets than go with them. I'm afraid he's going to freeze to death outside in this weather."

"They find people every morning. It's mostly the older ones, though, that freeze to death. The younger ones have more energy and keep moving. They cruise the convenience stores and the all night joints to stay warm and steal enough to eat and buy drugs if they're addicted. Was he what you would call a street-tough kid? Did he seem to have a lot of attitude?"

"Not all that much. He put on a little front but for the most part, I think he misses his mother and is scared to death. If I wanted to help him out, what could I do?"

"It should be obvious to you by now that most of these kids don't trust the authorities at all. And the ones that are straight are even more pissed off because they get treated like they're suspects of something everywhere they go. It's a result of the public's paranoia over crime. Any black kid with his hat turned backwards, baggy pants and big tennis shoes is just look-ing for a victim. That's pretty much how they're looked at. And don't get me wrong. It's not all that hard to become a victim here, either. That's the problem. Mistrust by everyone of everyone. Even the government with its scandal of the day isn't helping that image very much. I'd say, if you can get this kid to trust you, get him out of this environment and you might have a chance of straightening him out before he does get into trouble. Every day he's on the streets he's a day closer to getting into trouble. They go hand in hand. If you want me to come talk to him for you, just call me. Sometimes if they're black...he is black, isn't he?"

"How'd you know?"

"In D.C.? Give me a break. Sometimes they'll trust a black man quicker. I'll do anything I can to help you with him. Do you know his name?

"Marcus, Marcus Frye. His mother is Mary Frye. She's in a room just a few doors down from where Dwight was."

Meecham took out a pen and wrote the information that Oscar was giving him down on a menu. He folded it and put it in the breast pocket of his coat.

"Well, if you don't run into him before you get out of here; I'll see what I can do."

"I'd appreciate it Bob. I feel kinda bad for him."

"No problem. I get calls every day about kids like this. Well, you're not going to stay for the memorial service?"

"You know, I didn't plan on being here but just a day when I left the paper and it's already been two now. Where is it going to be held?"

"The body will lie in state at the Rotunda for two days starting tomorrow and a memorial service will be held the next day. The actual funeral will be in South Carolina on the week-end. I'll find out the exact time for you in the morning."

"If it's going to be back in South Carolina, there's no doubt I'll be there. How about you?"

"Absolutely! And more than likely the President or Vice President will attend. Dwight was a pain in the side of some President's consciences for a long time. But most of them genuinely respected him and the votes he represented. Besides, half the media in the country will probably be at the funeral. Any politician worth his salt won't miss it. Well, what did you learn after talking with Dwight for so long? I would expect it to be pretty earth-shaking if he spent the last two days of his life talking with you."

"Some of the most interesting moments I've spent in a

long time, Bob. Dwight told me about a number of events in his life that he felt were very significant to him and actually to the whole country. He wanted to make sure they weren't forgotten or overlooked when people started looking at his life."

"Things his friends already knew?"

"I'm not sure. Probably not. I imagine a lot of people are going to have some problems with what he said and I haven't decided yet how I want to tell the story. It was a pretty remarkable turn of events. I'll let you see what I do before I release anything. I'd like your opinion on it."

"Just let me know when you're ready."

"I'll do it. Well, what do you say we start heading back? I want to try and get a flight out in the morning and I'd like to go back to the hospital for just a little while and visit with Mrs. Frye. Maybe I'll run into Marcus again."

"Fine. I'll give you a lift."

It was after ten by the time Oscar got back to the hospital. Visiting hours were over but he nonetheless tried to look inconspicuous as he headed to Mary Frye's room. When he entered, she was awake, just staring at the ceiling. He walked over to her.

"Good evening, Mrs. Frye. Feeling any better?"

"Oh, I'm so pleased you came back to see me. I'm not gettin' better as quick as I needs to, Mister...I forgot your name."

"Oscar. Oscar Phipps. Just call me Oscar."

"I really need to get back to work so that I can get my boys back with me."

"Isn't there anywhere I could take them for you? Do you have any relatives that might look out for them who Marcus wouldn't mind staying with?"

"No, sir. There's just us. Their father run off when they was little and it's been just us ever since. We ain't had nothin' but they has always been good kids. I've been at work most of the time they was growin' up. Had to work two jobs just to keep clothes on their back and food on the table. We got food stamps and some kinda' welfare they give me every month and we'd been gettin' by all right. At least till my heart started givin' me problems. Now, it looks like most everything is just fallin' apart. It upsets me right smart that there ain't a thing I can do about it. I swear I would get up and leave if I could."

"I don't doubt it for a moment, Mrs. Frye."

"Mary. Everybody calls me Mary. Have you seen Marcus?"

"Just once after he left here. I did my best to get him to go see where Cody was staying but I couldn't get him to try it. He's pretty strong-minded, isn't he?"

"He's just scared. He's been as good a boy as I could have hoped for. And him havin' to grow up in the places we lived at. There's been lots of trouble he could have gotten into but he never did. He even done good in school. But now, he ain't been in six months or more. I'm afraid if he gets behind he won't want to go back. A lot of those boys he's hangin' around with don't go and they're not who he needs to be with. You hear what I'm tellin' you, Oscar?"

'I do, Mary. I wish there was some way I could help you but I'm afraid I've got to go home in the morning, back to South Carolina where I'm from. I spoke to a man I met here, though, a man named Bob Meecham who works for the President."

"The President of the United States?"

"Yes, ma'am. He's a black man and he says he's familiar with problems like yours and he might help if we could just get Marcus to trust him. I think he'd like Bob if he met him."

"Lord, I wish that would happen. I'd give anything to know they was goin' to be all right. It just ain't safe around here no more and I swear I can't hardly make enough money to take care of 'em. Do you think he would really help them?"

"I do, Mary. When I get home tomorrow I'll call him and get him to come by and see you. You tell him about your situation and I believe he'll help if he can. I'd better run now. I sure hope you get to feeling better soon, Mary. I'll check up on you in a few days."

Oscar leaned over and gave her a quick hug. He could not help but notice the watery glow in her eyes and it moved him to see someone needing help so badly to obtain the very minimum that life could offer. He turned and left.

Washington National was jammed as usual and Oscar looked forward to returning to a more sedate setting where life moved a little slower and people at least took the time to pretend to be courteous even if they weren't. The flight home was un-eventful and the bed in his small-framed home never felt more comfortable. He was glad his years as a journeyman reporter and traveling correspondent had come to a close. To be the editor of a small but well-respected newspaper in such peaceful surroundings was perfect for him now. He wouldn't trade places with the Edi-tor-in-Chief of the Washington Post or the New York Times. This was the time in his life to reflect and appreciate the simpler things life had to offer.

He slept in a little the next morning and arrived at the of-fice which was already at full speed by nine thirty. A few em-ployees nodded to him as he passed, but most of them were deep into the stories of the day and already off to beat the deadlines.

The in-tray on his desk which normally stayed at slightly below overflowing had swollen beyond its banks due to his brief absence and his phone was completely covered by post-its. His experiences the past several days had left more of an impression on him than he realized and none of the problems waiting for him at home seemed all that critical at the moment. Esther Holloway, his long-time assistant editor and confidante, came into his office with a cup of coffee knowing Oscar hated to go very far into the day without a caffeine fix.

"So, my big shot friend of the movers and shakers, how was your trip to Washington? Rub elbows with the Kennedys?"

"Why don't I ever get 'welcome home, Oscar, have a nice trip?'"

"Hey, we don't want to spoil you. So tell me. What excit-ing happened? Fred told me that a couple of self-important types hauled you out of here in a real hurry."

"It was interesting, Esther. Very interesting."

"That's it? Interesting? Come on, Oscar. I've been taking your calls and keeping this place afloat for you for two days and that's all I get....interesting?"

"I want to let it settle, then put some of it on paper before I even start talking about it. You'll be one of the first to read it, though. That's a promise."

"I'll hold you to it. Your messages are numbered in order

of who was screaming the loudest. Oh, and your friend, what's his name...the black preacher...Alfred?"

"Alonzo?"

"Yeah, Alonzo. He's been calling about every two hours. You'll probably get a call from him before you finish your coffee."

"If I do, put him through. I want to talk with him."

Oscar went through the most critical messages and returned the calls he felt could not wait, but his mind was anxious to start putting some thoughts on paper while Dwight's story was still fresh in his mind. Not that it would be easy to forget. By noon he managed to put an outline together and was deep in thought when Esther reappeared. This time she was truly impressed.

"Oscar, you have a FAX from the White House. From a Bob Meecham, the Chief of Staff for the President. Do you know him?"

"We go back a long ways, Esther. There's volumes about me you don't know. Hand it to me if you would be so kind."

True to his word, Meecham had sent the details of Dwight Morton's funeral. It would be held Saturday at 4 p.m. in Lydia. The President would definitely be there along with many other dignitaries and a seat would be reserved for Oscar in the section with the President and his staff. Having been in semi-withdrawal from the outside world in the insulated confines of Florence, Oscar was quite taken aback by the invitation. It crossed his mind that just his brief time with Dwight was already having an impact the way others said he did on their lives. What was the power of the man that was so pervasive?

Oscar knew a legacy as rich as Dwight's needed to be handled with a great deal of sensitivity. When the truth came out about the killing of Nathaniel Fulbright, all the good from Dwight's life would remain intact and yet the name of Pickle Mather would be cleared of the crime. Pickle would finally be appreciated for the sacrifice he made at such a tender age. After all, he thought, it was as much the legacy of Pickle Mather as it was Dwight Morton's. The course of Dwight's life was really the result of the actions taken by Pickle.

For the next two days, Oscar contemplated his task and slowly put words on paper, ever mindful of how detrimental they could be if he fell short in the retelling. He finally got through to Alonzo and promised to visit with him to discuss how the strike at the chicken plant was affecting the local workers. Alonzo pressed him hard to take up the worker's cause and embarrass the owners into a fair settlement. Oscar still felt uneasy about involving the paper in a labor dispute. He did promise to think it over and get back with Alonzo after Dwight's funeral.

By Saturday morning, Oscar was ready for a break and left very early in the day to attend the funeral. He would not only cover what would be the most newsworthy day in the history of Lydia, South Carolina for his paper and their related news syndicates, he would also try and find some of the places that Dwight had indelibly sketched in his mind. Oscar felt it would help him have a clearer picture of what occurred if he could visit a few of the spots Dwight had spoken of. Perhaps he would get a feel of what Lydia was like sixty years earlier. He knew a lot of the towns in South Carolina had remained virtually unchanged since their rebirth in the wake of the despised march of General Sherman and the armies of the North.

The town square was immediately recognizable from Dwight's description. Oscar parked his car and walked slowly down the street. It was only 8 a.m. but the street was humming with activity. The President did not visit there every day. Oscar thought this might be how it was on the day of Dwight and Dot's wedding when so many of the state's elite paid their respects.

One shop that looked particularly busy and interesting was the small red brick barbershop on one corner of the main square. Trying to soak in every detail and feeling that it brought with it, Oscar walked up to the door of the shop. There was an antique barber's pole, the red stripe quite faded but turning smoothly and the name Red's lettered on the door. Oscar pushed open the glass door and entered. A cow bell attached to the door announced his entrance. There was an interesting assortment of local citizenry populating Red's that morning. They were relating tales past, present and future and Oscar didn't have to be in attendance but just a few moments to hear the name Dwight Morton thrown about with great familiarity. It was apparent that to be a legitimate citizen, you needed to have had some personal contact with Dwight. That would establish you had been around for a while. Most told of brief encounters with him where he either assisted them with some sort of personal problem or he enlisted them to help someone else. Of those in attendance, all indicated that when approached for help, Dwight always came through.

Oscar looked around at the numerous faded photographs on the wall. One particularly caught his eye. It had the presence of Dwight standing in front of a T-model with Dot, Robert and Eileene Morton beside them. But of even greater interest to Oscar was the large, matronly black woman standing to one side of them and the young black boy to her side. Oscar stood directly in front of this treasure and studied it for at least five minutes before his unusual activity caught Red's eye.

"Can I help you, sir? You waiting for a trim? Sir?"

Oscar finally realized he was being addressed.

"Oh, I'm sorry. I was trying to identify the people in this old photo. Do you know who they are?"

"Of course I do. Everybody in town could pick out the folks in that shot. That's the Morton family. You know the young Morton boy, the tall one there. Well, he died just this week. In his eighties. The President of the United States will be here today for his funeral."

"Yes, I know. That's why I'm here. I realized it's the Mortons in the picture. Tell me, who are the black people in the photo with them? Do you know them?"

"Well, I know of them. Never met them. They was both dead before I come to Lydia. The woman was Dwight Morton's mammy. That's what they used to call a black woman who raised the kids for rich white families around here."

"And the boy?"

"From what I been told, he was the mammy's son. Not too long after that picture was taken, he was hung for killing a white man right here in town. A group took him out and lynched him is what I always heard. You a newsman or something?"

"Sorta. I'm Oscar Phipps, editor of the South Carolina Journal over in Florence. You get our paper here, don't you?"

"Sure do. Every morning. Read it myself, cover to cover. I think I recognize your name. You here to cover the going's on during the funeral, huh?"

"That's right. And I'm doing a story on the Mortons. Since I don't have any photos of the family like this one, I wonder if I could borrow it, just to make a copy? If I use it in the paper, I would put your name under it and give you credit for letting us use it."

"Well, sure, help yourself. And here, let me spell my name right for you. Every body can spell Red but my last name is tough. It's Thompson with a TH at the front. Not just a T. Some folks get it wrong. You'd put my name right under the picture, would you? Even if it was on the front page?"

"That's right, Red. Here's my card and don't worry, I will treasure this picture. You'll get it personally delivered back here to you in a few days, as quickly as I can get it copied."

"All right! Damn! Here that, boys? Name's gonna' be on the front page of the paper."

The group was amused at Red's sudden moment of fame. One tobacco chewing farmer squeezed out a spit of chew into his empty Coke bottle and shot back at him.

"Just like a damn rock star, Red. I swear you'll be pokin' one of them damn earrings in your ear next."

Everybody in the place broke up and Oscar was fascinated by the charm of the place. He could easily close his eyes and see Nat Fulbright striking up a deal with Bill Moore while a similar crowd filled the room. Oscar opened his small leather legal cover and gently pressed the old picture in between the yellow lined pages so that it would remain flat and not be damaged. With his treasure duly stored, he bid the group farewell and exited to continue his rounds of the city.

Lydia's isolation and distance to a larger city spared it the destruction of most of its commercial buildings in the name of progress. Oscar was convinced the town was, for the most part, the same as it appeared when Dwight and his family had the picture taken he found hanging in the barber shop. He tried to pick out structures that played some role in Pickle's story. He walked to the center of the block opposite the town square and continued up and down the street looking for a building with a particular characteristic. He examined each shop on the street looking for the same thing - bars in the window. He felt that the jail must still be standing but was perhaps being used for some purpose other than a prison.

In the Lydia Farm Supply store he inquired about the location of the old prison. The owner told him it had been an auto parts store for a number of years. It was the third store front down the street. Dwight walked to the building, taking in its appearance each step of the way. The small barred windows had been knocked out to make way for wide plate glass replacements that better suited a retail store. He pushed open the door and walked in. It was small, but painted a bright white and kept in a very orderly manner. It was clean and well-stocked. James Fenny, the owner of the store, came over to ask if he could help Oscar find anything.

"Mornin'. Somethin' in particular you're looking for? Got quite a bit of stock in the back. The showroom ain't too big so I have to store some of the bigger items in the back."

"Actually, I'm just looking around. I'm from the South Carolina Journal. I'm here to attend Dwight Morton's funeral after lunch."

"Nice to have you folks come pay your respects. Dwight was raised right here, you know."

"Yes, I did. I knew Dwight for quite a few years. He mentioned the old jail to me before and the man over in the farm supply said this used to be it. That so?"

"Yes, sir. The Lydia jail was right here. It ain't been a jail for many years, though. We used to have a sheriff and all right here, but a long while back, some of the town leaders, and I believe Dwight was one of 'em, decided we'd be better off just letting the county officers look out for us over here. There ain't much happens here and it probably saved the town a lot of money. But, you're right. This was the Lydia jail."

"Has all of it been gutted like the room we're in?"

"No. The cells are still in the back. They got shelves in them now. I just use them to store mufflers and bulk oil."

"Would you mind if I took a look? I'm doing a story on

Lydia back when Dwight was young here and I would sure love to get a look at it."

"No problem at all. Follow me. Watch your step though. Ain't much light back there and the hall is narrow."

The minute he stepped into the dark hall, Oscar could feel the ghosts of another, less cordial time. The hall was just as Dwight had described it. Along each side were two small cells and at the end on the right, up against the back wall was a single small cell. The bars were still there. The inside was not more than eight by ten feet and an antique wash basin was still mounted to the wall. It was full of cigarette butts as it had become a convenient ashtray in recent years. The room was nasty and reeked of spilled motor oil. Oscar could almost see Pickle doubled over on a cot in the corner, waiting for the help that never came. The cold damp room was a stark strong reminder to Oscar of that brutal evening, so many years ago. He grabbed two of the bars and tried to imagine what must have gone through Pickle's mind as the hooded mob tore him from the cell and pushed him down the hall on the way to his death. Dwight's accuracy in describing the jail certainly lent a great deal of credibility to the other aspects of his story, and Oscar was more certain than ever he had heard a very accurate accounting of the facts.

"I've seen enough. I sure appreciate you bringing me back here."

"I know it's not much to see, but this really used to be the main jail here."

"I'm sure you're right, Mr. Fenny. I don't doubt it for a minute. Very interesting."

"Well, come back and visit any time you want. It's not usually this busy 'round here. What with the funeral and all, the place is really hoppin'. Normally we've all got time to sit and talk most of the day if we want to. You just come back any time."

"I'm sure I'll be back and visit with you again Mr. Fenny."

"Just call me Jim. That's what folks around here call me."

"OK, Jim. Thanks again."

Oscar headed down the remainder of the street. The morning had created a very clear impression in his head that served to bring Dwight's story to life even more than before. The clock in Oscar's stomach was beginning to go off and he looked around until he spotted a small café. He decided to get a quick bite before he'd have to head towards the funeral. It was not quite noon and he didn't want to get there late.

The Main Street Cafe was packed. The out-of-towners had tracked down the best source of local home cooking and had wasted no time getting a booth against the wall or one of the stools by the counter. The grill was directly in front of those seated on the stools and they could watch the cook as he turned the grilled hamburger steaks and ladled out great heapings of bar-becue laden with an in-house sauce touted on the front window as the best in Lydia. That boast led Oscar to wonder how many other places in this one-block town were making a competitive product at that very moment. He chuckled to himself and stood in line at the order counter since all of the seating was occupied. He would get a hot dog and go on about his business. A hurried waitress in the traditional pink and white waitress uniform came over after five minutes or so to get his order. She was rather worn-looking with her gray hair in a bun and her face reflecting a lot of summers working in the fields. His attention was immediately drawn to her name tag which read Mildred Tanner. His curiosity overpowered him instantly. He had to ask.

"Are you related to Eloise Tanner?"

"Why, yes, she was my Grandmother. How did you know?"

Oscar pointed to her name tag.

"Did you know her? She died when I was small but I can still remember her coming out to my folks' farm. She worked at the bank in town and used to visit us every Sunday and help my momma fix lunch."

"I didn't know her, but Dwight Morton mentioned her to me the day before he died. He held her in high regard and said he owed her a debt of gratitude."

"Senator Morton? You're kidding!"

"Not at all."

Her face lit up as if she had been told that she had inherited the family fortune. She was anxious to hear more.

"Can you tell me what he said?"

The owner of the cafe, short-handed with the unusual crowd crowed at her from the far end of the counter.

"Don't go to sleep on me over there, Mildred! You got a line there."

Wanting to talk more, but also wanting to stay employed, she had to say to Oscar,

"Can you come back a little later, when it's not so busy? It's never like this here and I would really love to talk with you."

Oscar replied,

"Tell you what, give me two hot dogs all the way, a small soda to go and I'll give you my phone number. You give me a call in a few days and we'll talk about your grandmother."

Mildred took his order and returned with his ration of cholesterol and chili in moments. She had quietly put his order in before some others who were ahead of him. He handed her a piece of paper with his number on it as he had promised.

"So you work for the Journal? That's the paper I read. You will call and talk about my granny, won't you?"

"You can count on it. Thanks for the quick order. See you later."

Oscar turned and twisted as he made his way through the packed diner to the street. On this particular morning the cafe reminded him more of a crowded deli in New York than a hot dog joint in a sleepy southern town. When he got back to the car, he opened his bag and devoured the hot dogs. They were dripping with grease and chili to the point the buns were getting soggy and all in all he thought they hit the spot. After all, he was not at home and couldn't be held responsible for going off his diet in a strange city. He took the one napkin that had been shoved into the bag and cleaned himself up as best he could. In spite of his best effort he could not get all of the stickiness off his fingers. The typist in him got the shivers each time the sides of his fingers stuck together. He spotted a drinking fountain inside the city square and got out, quickly washing up and returning. As he was getting back in his car, he saw a satellite news van headed down the street and surmised it was heading to the funeral. He fell in behind and followed it for about a mile. Along both sides of the narrow asphalt pavement cars were parked on the shoulders and

Oscar pulled over to park in the first open spot. He got out and followed a group walking down the road. They turned into an open field and jumped a ditch, not waiting to get to a small wooden bridge that crossed it a short way further down the road. The crowd grew larger and Oscar passed several reporters who had stationed themselves at strategic locations they thought offered a view of the proceedings. He continued on through the crowd until he saw the tops of green funeral home tents just ahead. As he got closer he noticed a rather large number of dark-suited young men staring intently at the crowd and he knew they must be part of the Presidential entourage. One of the young men asked him for identification and he produced his press credentials and drivers license. After passing this test, he asked the man.

"Can you tell me where I would find Bob Meecham?"

"He's with the President's staff. They're seated in front of the largest tent. Is he expecting you?"

"Yes. Can I go over that way?"

"Wait just a moment if you would sir."

He pulled a walkie-talkie from under his suit coat and relayed some code numbers to the party at the other end.

"Your name again sir."

"Oscar Phipps. He'll know who I am."

"Yes, sir."

Once again he addressed his walkie.

"Phipps. Yes, that's affirmative. Mr. Meecham. Roger. We'll wait."

After a few moments, they were joined not by another guard but by Bob Meecham who walked over to meet Oscar.

"Oscar! Glad to see you. I've got a seat reserved for you over with us. Follow me. He's fine, Browning. I'll escort him over."

"Yes, sir, Mr. Meecham."

It was apparent that Meecham received a great deal of respect from those present. Everyone they passed spoke to him. Even though he'd met a great deal of people in high positions over the years, Oscar had never met a sitting President and he felt a rush of adrenaline shoot through him as he and Meecham drew close up to the President and First Lady. Meecham took him straight over to where they were seated.

"Mr. President, this is Oscar Phipps from Florence, South Carolina. He was a close friend of Dwight's and we have recently had several conversations about the Senator and what he meant to the country."

"Nice to meet you, Oscar. Your state has a great deal to be proud of in the man we're burying here today. Knew him many years and he was a statesman of the highest caliber. If I could pick anyone for our younger electorate to pattern their careers after, Dwight Morton would be at the top of the list. Well, it's a pleasure to meet you, Oscar."

"The same here, sir, ma'am."

Bob put his hand on Oscar's shoulder and guided him towards two empty seats only several away from the President and First Lady. Oscar looked around at the faces in the immediate vicinity and saw that Meecham had been correct. No politician or prominent public figure had stayed away. Even on Dwight's final departure from this world, there were many on his coattails, trying to grab a piece of the perception of virtue that surrounded Dwight for most of his life. What would the revelation that Oscar carried with him do to the reputation of a man whose name had not seen so much as a blemish since it first came to the public's attention over sixty years ago? Should the facts go to the grave with him? That was not his decision. Dwight had made it himself and entrusted him with its execution. He would do what he must and trust that the greater good would prevail. As the funeral began and members of the crowd came forward to present eulogies and accolades, Oscar looked beyond the gathering at three large columns that stood erect but alone as if supporting the sky. They could only be a remnant of the once grand home that stood on these grounds. They were the only surviving pieces of Fountainside. He continued to examine the area and found just to the rear of the gathering were a large number of children's swings and playground pieces. There was a wooden sign in front that read:

"Lydia Park at Fountainside: Donated to the city of Lydia for the benefit of all children by Dwight and Dorothy Morton. Dedicated November 23, 1947."

It was an immaculately kept park with grounds that looked

like a golf course. If it had Dwight's name on it, one could rest assured it would be done right. The small details never passed him by. Dwight's casket, draped with an American flag and covered with flowers, was only a few feet in front of him. There were soldiers from every branch of service in full dress uniforms to both sides. The speeches were eloquent and what everyone hopes will be said at their funeral. After thirty minutes of testimonials, a Baptist minister from Lydia said a prayer, and the Marine guards who were Dwight's favorite, folded his flag and carried it to Otis Peacock, the mayor of Lydia. Since Dwight was leaving no heirs, he asked that any such keepsakes be given to the town to display as best they saw fit. Finally, a twenty-one gun salute was offered and the service ended. The crowd began to drift back to their cars, though some remained to look at the grounds that once sheltered as magnificent a plantation as the South could offer. Bob Meecham said a few words to the President and then came over to join Oscar.

"A beautiful ceremony, don't you think?"

"Dwight would have been proud. He also would have been amused at the fuss being made over him."

"You're right. That was not his style."

Oscar was beginning to get the feeling that the attention he was receiving from the President's Chief of Staff was more than just 'Hey, we were both friends of the same great guy.' He truly liked the man but his time was obviously limited and what was the big attraction to a small town newspaper man? After a lifetime of reading people, he was not often wrong about such things. To Oscar, it was just journalistic intuition.

"So, Oscar. You heading back to Florence now?"

"Not right away. I want to see the area a little more. I'll probably head back just before dark. I'd like to look around the grounds here. From the size of these columns, it must have been a very imposing home."

"It was magnificent. Dwight considered rebuilding it for some time and then when his political career started keeping him away so much, he and Dot built a modest frame home back where the old slave quarters were. He never felt the need for personal luxuries. They also kept a place in Columbia near the State

151

House but he said it never felt like home. I was on the board of directors of his foundation and I can assure you that he could have had anything he wanted and I mean anything. I guess that's why it didn't matter much to him. All of his effort was directed to his work and the charities that he and Dot ran. You know Oscar, there's something I've been meaning to talk to you about."

Oscar felt like saying 'I knew it!', but he restrained himself.

"What's that, Bob?"

I'm the executor of Dwight's estate, and the remaining assets he had not already transferred to the foundation were willed to it. There is as I mentioned before, a board of directors that oversees all of their affairs. They more or less say who will receive what each year. They look at a lot of children and young people. They try to determine what sort of help and scholarships they should get. We also help a lot of troubled kids that other groups wouldn't think about helping because they don't consider them worthy or deserving. Dwight always felt that many of those kids could be turned around with a little help at the right time in their life. We will of course operate in the spirit he would want and do our best to continue his work. The directors are not paid anything other than being reimbursed for their expenses and there is quite a bit of travel around the country a lot of us enjoy. Get to see the real world, not the tourist's view of the different cities we visit. Anyway, you need to be a part of this. Dwight specifically requested that you play a significant role in these efforts after his death. He respected you and thought your heart was in the right place. So do I. How about it? Would you serve on the board as director? I'm going to oversee the trust fund and my job needs to be filled. The President has been good about letting me attend to the business of the Foundation because he believes in it too, but I'm really overloaded and need somebody to help fill the holes. What do you say?"

"To be honest with you, I am flattered. But in reality, I'm as bogged down as you are. I'm editor of the paper which is a full-time job and I've always felt there was a book or two in me and I'm just getting my thoughts together for one right now. It would be about Dwight and I don't want to make a half-hearted attempt. Besides, I'm no spring chicken myself. These are my 'golden years', Bob. You know what I mean?"

"I hear what you're saying, but for what I'm asking you to do, there's not a lot of people that could do it as Dwight wanted. He knew you could. And, I'll tell you something else."

"What's that?"

"Dwight promised me you were going to do it. He said 'don't worry about it Bob, he's going to be the one.' You're not going to make a liar out of a dead man, are you?"

Oscar's immediate thought was to decline gracefully but, he replied,

"You know that's not playing fair, Bob. I thought as much of Dwight as anyone and knew him longer than most people. I'd like to help but I swear I just don't think I have the energy to do it justice."

"Well, look, Oscar. Don't tell me 'no' right now. You just think it over for a while and let it sink in. There's a lot of problems in the country today and here's a chance to help in a significant way. I'll get back with you in a week or so. How about that?"

"Sounds reasonable to me."

Meecham put his arm around Oscar's back.

"Oscar, it's been good talking with you again. The President said to tell you it was a pleasure meeting you. We'll talk again, soon. See you later."

"Will do Bob."

Meecham turned and hurried off to rejoin the Presidential entourage. Oscar had to admit he was impressed by the man. Dwight had seen something in him and made sure he reached his potential.

Oscar began to look around the grounds. After Dwight's gift to the city of the land around Fountainside, he funded and supervised the building of the park. No town in the South, especially one as tiny as Lydia, had one any finer. It was superbly maintained and most of the jungle gym equipment and swings looked new. After walking the perimeter of the clearing, Oscar headed down the dirt road leading from the back of the ruined foundation of the house. After a few hundred yards, he came to a

couple of small shacks on either side of the road. He didn't have
to be told what they were. He wondered if one might have been
Momma Mather's. There was a historical marker in front indicating what they were but it gave no hint as to whether one was hers.
And, why should it. The names of Pickle and Momma Mather
had probably not been uttered in Lydia after their deaths. At the
present, he alone knew their significance. He felt that the shack
to his left was the place that Dwight had described to him in such
detail but in fact, it was almost identical to the others. Still, he
had a feeling about it. He looked in through the old bubble glass
window and saw a large single room with a fireplace in it. He felt
in his heart this was it. He stared into the room for several minutes and was overcome by a feeling of nostalgia and sadness.
After a while, he turned and made his way back to the family
cemetery. A crew was removing the flowers and seats from
around Dwight's grave and the crowd had disappeared. With the
area now open, he could see for the first time the other gravesites
adjoining Dwight's. There were Robert and Eileene Morton's
headstones to the right of where Dwight's casket was being low-
ered. To the left was a statue of a young woman sitting gracefully
reading a Bible. The inscription read:

DOROTHY MORTON
"DOT"
BELOVED WIFE OF DWIGHT MORTON
AN ANGEL ALWAYS
BORN 1911 - DIED 1973

It was not hard for Oscar to read the sentiment there.
There were older graves in the small square plot, but none that
reached out quite like the two headstones centered together at the
back of the plot, closest to the home site and directly behind
Dwight and Dorothy's. They were matching black, polished granite and as fine as any others in the cemetery. It was the resting
place for Momma Mather and Pickle. Compared with all the
sights stirring memories in Oscar's mind, nothing brought them
back as much as standing there staring at these two graves. They
had only their names and dates on them but their stark beauty and

position spoke a lot about the Mortons' regard for them. It was apparent they were considered family as only direct family members were in the plot. At that moment Oscar knew he would have to put forth the effort needed to make certain Pickle's story was told with heart and credibility so the full breadth of his actions would be appreciated. He committed himself to the project. He determined he'd seen enough for one day. He pulled out a cigar from the pocket of his tan corduroy jacket and started to his car. The drive back would give him time to put together in his mind how he would cover the funeral for the morning edition of the Journal. After all, that was why he was there.

CHAPTER ELEVEN

Two young men sat on the front steps of the dirty brownstone trying to outdo one another for the attention of an attractive young woman who sat a couple of steps below them. It was the poorest section of D.C. and predominantly black. These three did nothing to alter those facts. They were inner-city products with all of the problems and lack of prospects that accompanied their birthright. Nonetheless, they were preoccupied with the ancient customs of their age, rich or poor, black or white. Their words would have been considered a foreign language to an outsider. The slang was their own and the barrage of vernacular phrases and words could only be understood by others of the culture. They weren't much different than their counterparts in every urban area of the country. However, remove their uniforms and customs and they were no different in their basic pursuits than anyone. They were in the midst of boasting and laughter when a chopped '72 Chevy rounded the corner of their street, tires screaming and spinning as the completion of the sliding turn allowed more acceleration. As it approached the dilapidated tenement where the three sat, it veered sharply up onto the curb only twenty feet in front of the steps. In alarm they rose quickly, the boys jumping to either side of the porch and the young girl turning to run back into her home. Within seconds, automatic weapons protruded from the front and rear windows of the four door Impala. From the rear window on the far side another predator arose, seated himself on the base of the open window and leaned on the roof of the car. In the few seconds that passed, dozens of rounds of high powered ammunition found the front of the house. The two young men, used to such encounters, made good their retreat to the back alleys on either side of the building. The young woman was not so fortunate as several of the slugs found their mark, severing her spine and destroying her heart as they passed easily through her torso. She fell on the porch before reaching the front door of her home. Not waiting to even assay the carnage, the car sped off, tires still screeching as the youthful assassins retreated to the interior of the death wagon. Another drive-by shooting had been successfully rendered by those virtually no different than those they attacked. Their yelps of victory could still be heard on the street as the screams of the young woman's mother joined in to create a chorus of agony from the rotted deck where the young slain girl lay.

"All right man! You see those assholes diving? Man, they won't be back to our 'hood' no more!"

The driver of the shooters was delighted with the results of their actions. The other three youths were not all in accord.

"I don't know, man. I think we hit their bitch. I didn't want to shoot no girl, man. Ernie, the cops are gonna be all over our ass now. You know they're gonna know it was us. If anybody says anything, we'll get made. You hear me, man? This ain't gonna go away. Man, I hope she don't die."

Ernie showed little regard or fear for what might follow the shooting.

"You whimp. The bitch shouda' been more careful who she was hangin' with. She asked for it. I wish we'd hit 'em all. You got to get respect if you don't want them fuckin' with you. They know we're serious now. And nobody's gonna say a fuckin' word. Ain't that right, Bishop?"

"Yeah, I guess, Ernie. But I still don't like shootin' no girl. She was just at her house, man. They was visitin' her at her house. She didn't do nothin' to us."

"Look, just shut the fuck up about it. You gettin' scared, get out, anybody who's scared, just leave your heat and get the fuck out."

He pulled the car over to the side of the road and two of the boys got out. Ernie and Bishop continued on, spinning the wheels again as he floored the old Chevy down the street.

"Man, you believe those guys? They're homies, man! We look out for them, let 'em hang with us, join us. We stand good for them. Risk our lives for them and they fuckin' wimp out. I can't believe this, man. You got any more ice on you, man?"

"Back at the place I got some. We gotta' get off the streets anyway in case somebody made the car. Let's get some crack man."

"All right, Bishop, you're all right. Fuck those guys, we don't need 'em."

They continued on as the last remnants of the day departed and the street lights and liquor store signs began to light up. On the next corner, standing in front of a sidewalk grate with steam rising from it, someone they recognized waved at the car.

"Hey, man, it's the kid. Pull over."

"You want to get him lit up? You know it would be his first hit. Might be fun, Bishop. What do you say?"

"Do it."

Ernie pulled the car over to the curb in front of where Marcus was trying to grab some warmth from the steam leaving the grate. As they turned in, the warmth of the car seemed inviting.

"Hey, Ernie, what are you guys doin'?"

"Get in. We gonna take you for a ride and have some fun."

Marcus got in the back seat. He had to push a gun over to sit down.

"What are all these doin' back here?"

"We been doin' some tradin' to score a few bucks. You want to buy one?"

"I don't need no gun. I don't have any money, either, for nothin'. Where are we goin'?"

"Just over to Bishop's. He's got some shit over there. You ever try ice, man?"

Both of the older boys laughed at the thought of getting Marcus strung out. As they prodded him to go with them and try it out, an unwelcome sight appeared in the street behind them. The flashing blue lights of a police squad car filled the streets and bounced off the windows of the shops and row houses.

"Shit! We're made. Hit it, Ernie!"

Ernie turned around to see how far back they were.

"Fuck, they're right on our ass!"

He floored the car, its rear end sliding sideways as the old engine spewed out a black cloud of oil and unburned fuel from the exhaust. He straightened up the front end and stomped the accelerator pedal.

"Move, Ernie! Get the hell out of here!"

Confusion covered Marcus' face.

"Ernie, they might be after me. They want to take me to a detentions place or somewhere's while my mother's sick. Just stop and I'll get out. You're gonna get us killed runnin' from 'em. Just stop, man!"

"Shut the fuck up kid! It ain't you they're after. Tell him, Bishop."

"Hand me the gun, kid. They think we hit somebody."

"You mean they think you shot somebody? You didn't, did you?"

"They was in our turf, man. Now shut up and get down."

Marcus turned and looked out the rear of the car. There were now two police cars in pursuit. The first was less than twenty feet behind them with the siren blaring and its headlights flashing. Marcus was beginning to panic.

"Stop, Ernie, stop the car. You're gonna get us killed."

"I'm not tellin' you again! Shut the fuck up!"

Marcus laid over on the seat and hung on to the door handle. The shocks were old and the car so low that with each turn it would bottom out and grind its underside into the street shooting flares of sparks out in its wake. Seconds began to seem like eternity and it was not long before the lead pursuit car started to ram into the rear of the Impala.

"Fuck! Shoot 'em, Bishop! Give it to 'em! They want to crash my fuckin' car. Hit 'em!"

The sudden collision threw Marcus to the floorboard between the seats. He curled up on the floor and covered his ears to shield the sounds of gunfire bursts directly over his head. Shards of glass began to fall around him. All he could think of was getting out of the car. If it came to a stop he would open the door and run. He hadn't done anything. They weren't chasing him. If he could just get out of the car he would be OK. As they approached a forced turn directly ahead, Ernie swung wide to the left and then cut hard to the right and again gave the pedal a hard foot. Their pursuers had anticipated his direction and the road ahead was sealed by patrol cars, the sky lit up with continuous blue blasts from the lights. There was no retreat and no escape. Ernie made a desperate decision with no input from his passengers.

"Hold on, we're goin' through the roadblock!"

"You're crazy, man! It'll kill us! Just stop, Ernie. They got us, man. Just stop the fuckin' car!"

"No way, man. We'll make it. Hold on. We'll make it."

Police officers, kneeling behind the parked cars with their weapons drawn, waited until they realized the car was not slowing down and then simultaneously began to open fire. The windshield exploded in the first blast of bullets. The two young men in the front seat did not speak or scream. Ernie's head just slumped quietly forward and his hands fell from the wheel. Bishop appeared to just lean over against the door as if resting his head to sleep during a long drive. The car, with no control over the wheel, veered wildly to the side and slammed at full speed into the rear of one of the squad cars. The officers dived to avoid the collision and as soon as the cars stopped moving, they ran towards the overturned Chevy, weapons drawn. There was no movement, only the spinning tires and smoke from under the pile of oil-and gas-soaked metal. One of the senior officers cautioned the men who were moving on the car.

"It could blow with all that gas. Watch what you're doing."

As the commands to get out of the vehicle were ignored, a pair of patrolmen cautiously approached and looked into the vehicle, guns pointed into the dark, smoke-filled interior.

"Nobody's coming out of this, Sergeant. They're pretty young. Looks like twenty years old maybe. Two in the front. Looks like a kid in the back. Jesus, they're really torn up. Serves the little bastards right. So, that's four dead - over what? I just don't get it."

From inside the dark buildings, onlookers began to appear out of the darkness. In a short while, the previously deserted street had become entertainment for the dozens who wanted to get a closer look at the carnage. For most of them, it was only one scene in a continuing series of violent shows they had grown accustomed to.

Oscar arrived back in Florence around nine-thirty in the evening. After seeing the outpouring of emotion and the public's embrace of the life of Dwight Morton, concern for the responsibility he had accepted from the Senator was mounting. In revealing the truth, he'd reveal that though there were a great deal of extenuating circumstances, Dwight had broken into someone's home and killed him. Despite his own wishes, he had let a young black boy take the blame and resulted in his lynching. Could he take the chance on ruining the reputation of a man so well regarded by virtually everyone? Maybe it would be best to leave everything as it was and forget he ever heard of Pickle Mather. Then there was the promise he made to a dying man. Dwight insisted this be done. The idea sounded easy, but in reality, the doing would prove to be a test for Oscar on many fronts.

The day had taken its toll on him and he sought refuge under the covers as soon as he got home. As usual, when he left for even a short while, the light on his answering machine was blinking steadily. He would wait till morning to start putting out fires. The events of the past week had been troubling to him emotionally as well as physically and his fatigued body fell as much into a coma as a deep sleep. He awoke an hour after he usually arrived at the office. As late as he already was, he took a slow shower and stopped at a favorite greasy spoon for scrambled eggs and sausage followed by a two dollar cigar. After a while, he felt he had sufficiently recharged to attack the day. "Thank God I'm the editor now" he thought to himself. In days gone by, to arrive this late would have shown a particularly careless attitude he would never have allowed himself.

Esther was waiting at the door when Oscar entered.

"Don't even tell me, Oscar; I don't want to know. OK, what the hell is going on? Are you sick? You haven't been this late in fifteen years. I was about to call the cops to go see if you had been mugged or something. No, don't tell me. I don't want to know. You've got everybody and their brother calling. Alonzo called again, they're getting close to the edge down at the chicken plant and he thought you might want to pick sides. There's been some rock-throwing and the owners are talking about hiring scabs or closing the place. It could get nasty at any time. The bank called yesterday. You're overdrawn again and William said he covered three or four checks but you need to call and let him transfer some out of your savings account. You never told me you had a savings account."

"Well, what the Hell difference would that make to you?"

"Hey, I might have considered giving you a little more attention if I had known you were a man of means. A gal's got to think about those things, you know."

"Trust me, if the checks are over a hundred bucks, the savings account will bounce, too."

"Figures. Where was I? Oh, I remember. Doctor Meadows called; you're three months late for your physical. He asked if you were still smoking those damn cigars."

"What did you tell him?"

"I lied, of course."

"Good girl. Anything else?"

"Some woman named Robinson called you a couple of times last night and once already this morning."

"Robinson? I don't know any Robinson. Say what she wanted?"

"Nope, said it was important and she would keep trying till she got up with you. You sure you're not seeing somebody? I mean you sure aren't hanging around the office all of a sudden and now a young woman is calling and won't leave a number. Looks bad Oscar."

"You know I am not seeing any young woman. I haven't got a clue what she wants. Probably calling to get me to switch long distance phone companies again."

"Well, it's not my business, but she said it was something social."

"Social? What the hell does she mean by that? Was it a local call?"

"I think not. She's calling in on the 800 number."

"Social? I know! I bet she said Social Services."

"Might have. But that sounds worse."

"Esther, you have a dirty mind. If she calls again, get me. I'll be wading through the messages on my desk which I'm sure are to the ceiling."

"You're right there."

Oscar, enjoying the sparring with Esther as part of his morning ritual, made his way through the crowded main office to his own office. The first message was from Alonzo and he felt he owed him a return call so he proceeded to try and reach him. The number rang at Alonzo's church.

"I'm sorry; Mr. Chavis isn't here right now. He's down at the picket line."

"Can you get a message to him?"

"If it's important, I'll send somebody to tell him. Who's calling please?"

"Just tell him that Oscar called and I'm back in the office. I'll be here all day if he wants to get back up with me or drop by."

"Yes, sir, I'll tell him."

Oscar picked up the previous day's paper and scanned the front page. He was actually pleased how everyone functioned whether or not he was there. For the most part, the staff was competent and motivated. Many were young and hoping that a stint on a small daily like the Journal would be their ticket to a big city paper. He didn't mind that fact at all as he had been there himself and knew the nature of the business. If he were twenty again, he would be doing the same. As he turned the pages, Esther came into the office.

"It's your young lady friend. I'll just shut the door and give you your privacy."

Oscar threw the paper at her.

"You are a troublemaker!"

On the other end of the line was Betsy Robinson, the social worker helping Mrs. Frye and Cody. He hoped this was not bad news about Mrs. Frye.

"Good morning, Miss Robinson. This is Oscar Phipps. How are you today?"

"To be honest with you, Mr. Phipps, I'm very upset right now."

"It's not Mrs. Frye, is it?"

"No, she's getting better every day. It's her son, Marcus. He's in very serious trouble."

"What's the problem? Is he still running from you?"

"He's not running from anybody now. He's in jail. He was involved in a drive by shooting where a young girl was killed. The police identified the car and the driver. They chased

164

them till they rammed a police roadblock. Two older boys in the front seat were killed. Marcus got cut up but that's the least of his problems. He's been booked for murder and they're wanting to try him as an adult. I spoke to the District Attorney's office and they're ready to throw the book at him. He's scared to death and you're the only one he knew to call. I told him I'd try to get up with you."

"What does he think I can do?   Really, I'd like to help, but I'm in South Carolina and I barely know him. I just met him and his brother, Cody in the hospital a few days ago and to be honest with you, he's not the easiest kid I've met to get along with. He struck me as a problem looking for a place to start."

"Listen Mr. Phipps, I know what you're talking about, but I work with a lot of kids and I know he's not capable of a drive by shooting. He's been raised well by his mother and I don't believe for a moment he had anything to do with it."

"So why was he in the car?"

"He says he'd been staying some with the older boy and they just asked him if he wanted to go for a ride with them. He said they told him after he got in the car they had shot somebody and just a couple of minutes later, the Police were after them. He said he wanted to get in the car because he was cold and didn't have anywhere to go. Mr. Phipps, I'd been trying to get him to let me place him in a foster home all week. He'd been hanging around the corner where he says they picked him up and I believe him. Practically every time I'd pass that way after visiting his mother, I'd see him standing there over a steam pipe trying to stay warm. I know he didn't take part in a shooting. Would you consider trying to help him? If he has to settle for a Public Defender, I guarantee you he'll wind up in a correctional facility of some sort and it'll ruin his life. He deserves a chance. Won't you come talk with him?"

"I just don't know Miss Robinson.   I'm not sure I could help at all."

"You're the editor of the paper there, aren't you?"

"Yes, but we're in South Carolina, don't forget."

"Don't you know anyone here who might have a little pull?"

After her prompting, one name did jump into Oscar's head.

"Well, I might know someone. Give me your number and I'll make a call and see what I can do."

"Thank you, Mr. Phipps. Believe me, it's the right thing to do. He's a good kid and he deserves some help from somewhere."

"I'll see what I can do. And call me Oscar. Nobody calls me Mr. Phipps."

"Thank you, Oscar. I'll be waiting to hear from you."

After turning down Meecham's request to work with the Morton's trust fund, Oscar felt a little odd about calling him back so soon to ask for a favor. He made the call anyway. He figured pride should certainly be a small concern at a moment like this.

"Is Bob Meecham available?"

"Who's calling, sir?"

"Tell him it's Oscar Phipps from South Carolina."

"Yes, sir. He's in a meeting at the moment. I'll get a note to him. Can you hold for a moment?"

"Of course."

Only a minute passed before the familiar, amiable voice came on the line.

"Oscar! You're going to take me up on the director's job, aren't you? I told you. A conscience is the heaviest weight in the world."

"Good to speak with you, Bob. Actually, I haven't really come to a decision on that yet. I was calling to see if you would consider helping me. You remember the young boys I was telling you about I met in the hospital?"

"Right. What's the problem?"

"The older one is in some pretty serious trouble. Seems he is implicated in a drive-by shooting. The social worker who is helping them swears he's not involved but the police have him in custody and are charging him. I guess he's going to need a half-decent lawyer and somebody to go his bail. He doesn't have any money so it's going to take an organization of some sort to underwrite him. I think the social worker is right; he probably had nothing to do with it. He didn't seem the type. Any suggestions on where I could go to find him some help?"

"Tell you what, Oscar. I'm in with the boss right now. You come on up in the morning and we'll take a closer look at the problem when you get here."

"I knew it. You're gonna make me come up there. You're not just going to give me a name, are you?"

"Call me when you get to the airport and I'll send over a car. Talk to you later."

The line went dead on the other end and Oscar began to understand fully what a pro he was dealing with. Here was a man who could call the shots, get things accomplished and not offend you in the process. As bad as he hated the thought of it, Oscar was on his way back to D.C. He called Esther and told her he had to leave and for her to cover for him. She exploited the young social servicer issue to the fullest again. He finally told her she was right, he was seeing a younger woman, to keep it to herself and have his ticket waiting for him at the airline ticket window.

"I'll be back in the morning. Try and keep your mind out of the gutter, Esther. I swear sometimes I think you should be an editor for one of the grocery store tabloids."

"Hey, I guarantee you I could dig up enough dirt I wouldn't have to make up stories like Elvis was an alien."

"No doubt, Esther. Anyway, I'm out of here. I'll call and let you know I'm alive. Alonzo is going to swear I'm dodging him but just make my apologies and tell him that I'll be back shortly and I'll get up with him. You know, standard apology number four. Oh yeah, call back my young lady friend at this number and tell her I'm on my way to D.C. and I'll call when I get there. You got all this?"

"Got it!"

"OK, I'm gone."

"Hey, Oscar!"

"What now?"

"You didn't lie to her about the savings account, did you?"

"When I get back, I'm going to try and have you placed in a nice quiet hospital Esther, where you'll get the help you need."

Not looking forward to such a quick return trip, Oscar made a hasty round of the main floor so the staff would know he was still alive and then he made a quiet exit for the airport. The flight this time was less turbulent and he managed to relax a little on the way. Washington National was swarming when Oscar arrived. He had not made arrangements for a rental car and decided to just call Meecham and take him up on his offer of a ride. Always preferring to travel light, he had only a carry-on bag and no need to wait for any luggage in the baggage claim area. He walked over to one of the many exits from the main lobby and was startled to hear his name on the loudspeaker.

"Mr. Phipps, please meet your party at shuttle parking."

Oscar wondered if there was possibly another Mr. Phipps in the airport but figured he should proceed to the shuttle area just to be safe. He was surprised to find Betsy Robinson waiting on the sidewalk.

"Mr. Phipps, I'm so glad you came. The kind lady that you work for told me that you would be arriving now. I hope you don't think I'm being pushy, but I just couldn't wait to get up with you. I'll be glad to drive you to a hotel and then over to talk with Marcus.

"She told you she was my boss, did she?"

"Well, not in so many words, but she indicated that she pretty much kept you 'in line'."

"I can't wait to get back now."

"Mr. Phipps, did you have any luck with your contact?"

"Please call me Oscar. I spoke to my friend here and I believe he'll do what he can. I haven't made any hotel reservations yet, I left so quickly to catch my flight. Florence doesn't have a flight leaving for here but twice a day and I wanted to catch the early one. Why don't we just go on over where they're holding the boy and let me talk to him. I need to understand exactly what we're up against before I try and take any steps to help him. You ready?"

"Yes, I'm parked right over here in the hourly lot. That's all you brought?"

"This is it."

"Great; follow me to the car. You want to drive?"

"Not a chance! I don't even like the traffic in Florence so you can imagine how well I'd do up here."

"I don't like it, either, but you get used to it. We're just ahead of the rush hour. We can get there in about a half hour."

"Lead on, Miss Robinson."

While the young woman drove, Oscar studied the streets and neighborhoods they passed. This was definitely not the tourist route. You didn't have to get far from the nation's capital and the glistening government buildings to be in the middle of depression and poverty. The streets and corners were filled with an array of characters that made you wonder if they would do you harm. The buildings were filthy and the storefronts covered over with plywood where windows had been. The places that adapted and survived looked more like prisons than stores. The windows and doors were heavily barred. Security cameras and alarms occupied every possible corner and eave of the buildings. A trading post in Indian Territory during the Indian wars would not have had more protection. Of course, back then the Native Americans wielded bows and knives, not automatic weapons with multi round clips. Oscar couldn't imagine anyone actually calling such a place home. How could anyone live like this? Didn't they realize there were still some decent places where you didn't live in fear of being shot or mugged with every step outside? Of course, he also would not want to see any influx of such characters into his hometown. Florence was already finding itself with some of the problems that had been the sole property of the bigger cities for so long. Violence and drugs had invaded every part of the country now even though nothing in his state could begin to compare with what he was seeing on this short journey.

Through several commercial districts and mile after mile of low-end housing they continued until a huge expanse of twelve-foot tall chain-link fence topped with glistening razor-wire appeared ahead. There were towers at each change of direction in the perimeter fence and armed guards were readily evident. Betsy Robinson had visited a large number of her clients here over the years. She knew exactly where to go and the guard at every checkpoint spoke to her by name.

"It seems to me you would have as much influence here as anyone. Everyone is treating you more like family than a visitor."

"I have been here an awful lot, but I assure you I carry no

weight with the district attorney's office. I'm looked at more as an arm of the Court than a friend to whoever winds up in here."

"Why such a concern about Marcus, then?"

"Most of all, I know he's not guilty. His mother has put her entire life on the line for her sons and I can't just sit by and see her dreams burn up in front of her. I don't doubt Marcus is heading for trouble if there aren't some pretty significant changes made in his environment soon, but right now, he's just a big kid. He doesn't have any meanness in him. His mother has loved him and tried to keep him from filling up with anger and bitterness over their situation - the poverty and uncertainty. I want to try and keep him from breaking her heart. You know what I mean, don't you, Oscar?"

"Yes, I guess that's the reason I'm here, too. I see exactly what you're talking about. I'm here as much for Mrs. Frye as for Marcus. Maybe we can do something together to help them."

"I really do hope so. I've seen it work in the opposite direction so many times that I feel like I want to make a stand on this one and see if I can make some kind of difference, just once."

"Very commendable, Miss Robinson."

"Call me Betsy, OK?"

"Of course, Betsy."

"We'll park here and a guard will escort us inside."

"Is this a juvenile detention center?"

"No. This is a regional correction center where prisoners are held until they are either tried and released or convicted and sent to a permanent jail. There's not many youth here. They're sent here if they're being tried as adults or if they're so dangerous they don't want them around other youngsters. I've met some people in here that would scare you to death to talk to for five minutes. If you start to feel sorry for the people behind these bars, you need to meet a few of them. Thank God most of them wind up in places like this. I couldn't sleep if they didn't."

"I've met a few over the years myself."

"I can't believe they would have a kid like Marcus in here with career criminals though. Doesn't make sense. I thought they had rules against that sort of thing."

"Doesn't apply here. They say this is just an interim holding facility but as long as it takes to go through the court system, some of the inmates spend several years here before they get sent to a permanent correction center. By that time, you can imagine the impact an environment like this can have on a young kid like Marcus."

"Pretty depressing. Well, let's see if we can get him out of here before they have a chance at hurting him."

A large burly guard with a sour expression on his face came over and motioned for Oscar and Betsy to follow him. Oscar wondered how anyone could work in a place like this for long and not become completely embittered at the human race.

"Good afternoon, Ms. Robinson. Is this gentleman with you?"

"Yes, Mr. Ahearn, we're here to see Marcus Frye. Could you have him brought to the visiting area?"

"Will do. Follow Officer Jennings here if you will. He'll take you through the gates. Oh, nice to see you again."

"Thank you, Mr. Ahearn."

The visiting area was large and looked as warm and inviting as a morgue. The furniture was cheap and worn and the floor was the typical large colored squares of linoleum that had gone out of style in the fifties, about when the prison was built. There was a long divider with chairs on both sides and a Plexiglas screen at the top.

"Do we have to talk to him through this?"

"Normally you would, but they let me go to a meeting room on the other side of the wall. That's where they'll bring him."

Oscar saw Marcus enter the room. He was wearing bright orange prison coveralls and was being led by a huge guard. Marcus stared at the floor and walked like a man going to his execution. After they shut the door behind him, the guard came over and escorted Oscar and Betsy back to the same room. As they entered, Marcus looked up and Oscar could see the hope wash across Marcus' face.

"Mr. Phipps, you came. You got him to come, Miss Robinson, just like you said. Did she tell you, Mr. Phipps? I didn't do nothin' and I can't stay here. I just can't."

Oscar walked over and held out his hand to shake with Marcus. As he walked over, the boy stood up and after a brief pause he instead hugged Oscar. It was a spontaneous action that caught the very reserved Oscar completely by surprise. Tears filled the boy's eyes. There were bruises and small fresh cuts on his face. Oscar hoped that they were all a result of the wreck and not souvenirs of his brief stay in the prison.

"Mr. Phipps, please get me out of here. I ain't done nothin'. There are some people here that are bad. I mean really bad. I don't want to stay here with 'em. Can I go with you today? Are they gonna let me out now?"

"I don't know what's going to happen, Marcus. I've come to see what I can do. I want to help you and so does Miss Robinson. Sit down and tell me exactly what happened."

Betsy pulled out a small cassette recorder and set it on the table. Then she got out a yellow legal pad to make notes on. Marcus told them in great detail what he remembered of the events leading up to his arrest.

Marcus' spirits seemed to be improving and the presence of allies had done a lot for his state of mind. Oscar didn't doubt any of what Marcus told him. It made sense and he felt confident Marcus was not lying. The only thing Oscar didn't clearly understand was how he had gotten involved and what he should do next.

"Has anyone treated you badly or hurt you, Marcus?"

"No, sir. They haven't had a chance yet. I ain't even gone to the shower. Several of the men have said a lot of shit that I don't like."

"Like what, Marcus?"

"Like what they was gonna to do to me when they got me alone and stuff like that. They're really starting to bother me."

"Well, I don't know how long it's going to take to get you out but I promise you no one is going to harm you. I'm going to speak to whoever is in charge as soon as we leave you. I'm going to see what has to be done to get you out on bond or if they'll release you in my custody."

Betsy, speaking as the voice of experience, added,

"That's very unlikely, Oscar. If they set a bond, they'll let you put up collateral for it but they don't let any capital offenders out with just a signature or personal recognition."

The worry was coming back into Marcus' voice.

"What does that mean? Please don't make me stay here any more. This place is terrible, Mr. Phipps."

As he sat across from the young black boy, a vision of a bygone day and another young man in a similar circumstance flashed into his mind. He remembered sitting in the small cell in Lydia and getting a sense of the terrible ordeal that Pickle had been through. He stiffened himself and at that moment made up his mind Marcus would receive whatever help he was capable of providing.

"Look, Marcus, I've got to talk to a few people about you right now. You will hear from me before the day is over. That's a promise. Try not to worry and just stay put wherever they've got you. Don't go anywhere without a guard. I'm going to tell the warden you are to have an escort to the shower or anywhere you're allowed to go. You could get a shower or go to the toilet and it would be safe. We're going to go now so we can get up with these folks before they leave for the day. You going to be okay?"

"Yes sir...I guess so. You're going to do all that for me? Why?"

"It's not just for you, Marcus. It's for me, too, as well as your mother and a lot of other people. We've got to go now. Take care."

"Yes, sir. Please don't let this take too long."

Betsy motioned to the guard. He came over and escorted them from the room back to the lobby and then left to take Marcus back to the cell block area. Oscar approached the supervising guard in the lobby.

"Excuse me, officer. I would like to speak with the warden if that's possible."

"You mean the superintendent?"

Betsy spoke up.

"Mr. Ahearn, can you call Mr. Betts and tell him I need to talk with him?"

"I will, Miss Robinson, but you know he usually just sees

people with an appointment."

"Well, call him just the same and tell him I said it's important that I speak with him right away. Let him know it's kind of an emergency. OK?"

"Yes, ma'am."

After a few minutes in the small room that served as an office, he returned.

"He wasn't happy about it but he said to come over to his office right now. I think he's trying to get out of here early today. Said something about going to the show with his old lady."

"We won't keep him. Thank you Mr. Ahearn."

"Yes Ma'am."

The thing that immediately struck Oscar about Superintendent Betts was that he instinctively did not like him. His first glance of the man reminded him of the many small minded bureaucrats he dealt with during his years as a reporter. He was short, fat, wearing a cheap, ill-fitting suit and a plaid shirt with a prominent stain just under the collar. He was almost completely bald on the top of his head. He tried to hide the fact by combing ten or so long strands of greasy brown hair from the side across the top extending to the fringe on the other side. He had stained teeth and apparently was unaware how gross they looked since he kept a patronizing politician's smile fixed on his pale fat face. Oscar was afraid that his own face was radiating a disdain for him.

"Ah, Miss Robinson. How are you today?"

As was his self-important custom, he did not wait for a reply.

"I guess my man told you I have a previous engagement this afternoon but I can always spare a moment for a fellow employee of the district. How's old Bob Bridges over at the main office? I'm sure he's up to his ears, right? Well, what can I do for you and your friend here, and who are you, sir? You work with Miss Betsy, do you?"

Oscar now knew his first impression was on target.

"Phipps, Oscar Phipps."

"Good, good. Phipps; don't recognize the name. You with the local office of Social Services?"

174

"No, I'm not. I'm the editor of a paper in South Carolina. I'm here to speak with you about someone you have in custody."

"I don't generally talk with the press, Mr. Phipps. Phipps, that correct?"

"That's correct. I hope you can make an exception this time. Miss Robinson has gone to a lot of trouble to bring me here and I have a number of previous engagements myself."

Oscar thought the last statement might have been a little too obvious but he was having trouble being nice to the pompous ass.

"That so? You know, Miss Robinson, it's not a good idea to bring a member of the press into my office without giving me some sort of idea what this is all about. To say the very least, I'm a little shocked by your actions. That's not to say that I am not appreciative of the fine job that members of the press do. Just what story is it that you're after, Mr. Phipps?"

"I'm not here about a news story, Superintendent. I'm here to see about an inmate you have in here who really should be at a juvenile detention center. I'm a little dismayed he would be in here with adult offenders."

"That so? Well, I don't send them here. I just keep them here after the decision has been made. I'm not aware of any particular problems this has caused any incarcerated individual under our supervision. Has someone made some sort of accusation to the contrary I should know about?"

"Not that I know of. I'm only concerned about one young man who's here now."

"Well let's get down to business then, Mr. Phipps. What can I do to help you and Miss Robinson?"

Betsy felt that Betts was going to need some pushing from her to get a response.

"The young Frye boy who was in the car that crashed into the police roadblock. We know he was not involved in the drive-by shooting and we want to expedite getting him out on bail."

"So, why not go see the judge just like you would for any other prisoner?"

"We will be doing that first thing in the morning. Our main concern is that he is young and not worldly. We don't want anything to happen to him before we can get him out on bond."

"We take very good care of our prisoners here, Miss Robinson. Nothing is going to happen to the boy. Are you requesting some sort of special treatment for him?"

Oscar interrupted.

"That is exactly what I'm asking, Mr. Betts. I'm requesting that you segregate him from the other prisoners until we can make the necessary arrangements."

"That's just not possible, Mr. Phipps. We treat everyone the same here. He'll go to recreation with the others, as well as meals and showers."

"And he'll probably be assaulted before twenty-four hours pass."

"That will not happen here, Mr. Phipps. Our prisoners know better than to engage in that sort of conduct."

"Sure, and the Easter Bunny lives next door. You know as well as I do what will happen to an inexperienced fifteen-year-old who's never been away from home before in his life."

"Hey, he's the one that got in the car. If he didn't want to be in jail, he should have stayed out of trouble. I don't know how you people do things down South, Mr. Phipps, but up here we go by the rules. Treat everybody just the same. He stays at my prison, he does what I say and I say he gets no special treatment. Have I made myself perfectly clear? You can write in your paper what a hard-ass I am if you want, but up here people are getting tired of things like drive-by killings. We don't have a lot of sympathy for criminals. They pay me to keep 'em locked up as long as the Court says and that's what I do. What goes on once they get behind these bars is up to me. We follow the law, mind you, but no special treatment is given to anybody. Anything else I can help you nice folks with?"

Oscar fumed inside. His blood pressure was approaching an all-time high.

"Betts. Granted, I'm from a small southern town, but I'm a pretty well-traveled guy. I've dealt with people like you an awful lot over the years."

"Is that right?"

"Yes, and I gotta tell you Betts, I'm real good at it."

"That's very interesting, Mr. Phipps. But it's of no concern here as our dealings are all over right now. Ahearn will show you folks back to your car."

"One last thing, Betts. If anything happens to that boy, you won't believe the amount of investigating that's going to happen here. Any 'i' that wasn't dotted, any 't' that wasn't crossed and you, my friend will be amazed at how quick I can fill your life with problems."

"Are you threatening me?"

"I never make threats. You better keep him away from the other prisoners and that's all I'm going to say to you."

"Miss Robinson, you'd best take your friend here and leave. I'm sure the Director of Social Services would be interested in what was said here this afternoon."

Betsy was very nervous by this time. This was not what she wanted and she knew she had no weight to throw around here or in her own department. She knew she would be hearing more about this confrontation. Betts called for a guard.

"Mr. Ahearn, they are ready to leave now."

"Yes, sir."

As they left, Betts went over to his desk and stood between it and his chair. His face was red with indignation. He turned, picked up his foot and shoved the chair into the wall of the office, the impact knocking a couple of pictures from the wall. He picked up the phone and pressed a code number.

"Sergeant, you have a prisoner named Frye in your area?"

"Yes, sir. Block two. What's the problem?"

"I've just had a couple of visitors who told me that we'd better give special care to Mr. Frye. Keep him segregated from the bad men on his block. I was offended someone would think we wouldn't take good care of him. I know he'll be just fine if he mixes with the rest of our guests. See to it he gets every opportunity to meet some of the fine people who are staying here with us. Do you understand, Sergeant?"

"Exactly, sir. I'll see to it."

"Very good, Sergeant."

As he hung up the phone, a smirk took hold of his yellow teeth. Proud of himself, he threw on his overcoat and left the office.

By now, Marcus could recognize the sound of the guard's hard soled boots on the concrete gangplank that ran outside of his cell.

"All right, Frye, chow time. On your feet. Don't make me angry, boy. Get a move on."

Marcus was hungry but he knew he did not want to go to the chow hall.

"I'm not hungry right now. I'll just stay here if that's all right."

"It ain't all right. I'm responsible to see you stay in first class condition and you can't do that without eating. Get up and moving."

Marcus sat on the end of bed and did not move. The guard opened the cell door and moved over so close to him that his legs pushed up against his own.

"Don't upset me, boy. Get up now! If you don't move right now it's not going to be pleasant."

Marcus kept looking down at the floor. He didn't respond. He would be safer with a guard who was mad at him than with the pack of animals that had been making catcalls and smartass remarks to him all day in the cell block.

The large aggressive guard grabbed the end of the nightstick from his belt and without another word; he bent over and placed Marcus in a headlock using the stick as choke bar on his neck. He squeezed till Marcus could barely draw a breath.

"How'd you like this, boy? I handle men, grown men all day long and don't none of 'em tell me no. You think I'm going to take it from a punk like you? I'm real good at pressure points. Spots that hurt a hell of lot and almost never leave a bruise. Kind of a specialty of mine. How's this feel?"

Marcus was straining to breathe. The guard continued the pressure until Marcus was only a few seconds from passing out. He then roughly pulled the nightstick back from Marcus' head, allowing him to fall back on his bunk.

"You feel like a nice hot meal now I bet, don't you?"
"Yes...sir. I'll eat if I have to."
"That's the spirit. Now get your scrawny ass moving."

Marcus moved in front of the guard who followed him every step towards the mess hall. Marcus thought if the guard was going to stay with him at least he would be safe. He might not like him but it was his job to keep order.

As they entered the dining area, scores of prisoners were already seated and many more waited for their meal in the food line. With his own personal escort, Marcus drew attention entering the hall. Except for the few prisoners who had cells adjacent to where he was being held, this was the first time most of them had noticed there was a young, new resident in the prison. Each table they passed had at least one and more often than not several cat-callers and whistlers expressing interest in him. Undoubtedly, some were only being smart or trying to intimidate the kid but there were some whose interests were more than that. They knew he was bound to be scared out his mind in such a place and there was enough venom there to find its way to him.

"Hey sweetheart! Come sit with us."

"You are one fine-looking thing, sweet cakes. You'll like it over here. Bring your fine self right on over. We won't bite."

Each remark was followed by outbursts of laughter from the general populace and Marcus wanted badly to be anywhere in the world other than here. The freezing street corner he had practically been living on would seem like a safe haven compared to this. The guard escorted him over to the end of the food line.

"Now get your food and find a seat. I'm not takin' any more crap off you today. When you're through, go back to your cell before the locks are set off. You understand, boy?"

"Yes sir. You won't be coming with me?"

"What the hell do you think this is, boy, a cruise ship?"

He was finally alone in the crowd. With no guard and no place to escape to he knew he wouldn't leave the large eating hall without a confrontation. He went through the motions but was too nervous to eat. He grabbed a container of milk and an apple and tried to find a seat away from the name-calling and intimidation being thrown his way.

In a corner of the room he found a small table that was vacant except for one older man. He was a black man, just like ninety per cent of the prisoners. He was pushing sixty years in age if he wasn't already there, with gray hair and the look of resignation that appeared on the faces of many old-timers who'd spent most of their lives in jail. He didn't speak a word as Marcus sat across from him. Marcus refused to look around and stared at the table directly in front of him. He took a few bites off the apple and a couple swallows of milk. He hoped Oscar and Miss Robinson would have him out of there by morning and he could worry about eating then.

"Hey, boy. Mind if I sit down with you a while? You look real lonesome sitting there. I'll give you a little company. What do you say to that, sweet thing?"

Marcus remained silent and refused to look at the large young black man who sat down to his right. Two others had followed him to the table and most of the prisoners in the mess hall were watching or egging them on.

"What's wrong? You ain't being too neighborly now, considering my cell is just a couple of doors down from yours. Why, we're neighbors, bro'. We live in the same 'hood now. Don't you wanna be friends? I think I could be a real good friend to a fine young man like yourself."

The crowd roared and Marcus was so scared he was beginning to shake. He didn't know how to respond. They were all much larger than him and obviously hardened to this environment. He knew he had to get out, and soon. He just wanted them to go away and leave him alone, but he knew it would not be that easy.

"What's wrong boy, cat got your tongue? I'm speakin' to you. Are you deaf?"

When Marcus didn't answer again, the seated youth slid his foot under the leg of Marcus' chair. He then took his hand and pushed the top of the chair until it fell over, sprawling the boy on the floor, milk all over his face.

"My gracious, you've taken a nasty fall there, young man. Here, let me help you up."

As he grabbed Marcus' arm and lifted, he took his other hand and grabbed directly at Marcus' genitals. The crowd exploded again. Marcus' mind reeled, wondering what this idiot was doing and why was everyone going along with something so crude. He took his own hand and pulled the man's hand away from him.

"Now that's not real friendly. I'm beginning to think you don't like me very much. Correct me if I'm wrong. Or maybe you're just shy. Yeah, maybe that's it; you're just shy. Here, sit back in the chair and let's get to know each other a little better, brother."

The moron was still being encouraged by the crowd and he was enjoying being the center of attention as he spent his cruelty on the frightened kid.

"Now, that's better. I know we're gonna' be the best of friends. My name is Tompkins. I'm pretty well-known in here. You could say that people here respect me. They don't give me no shit. Get the picture? I'm a real good man to know. I can make your time here real easy, or.....I can make you wish you just never been born."

As he reached over to touch Marcus again, his own chair went out from under him and he in turn crashed to the floor. Surprised, he looked back to his other side where he was confronted by the old man at the table who had seen enough. Neither of Tompkins' buddies made any attempt to come between the two men. They understood the special position the older inmates held in the jail.

"Get the hell out of here, Tompkins. I'm eatin' and I don't need your shit. You understand, boy?"

The thug knew better than to directly confront one of the old-timers. They knew the ropes and were generally supported by the prison staff. Not to mention the older men stuck together and had their own kind of hierarchy based on seniority. If you messed with one, you would have to deal with them all.

"Listen old man, I was just trying to be friendly to the kid here. We was just playin' with him."

"I don't give a shit about the kid. You're bothering me. Now get the hell out of here before you upset me."

Now, his own stature confronted head-on by the older man, he pushed a point by standing up against him.

"You got no cause to talk to me like that. I don't give a shit how long you been in here or if you die in here. You touch me again, old man, and you'll wish you had stayed the fuck out of this."

"You're scaring the shit out of me, Tompkins. Now get the hell out of here before I personally kick your sorry ass."

"You want to try and do that right now, old man? I'm standin' right here waitin' on you. I don't think that kid is gonna' be helpin' you none. Let's do it, old man!"

The night stick came crashing down on the back of the legs of the loudmouth. He turned to see the guard staring at him.

"Tompkins, leave Perkins here alone and get back to your cell. Your meal is over. You need another shot of this to get your attention?

"I'm goin'. I see what's goin' on here. Watch your back, old man. You won't get away with this shit. And kid, you better stay in your fuckin' cell. I see you out here again, you're mine!"

The guard took the point of his night stick and shoved it into his back.

"Leave! Now!"

Glaring every step of the way, the crowd quiet again, he sauntered out of the mess hall. Marcus now had an enemy. Why couldn't they just leave him alone? Tears welled up in his eyes but he determined not to touch them or let them know they'd gotten the best of him at all. He was grateful to the old man.

"Thanks. I'm sorry they bothered you."

"You're the one who best watch his back around here, boy. Most of the young people in here are just trash. They got no respect for nobody or nothin'. He's a particularly hard ass. He'll hurt you if he gets the chance. You know, I got a boy at home, back on the outside. He's just about your age. About fifteen, I guess."

"That right? What are you in here for?"

"Got drunk one night, stole a car. Didn't mean to hurt nobody. Police started chasin' me and I run over somebody. Didn't mean to do it. It just happened."

"How long have you been in here?"

"Twelve years. Couple more and they'll probably let me out. Might as well. I'm too old and worn out to cause anybody a problem. Listen to me, boy. You get out of here, you get your life straight. Get you some education. It's the only way to survive. Then you can get a job and some respect. You got no job, no money, you got no respect. I can tell you one thing, you don't want to spend your life like I been doin'. It's just like you're an animal in a cage. No life at all."

Marcus could see the despair in his face. A loud buzzer went off and those who had remained in the dining area, either eating or just talking, all stood up and started back to their cells. He figured that must be the signal to leave. As he walked back to his cell, he passed the cells where the trouble maker and his friends were waiting.

"I see you, boy. You'll be remembering this day for a long time. You just wait and see what happens, you little shit."

Marcus did not look their way or respond. He continued on to his cell. Once inside, he laid on the hard cot and pulled the stiff army blanket up over most of his face. He dreaded what would happen if he weren't able to get out before the next meal or exercise period. By lights out, the smart remarks and the thinly disguised threats were getting more frequent and disgusting. His tormentors were enjoying themselves too much to let up now. Just before he fell asleep, the guard came to the front of his cell.

"Hey, kid, good news. Well, I guess it's all in how you look at it. The warden left word that you don't get a private room no more. So, in the morning you get a roommate. Ain't that nice? And, guess what? It's somebody you already know."

The guard laughed sardonically as he walked off. For hours Marcus lay awake listening to the idiots a few cells down trying to scare him. He knew too well what the guard meant. Why would they do this to him? What had happened to Oscar? Why hadn't he heard from him? One thing he knew for sure, he would not be put in a cell with one of those men, no matter what he had to do. He would rather be dead.

While Marcus waited anxiously, Oscar continued his efforts on the boy's behalf. The White House looked like a post card. As Betsy Robinson drove up to the guard house, she was more than a little surprised at where Oscar had asked her to take him.

"I'll get out here, Betsy, I've got your number and I'll call

183

you as soon as I find out what can be done. Will you be all right driving home by yourself?"

"I do it every day. Please try and get him out tomorrow. Staying in that place could do a lot of harm to someone like Marcus. He doesn't need or deserve this."

"I'll do what I can. Goodnight."

"Oscar..."

"Yes?"

"I just have to ask. You're not going to see the President, are you?"

"Let me assure that I'm not nearly that well-known here, Betsy. Just someone on his staff that might be able to help Marcus. I'll let you know how it went."

"I'm impressed. See you in the morning."

Oscar informed the guard he wished to see Bob Meecham and showed him his identification.

"Yes, sir, Mr. Phipps. He's called out here a couple of times to see if we'd heard from you. He seemed to think you'd require a ride from the airport."

"I know, but a friend picked me up. Is he still here?"

"You'd have a difficult time finding him when he wasn't here. Biggest workaholic I've ever seen and this place is like a nesting ground for them. Give me a minute."

In just a short while, an aide in a suit and overcoat came out and escorted Oscar into a waiting room in the White House. In all his years of covering stories about the government, this was the first time Oscar had been into the home of the nation's President. To think it had come about not so much from anything he had done in his life but from the strange turn of events set off by the death of Dwight Morton! It seemed that just knowing the man had great impact on the course of people's lives. One week he was at home in semi-retirement, enjoying the quiet life afforded the editor of a small-town newspaper, and the next he was in the White House fighting to protect a young boy he barely knew.

"Oscar! Glad to see you."

Meecham walked over and warmly embraced Oscar. There was that ever present Cheshire cat grin that nagged at Oscar because it seemed as if Meecham was leading him in a direction that only he was privy to.

"In here, Oscar. I've got a small office where we can talk."

He turned to the young aide who had accompanied Oscar inside.

"Thanks, Browning. I'll take it from here. Hold my calls, please, unless it's the boss."

"Yes, sir."

Meecham never seemed to require unquestioned authority but it was given to him by everyone in his presence. He had a bearing about him that commanded respect.

"Now, what's the story on the youngster you were telling me about?"

"He's in prison. Being held for taking part in a drive-by shooting which I know he didn't participate in."

"You sure he's innocent?"

"Not a doubt in my mind. His social worker feels the same way. I want to get him out tomorrow morning at the latest. It's not a decent place and the Superintendent is a first-class idiot. Can you arrange for him to get bond somehow?"

"Well, I don't practice law but I imagine that you would have to get an attorney and go before the district judge. He would be the one to set bond. With a capital offense like this, it could be fifty thousand, maybe even more. Have you got some collateral you could use to secure it?"

"Just my house in South Carolina."

"I doubt they would consider that, Oscar, what with the house being in another state and all. How about cash?"

"For crying out loud, Bob, I'm a newspaper man. I never made any money. I'll be working somewhere till I drop. Would you consider signing for him?"

"Well, Oscar, I'm kinda like you. I'm just a government worker and I rent; no collateral to sign over. It's a shame we can't get Dwight's Foundation to secure his bond."

"Can they do that? Is there enough collateral to cover it?"

"Are you kidding? There's millions in the trust fund. Plus tons of real estate and stocks. Dwight left everything to the Foundation."

"Well, why can't we just do that?"

"Has to be approved by the director."

"Let's call him, then. How do we get up with him?"

"That's just it, Oscar. There isn't a director now. Like I said earlier, I resigned to become the executor of Dwight's estate and can't serve in both positions because of a conflict of interest situation. Dwight left a number of businesses that are still strong and I have to oversee their administration. So there's no director right now. The person Dwight insisted would take the job didn't want to do it."

"Who was that?"

"Why, you, of course. It's really a shame, too. As director, you could just make one call and the Foundation's attorney would be on this so fast you wouldn't believe it. Yes, sir. But hey, I understand. I know how busy you are and everything. It's not like you work here in the White House and have all kinds of free time like myself."

The Cheshire cat grin broadened. The full extent of Meecham's charade to enlist Oscar in the cause was now apparent.

"You know, Meecham, this sounds a great deal like blackmail to me."

"Blackmail? What a colorful, descriptive word, even if it does have a certain air of prejudice about it. Let's just remember what Dwight always said. Everything works out the way it's supposed to. We just try and keep it headed in the right direction."

"He always got what he wanted, didn't he?"

"He was a very convincing fellow. He liked you a lot. Trusted you. Had the South Carolina Journal delivered to his office every day and always read your column."

"You're kidding."

"As God is my witness. He thought you were the most honest journalist he knew and he agreed with you on almost everything."

"And so, here I am. Right?"

"You would be amazed at how often this kind of thing happened with Dwight."

"I don't think I would. What's the bottom line here?"

"You agree to be the director. Become Editor Emeritus or Editor on Sabbatical at the paper. We rent you a place in D.C. and you spend a week or so here each month. There's a lot of travel involved, and a lot of the finest folks you ever met. I'll lead you along till you get your wings. And Oscar......"

"Yes?"

"I promise you, you will enjoy yourself and sleep better than you ever have in your life. You will be making a difference in people's lives. Just like this young boy. You will have the means to make a difference."

"You don't leave much room to refuse."

"A conscience is a heavy load if it's never emptied. So you'll do it?"

"I'll do it. But first, before we even get started on what in the devil I have gotten myself into, let's make that call to get Marcus out in the morning."

"Great! I'll see what can be done right now."

Meecham picked up the phone on a desk in the small office.

"You know the attorney's number? Is he going to be in this late in the day?"

"Well, there's usually someone there who can help."

"That's great."

Meecham dialed the number from memory.

"Good evening. Yes, this is Bob Meecham. Fine, thank you. Listen, there's a young man... What's his name, Oscar?"

"Marcus Frye."

"Marcus Frye. He's in a detention center here in D.C. awaiting trial. I have it on the highest authority that he is completely innocent and will be cleared of all charges. I would like for you to arrange a personal recognizance bond for him before the sun is up in the morning and release him into the custody of a Mr. Oscar Phipps who will be there to pick him up before nine A.M. Nine OK, Oscar?"

"Nine would be wonderful."

"Yes, that's perfect. Great. Thank the Attorney General for me. Same here. Good evening."

Meecham hung up and Oscar could not wait to express his thoughts.

"I see how terribly difficult that was for you to accomplish Bob. Why do I feel that somehow I've been had?"

"You shouldn't at all, Oscar. The fact is, favors of this sort have a price, especially in this town. I can't do that for just anybody, not even for Oscar Phipps from South Carolina. But, I can and I will for Dwight. That's who I did it for. The Foundation will always be his and when you're running it, you'll be surprised at the doors that open for just such things as this."

"Now I'm impressed."

"Good! How about a coffee? Where are you staying?"

"Nowhere yet."

"Then it's settled. You'll stay at my place. I'll have a car and driver at the front door when you wake up. You can be at the prison when the sun comes up. And by the way, Oscar..."

"Yes?"

"Welcome aboard."

The lights came on simultaneously with the intercom in the prison.

"Six A.M. mess call. Ten minutes."

Even though he had barely slept, the noise woke Marcus from a fitful sleep. In minutes he would be back in the general mess hall and then he would have to go outside in the courtyard with those maniacs. Panic was beginning to build. What could he do? What if Oscar hadn't been able to get him out? He couldn't go through with this. If they bothered him at all, he wouldn't finish the day under this constant fear. Better to be dead than continue living the way his life was headed."

"All right, shithead! Let's go!"

The guard was back. He didn't understand what they were all getting out of doing this to him. He finished pulling on his shirt and fell in behind the group making their way down the cell row to the mess hall. The jeers started immediately.

"Morning, darlin'. The guard says me and you gonna be sharin' a cell by dark. I just can't hardly wait to tuck your little black ass in tonight. We're gonna be just like brothers. I swear we are."

"You stay away from me! I'll never have anything to do with you and they'll never put me in a cell with you!"

"Never is an awfully strong word. We'll see."

"Yeah, we'll see."

As they entered the dining hall, Tompkins fell in line directly behind him. He pressed up close behind Marcus and kept rubbing at his butt as they went down the line. He was eliciting a good number of laughs with all this. Marcus picked up milk and a box of cereal and then as an afterthought, he slowed and loaded up his tray with fruit juice and one of practically everything that would fit on the tray. He tried to walk fast as he left the line and find a table away from Tompkins. The taunting followed close behind.

"Hey roomy, you ain't tryin' to run away from me, are you? We need's to get to know one another, my man. Get us a table."

Marcus looked around the room for any sign of help, but none was offered. Tompkins was generally feared by most of the inmates. He was just crazy enough to hurt someone. Then, Marcus spied the man who had saved him the night before. He quickly went to his table.

"Sir, can I sit with you again?"

The old man was slow to respond or even look up for that matter. He had spent years learning how to avoid trouble and he knew this situation could only end on that note.

"If you gotta. But keep your mouth shut, no matter what."

"Yes, sir, I will."

Tompkins, no longer respecting the old man, came over to the table and pulled out a chair.

"Good. You saved me a seat after all."

The old man looked up at Tompkins.

"That seat is taken. Ain't no seats left here at all. Find yourself another table. There's plenty of 'em around."

"But I like this one, with my little friend here. We're getting real tight, ain't we homey?"

Marcus didn't respond. As Tompkins tried to pull the chair, the old man stood up.

"Damn it, Tompkins, leave this boy alone. You ain't

gonna' mess with him no more, not unless you mess with me first."

"Well, old man, that's just fine with me. I never did like the way you old shits think you're special and that nobody's gonna' fuck with you."

Without warning, a hard right hand landed square on the old man's jaw and he tumbled hard to the floor.

"You wanted it, old man, you got it. Now punk, pick up your tray and follow me. You're my personal property now. Do what I say or you gonna wish you was in hell. I ain't gonna' tell you nothin' but one time. Now get movin.'"

Tompkins reached over to pick Marcus up by his shoulder and instead he caught a face full of milk and fruit juice as the boy threw the tray in his face. The crowd roared with laughter and approval as if that was the show of strength they had been waiting for from the kid before they could sympathize with him. Tompkins didn't find it amusing at all. He dove for Marcus in earnest, mouth snarling and eyes burning with the bright light of animal rage behind them. As he grabbed Marcus, the old man stood up and responded to his bloody lip by smashing Tompkins on the side of his head with an equally hard punch. But Tompkins didn't fall. He instead reached in his shoe and pulled out a small but deadly-looking homemade knife, courtesy of the prison shop. Many of the inmates had such devices squirreled away in case of situations requiring an armed response. The old man immediately saw what he had in his hand and attempted to back off. Tompkins followed after him, waving the knife menacingly at him. From behind, Marcus tackled him around the waist in an effort to defend the old man. Tompkins swung the knife backwards and cut Marcus on the arm, blood flowing profusely from the moment of impact. Not wanting Tompkins to take another shot at the boy, the old timer grabbed for the knife hand. Tompkins saw him coming and turned to greet his movement and thrust the knife forward into his belly as he lunged. Gravely wounded, the old man fell to the floor. By this time, guards near the entrance were moving in that direction. It had taken only seconds, but the actions had been severe and Tompkins was now out of his mind.

"It was the kid. He pulled the knife on me. He stabbed

the old man. The little shit is crazy!"

Even though he was proclaiming his innocence, Tompkins wouldn't drop the knife. Finally, two guards pummeled him with night sticks till he fell to the floor beside the old man and the guards removed the knife from his hand. Marcus looked at the cut on his arm realizing that it would probably require stitches, but was still relieved the episode had ended. At least he thought so. From behind, another guard put a half nelson on Marcus using his nightstick for a choke hold.

"OK, wise ass. You like to fight with knives huh? You're gonna' pay for starting this shit!"

The nightmare was continuing. What more could they do to him? They would not have the chance to find out to what depths they could drop. For as the words left his mouth, he could hear the superintendent's voice behind him.

"Let the boy go! What on Earth possessed you to grab him that way?"

"But sir, you said...."

"Shut up, Norris. Speak when I ask you a question. Not until then. Got it?"

"Yes, sir."

The guard turned to see the red-faced superintendent flanked by a half- dozen dark-suited officers from the Justice Department. They were not smiling, either. Betts kept his mouth shut as the agents of the Attorney General's office took over.

"Get this man to the hospital immediately, and not the prison hospital", one of the officers ordered. Everyone else in here, all of you inmates and guards, sit where you are. No one leaves this room until I say so. Do it now."

Marcus felt weak and almost ready to pass out. Between what he had just witnessed and the continual stream of blood down his arm, it was overpowering his ability to cope. He reached for a seat. A hand pushed it to him and then reached around his back and helped him sit down. It was Oscar.

"Mr. Phipps! You made it! You came back like you said you would."

"Looks like I was almost too late, son. You sit down. We'll get you to the hospital and have that arm taken care of in just a few minutes. There's an ambulance on the way."

"Take Mr. Perkins first. I'm OK. I'm gonna be fine now. Are they gonna let me out?"

"You can count on it. You're leaving with me today. There might still be a hearing to come back to court for, but you're going to be fine. So are Cody and your mother."

Marcus fell forward onto Oscar's shoulder and tried his best to stifle the sobs of relief that were flooding his eyes. Oscar's eyes were fighting a great urge to do the same. He felt as big a sense of relief as Marcus. Betsy Robinson came up and hugged Marcus, too. While they watched, uniformed police entered the room and note pads were showing up everywhere, taking statements from everyone in the room. Oscar could not resist the temptation any longer. He looked over at Superintendent Betts, sweat pouring off his pompous brow with every breath.

"Betts, I'm going to enjoy seeing you in the unemployment line. You aren't as decent as the worst criminal you've been in charge of here. You're in for some dramatic changes in your lifestyle."

One of the Justice Department officers came over to Betts and informed him of his rights to an attorney. Oscar, Betsy and Marcus walked out of the guard's entrance to the Mess Hall and outside to a waiting ambulance. Mr. Perkins was on a gurney being moved into the rear of the vehicle. Oscar asked the attendant,

"Is he going to make it?"

"I think he'll be OK. Lost a lot of blood but I don't think the cut got any organs. We'll keep him on an IV till we get him over to the hospital and I think he'll be good as new in a few days."

"Thank you."

"Yes, sir."

"Oscar, he got cut because he was trying to help me. He kept them away from me last night too. Can we help him get out of here too?"

"I don't know, Marcus. I'll see what I can do."

Oscar noticed once again the increasing circle of involvement. Once he was inside, it seemed to grow without any outside push from him. There was no way to stay neutral or apart from all of the problems. He would do what he could, and even more significant, he would discover what he could do.

CHAPTER TWELVE

The winter cold was finally relenting. The first few warm days of the approaching spring were causing the azaleas to bud. For Oscar, warm weather meant he had made it through the portion of the year that he'd never been able to get comfortable with. Cold went right through him during the winter and he hated the first blast of wind that struck him as he went outside each morning. To feel the sun on his bald head caused his spirits to soar.

He was headed down to the office of the Journal to break the news to everyone that he would be backing off quite a bit and would be more or less a contributing editor when he was able to spare the time. He knew someone else needed to be at the helm. He realized there were plenty of young thoroughbreds champing at the bit down at the paper just waiting to hear such news. Of course, there would be the obligatory "hate to lose you chief" lines passed around for a few days, and then the bloodletting until the reorganization was in effect. Then everyone would settle back into their work mode until the next turnover occurred. He kind of hated he wouldn't be there to see what went on when he left. He thought it would be a lot like being able to attend your own funeral.

Knowing he would be stepping down, there was one story he wanted to get in the paper before he pulled out. In pursuit of the facts he needed to undertake the article, he pulled in front of the chicken plant and looked around till he located Alonzo Chavis.

"Got a minute, Alonzo?"

"You're not ducking me still, are you, Oscar?"

"Get in the car. I haven't been ducking anybody. I've had problems of my own to take care of. As a matter of fact, that's why I'm here."

"What's that?"

"I'm stepping down at the paper to run a Foundation that Dwight Morton ran before he died."

"You've got to be kidding. You've been in the newspaper business ever since I can remember. What brought this on?"

"To tell you the truth, I don't understand it all myself. I

195

guess I was just ready to try something else. I never wanted to die in front of my typewriter, anyway. I was thinking you could be a big help to me."

"How's that?"

"I'm going to be traveling quite a bit and I sure don't want to overlook anyone in our own area needing a little help. The Foundation's purpose is to help the underprivileged and their kids get into college and break out of the poverty chain. Dwight had been doing a pretty good job of it and I want to try and keep it going at least as well. You probably have a better grasp than me of who around here deserves a little help. You interested?"

"Of course I'll help. But tell me, why can't we help the people you see right here on the street with me? They've been on strike for a couple of months and a lot of them don't have much to eat at home. The church has been doing what it could but we're all running pretty thin right now."

"That's the first thing we're going to tackle."

"You're kidding?"

"Nope, come on with me to the office. My last story is going to read something like, "Outside Owners Chicken". What do you think of that? I'll see to it that my friends on the wire service pick it up. This isn't their only processing operation and they won't want their plants in the other parts of the country to see what's going on here."

"Now you're talking, Oscar. We're gonna do just fine together. Always something about you I liked."

Before they reached the office, the two men had pretty well finished the article and were planning how to administer the Foundation in the area. Oscar had to admit that bringing people some good news beat the hell out of always reporting the bad. Whatever it was Dwight had noticed in him, he had never been able to find it in himself. He was pleased with the turn of events in his life. After a day of farewells and promises of keeping in touch and all the other things people say when they think they won't see you again, Oscar dropped Alonzo back at the picket line and made his way to the small frame house he had lived in for over thirty years. As he got out of the car and walked to the front porch he began to laugh out loud at how things had changed so dramatically for him. He opened the door and entered his home.

"Oscar! Momma, Oscar's home!"

Before he could even bend over completely, Cody was rocketing upward expecting Oscar to keep him from returning to the floor.

"Easy, Cody, you'll break my back. I'm too old to catch you like that."

"Momma has fried chicken tonight. We're gonna have chicken. That's two times this week. I love chicken. It's my favorite."

From the kitchen Mrs. Frye called out.

"Evening, Mr. Phipps. We're almost ready to eat. You just sit yourself down and read the paper. I'll call you when it's all ready. Won't be but just a few minutes. Cody, you leave Mr. Phipps be now. He's been workin' all day and he needs a break. You go get Marcus."

"He's still cleaning out the gutters, Momma. He's all dirty and everything. He looks really nasty."

"Well, tell him to come on in and clean up."

The smell of fried chicken and fresh vegetables completely filled the house. Marcus and his family were going to be the first recipients of a new program that the Foundation was starting. Oscar thought it would be a good idea to help inner city families get settled in smaller communities where the children would have a better chance of having a decent childhood without being afraid to walk outside. They would have a small house on the same street as Oscar's. It was already being remodeled for them. There were any number of such homes that could be bought that were a little outdated and small for the current market but were a palace to a family such as the Fryes. Meanwhile, they had the run of Oscar's place and he had to admit he was getting awfully attached to Mrs. Frye's home cooking. She was starting a new job in a few days; helping to manage a kitchen at the shelter Alonzo's church was starting. Alonzo was already living up to their agreement.

Oscar thought maybe he could go over to their place once in awhile and eat some of Mrs. Frye's fine cooking after they got settled. The boys were already back in school and both were ecstatic about their new environment. Marcus came in from the back yard, as dirty as Cody had said he was.

"Hey Oscar! I almost got the gutters clean. The garden hose washes 'em pretty good once I get the heavy stuff out. You know, Oscar, I got a question for you. You don't have to if you don't want to, but I was just wondering something."

"Well, go ahead. Ask me."

"What if I wanted to write? You know, work at a newspaper like you do. Do you think that would be possible? Is that something I could get into, I mean if I could do it and all?"

"Marcus, I promise you it's something you can do. You do well in school and I'll have you working there part-time before summer. But you're staying in school and going to college. You can work summers till you graduate. Then, if you find that's what you really want to do with your life, you'll have the education it takes to be successful at whatever you do."

"Really? You hear that, Momma? Oscar's gonna hire me at the paper."

Mary Frye came into the room. Her face radiated the relief that Oscar's help had given her.

"Marcus, you do just what Mr. Phipps says and show him you're gonna' do your part."

"I will, Momma. I'm doing good in school already. I like it there. The teachers will even help you if you need it. It's a cool place."

Oscar cut in.

"Mary, please call me Oscar."

"Yes, sir, Mr. Phipps... I mean Oscar. Dinner is ready. You boys wash up and get on in here."

As they ran to the bathroom, Mary Frye came over beside Oscar.

"Mr. Phipps. I want you to know that if I were to die tomorrow, you have made me the happiest I have been in my whole life. It's real hard when you don't know how you're gonna be able to take care of your kids. No matter what, I will always love you for what you has done for me and my boys and will mention you in my prayers every night for as long as I live and that's a promise."

"Well, Mary, I want you to know that I'm just as pleased about this as you are. It makes me want to try and help some other families. And that's what we're going to do."

"That's a fine thing, Oscar. Now come try some of this chicken while it's still hot. Oh, by the way, a package came for you here this morning. A man in one of those overnight trucks brought it right after you left. It's sitting over there on the dining room table. Put it in there where it wouldn't get broke."

Oscar walked over to the table, picked up the package and peeled open the overnight envelope it was mailed in. Inside was a small cardboard container marked 'fragile'. Carefully, he opened the package to reveal a small wooden box. It was of very dark, highly polished wood. About six inches square, it was delicate and appeared to be quite old. He carefully opened the lid and found a small note addressed to him. It simply read:

"Oscar,
Dwight said the last night that I was with him that when you took over the Foundation I was to give this to you. He said you would understand.
Bob Meecham"

Now, realizing what he held in his hands, he turned the small box over. There on the bottom, still embossed beautifully in the finish were these words:

"For Dorothy, thanks, Pickle, 1928"

There were several black spots on it and Oscar could only guess that somehow it had survived the inferno at Fountainside. He fully understood the meaning this small box held for Dwight and the thought that he would entrust it to him was overwhelming. In a lot of ways it meant more to him than trusting him to run the Foundation. It was an actual physical link to the young man whose sacrifice had meant so much for so many others who never even heard his name. He placed the box in a spot in the china cabinet. He would treasure it more than anything else he would ever own.

After the boys and Mary Frye settled into their beds for the night, Oscar went into the den and started a fire in the fireplace, not for heat but just because he loved to stare into the flames as he thought, especially when he was writing. It helped to wipe the slate in his mind clean so he could think more clearly and organize his thoughts. He was ready to undertake the portion of Dwight's request that had started him on this new and untried path. He felt the words must be just right and as much as he had worried over how he would handle this task, it had now crystallized in his mind and he knew what he would do. He could never recount the events any better than they had been presented to him. And so, with the fire crackling and the house still smelling of southern fried chicken, he began to type on his old manual Royal typewriter.

PRIDE AND PRIVILEGE

Nineteen twenty-eight was a good year in the South. Just enough rain and sun to bring in a good crop. The war in Europe was over and America was in a good frame of mind......

The End